Kate's Song

Forever After in
APPLE LAKE

Kate's Song

JENNIFER BECKSTRAND

summerside
PRESS™

Summerside Press™
Minneapolis 55438
www.summersidepress.com

Kate's Song

ISBN 978-1-60936-639-1

All scripture quotations are taken from the King James Version of the Bible.

This is a work of fiction. Any resemblances to actual people or events are
purely coincidental.

Cover design by Lookout Design | www.lookoutdesign.com
Interior design by Müllerhaus Publishing Group | www.mullerhaus.net

*Summerside Press™ is an inspirational publisher offering fresh,
irresistible books to uplift the heart and engage the mind.*

Printed in USA.

Dedication

To my six amazing children and one son-in-law for constantly reminding me of what is really important in life. (Zach, I hope you get your tennis court.)

And to my husband, Gary, for being my greatest support and biggest fan. I love you with all my heart.

Acknowledgments

I express my deepest appreciation to Mary Sue Seymour for believing in me and my writing, and to Lindsay Guzzardo for her gifted editing of my work. I am enormously grateful to Priscilla Stoltzfus, Sam Riehl, and their families for welcoming me into their homes and correcting my Englisch mistakes. My five beautiful and intelligent sisters give me constant encouragement, especially Dr. Allison Sharp, my alpha, beta, and zeta reader, into whose skillful hands I trust all my work.

Chapter One

"Is he dead? Please tell me he's not dead!"

Kate limped through the muddy field carrying a bag filled with most of her earthly possessions. The torrential rain pelted her face and rendered her nearly sightless. Her clothing, soaked and dripping, molded to her like a second skin, offering no defense from the biting wind. She chided herself for being so unprepared on just another refreshing Wisconsin spring evening. *Ach!* The shortcut to her home, which had made perfect sense an hour ago, now seemed *deerich*, foolish indeed.

And still the rain came. Kate might as well have been standing under a waterfall. Wiping her eyes so she could see her path, she trudged on stoically, never pausing to catch her breath or nurse her swollen leg and aching back.

The overwhelming darkness was dispelled intermittently by violent explosions of light followed by deafening cracks of thunder. Even though she knew they were coming, Kate still jumped like a skittish heifer at milking time with each earsplitting roar. The noise brought back the all-too-vivid memory of that horrible night she wanted so desperately to forget.

"Kate, get out of here."

"No, I won't leave you."

"He'll kill you."

Shivering uncontrollably, Kate climbed over the short wooden fence that separated the Yutzys' pasture from her *dat*'s orchard. Her foot jammed into the ground on the other side, and she groaned in pain and grabbed her knee. A wave of despair washed over her. She crouched with her back against the fence and began to weep.

"Kate, are you all right? Where did he hurt you?"

His face...

"Come away. Don't look at him."

"Dear Heavenly Father," she prayed, the storm drowning her words almost before she could form them. "I am so afraid. Please send me Thy peace." She gasped as she slowly flexed her leg. Eyes closed, she turned her face to the sky. "And if that is too much to ask, please just help me to stand up."

The thought of crawling on her hands and knees through the apple trees made her want to laugh in spite of herself. "Would it be too much trouble to send Dat with a buggy and a warm blanket, Lord? And a cup of Mamma's hot cocoa?"

No answer.

"I know, I know," she said wryly. "Faith without works is dead." Grabbing a fence post, she pulled herself up and squared her shoulders. The whipping wind sliced into her face like a thousand shards of ice. Her jeans were drenched and heavy, her already-aching body stiff with cold. How many more steps could she take before she froze solid right where she stood?

Keep moving, she told herself. Less than half a mile and she would be warming herself at the big stone hearth in the front room. Even after a two-year absence, Kate remembered the interior of her home in vivid color, and she could almost smell the lavender Mamma hung near the fire and taste the hickory-smoked venison Dat cured after hunting. And the apples—apples everywhere. Even at the academy, Kate never ate an apple without being immediately transported home to the middle of the orchard.

Her younger brothers would study her face with morbid curiosity. Elmer would be the first to bring her a blanket, because he always noticed the need. Mamma would try valiantly to hide her distress at seeing her middle daughter in such a state, but she would fuss and fret over Kate as if she were a newborn *buplie*.

Dear Dat would be overjoyed to see her, although he would not let it show on his face. But his delight would evaporate the minute he saw the blackened eye and swollen lip. Kate could picture Dat clutching his heart then getting that look on his face that said he was ferociously angry but refused to respond in any way that would shame him before his family. "Are you finally going to stay home for good?" he would ask. "This is what happens when you leave to see the world."

Kate slogged on, the promise of a warm bed the only motivation she needed to keep moving. Questions and answers could wait.

The lightning momentarily illuminated her childhood home through the bare trees, the rust-red roof in vivid contrast to the bright whitewash. Kate saw no light within or without. Her family retired early. Perhaps if she entered as quietly as possible, she wouldn't have to wake anyone.

Who did she think she was fooling? She would wake everyone.

To her relief, she found the door well-oiled, and she slipped into the front room and let the warmth wash over her like a hot shower. After the clamor of wind and rain, the stillness of the house attacked her ears, magnifying every sound. The floor creaked softly where she stepped, the grandfather clock tocked its eternal cadence, and the glowing embers of the dying fire crackled in the hearth. Kate swayed unsteadily, dripping wet and dizzy with pain.

As she expected, she woke Mamma. "Elmer? Is that you?" her mother whispered as she came down the hall holding a kerosene lantern. When she caught sight of Kate, her eyes widened. "Well, bless my soul. It is my little Katie." After quickly placing the lamp on the table, Mamma threw out her arms and, despite Kate's dripping clothes, enfolded Kate into a welcoming embrace.

Mamma pulled away and put her hand to Kate's cheek. "My poor buplie," she said. "My poor baby. Solomon, wake up now and come," she called down the hall, not bothering to muffle her voice in the still of the night. She took the bag from Kate's arm and placed it on the table. Then she slipped the waterlogged sweat jacket from Kate's shoulders.

Dat appeared, pulling up his suspenders and looking like he had been awakened from the sleep of the dead. He rubbed his eyes then focused on the girl before him. "Katie," he said softly, "you are home."

Overcome with relief, Kate couldn't make her lips form a reply. Her mother, almost in tears, wrapped her in a blanket. Her three brothers came out of nowhere and stood dumbfounded, staring at her.

"Elmer, Ben, give her some room," said Mamma, her voice trembling. "Oh, *leibe*, you are so cold. Like an icicle. Joe, put in more logs and build up the fire." Mamma pushed the boys out of the way and pulled Kate to the hearth.

Dat said nothing, just looked at her face with eyes wide.

"What happened to Katie, Mamma?"

"Leave her be, Ben. She must get warm first."

"How did you get hurt?" Elmer asked.

"*Oy*, anyhow, you look very bad, sister."

Kate could not answer. She put her hand to her forehead as the room began to spin. The floor seemed to rush toward her, and the world descended into blackness.

Chapter Two

Kate awoke with a start, the terrible dream that had seemed so vivid disappearing from her memory. Her wet clothes were gone, replaced by a soft flannel nightgown that gathered tightly around her wrists and neck. Lying in the bed she used to share with Hannah, Kate inhaled the fresh scent of pine and newly scrubbed floors. Dat would never approve of her recently acquired habit of sleeping in—too many late-night study sessions proved her undoing.

Kate gingerly rolled onto her back and closed her eyes, considering the damage to her body. She knew her right thigh sported a nasty purple mark the shape of a football; her left knee felt stiff, the bruises on her neck throbbed beneath the collar of her nightgown, and her lower lip seemed to be the size of a crabapple. Poor Mamma had probably gone into apoplexy when she saw all the injuries.

The nightmarish events of the last week rattled loudly in her head. She had stumbled into someone else's problems and been swept away. The memory of the ordeal left her shaky and ill.

Still, she felt no remorse for what she had done. She wished to heaven that her hand had not been forced. But given the choice, she would do the same thing again—even though the violence went against everything her people believed in. She had saved a woman's life, and Kate could not condemn herself for that.

Her old emerald-green dress and soft black apron hung on the peg next to her bed. Had they patiently waited there for two years, knowing she would return? She lifted the dress from its resting place and buried her face in the fabric. It smelled like church and Christmas, apple cider and fresh cream all at the same time.

Home. It smelled like home.

When she put it on, the knots in her shoulders untied themselves. She marveled that an old dress could have such a calming effect. After fashioning her hair into a bun, she fastened her *kapp* on her head and made her way down the stairs to the kitchen.

Mamma was bent over the cook stove, tending to a steaming pot. When she saw Kate, she bustled over to her with arms outstretched. "*Cum*, cum. Oh, look at you, you poor thing," Mamma cooed and held Kate's chin in her hand. "Such sorrow in your eyes. I cannot bear to think my child has suffered so." She wrapped Kate in a hug and held on until Kate wondered if they were going to stand like that forever.

"Cum," Mamma said. "Come and eat some breakfast." She led Kate to the table and seated her in one of the chairs. "I will cook some eggs, and there's bacon back yet."

"No, Mamma. You have just cleaned up. I will have some coffee soup."

Mamma shook her head and put her hands on her hips. "No daughter of mine is going without a good breakfast, especially my Kate. You are too *din*. A stiff wind could blow you into the next county. Did you eat nothing at that school?" Not waiting for an answer, Mamma went to the icebox and pulled out four thick slabs of bacon and three eggs.

Kate stood up. "I will help, Mamma."

Holding up her hand, Mamma said, "No, rest."

"I can help."

"If you don't rest, you might as well go lie in the road and let the buggies run over you, for all the good it will do you. Listen to your mamma and stay put."

Kate sank into her chair. She had to admit, it did feel better to be still.

Mamma clunked the heavy metal skillet onto the cook stove and arranged the bacon like a sculptor. "How far did you walk last night? You were soaked clear through."

"The bus dropped me off at the new grocery store."

"At Central and Ivy?"

"*Jah.*"

"Oh, *leibe*, you should have hired a driver. That is a long way."

"Not too long in nice weather."

"And you thought you were going to find nice weather in the middle of April? It made down heavy yesterday."

Kate had fled Milwaukee hastily and barely collected enough money for the bus fare. Paying a driver would have been impossible. But she would not trouble Mamma with the details.

"I hung your *Englisch* clothes in the washroom," Mamma said.

"*Denki.*"

"Do you always dress like that at school? Like a boy?" Mamma said, with a bit of scold in her tone.

"Mamma," Kate said, ready to defend herself, "if I dress Plain at school, I attract too much attention. Like a police car with the sirens going. Then the people stare at me or try to shame me. I always dress modest at school, Mamma. Just not Plain."

This answer seemed to satisfy Mamma, and she changed the subject. "The family will come tonight."

"Jah, I will be happy to see the new baby."

"They will want to know about the bruises," Mamma said quietly.

"Jah, I know that too."

Mamma studied her daughter's face. "And what will you tell them?"

"You and Dat will want to know also," Kate eyed her mother doubtfully.

"Your father will want to know the name of the man who did this, jah. But me? I believe bad tales are better buried with the dead." She turned and tended the bacon just beginning to sizzle. "All I want to know is if you will be leaving us again."

Even though Mamma did not look at her, Kate could feel the intensity of the question. Mamma never expressed her true feelings if she thought she was going to upset anyone, and she wouldn't tell Kate how badly she wanted her home if Kate was determined to go. Mamma was the most unselfish creature Kate had ever known. And in an Amish community, that was saying something.

Kate sighed. She stood, went up behind her mother, and put her arms around her shoulders. "I know what you are thinking—that your *madle*, daughter, went to school in search of God's will and came back with a black eye."

Mamma turned and looked at Kate, eyes moist. "Jah, that is what I was thinking."

Although Kate hated the thought of giving her mother something to cry about, she had to tell her the honest truth. "I am sorry, Mamma," she said. "I do not know. God has not made Himself clear yet."

Mamma buried her face in Kate's neck. "Your dat said it would be so. He said we cannot be impatient farmers with our Katie. You are our walnut tree, and we must not rush your growing season."

Wiping away a tear before it could escape, Kate held her mamma and savored the sweet reality of a mother's love.

"I—I will be here at least until the new term starts in September."

"That is a piece of good news, then." Sniffing twice, Mamma wiped her eyes then took Kate by the shoulders and steered her in the direction of the chair. "Sit, sit. My bacon is burning."

Kate shrugged and returned to her perch at the table. If she didn't have the damage on her face, she could pretend that nothing horrible had happened to her. Her arrival was only a week earlier than expected. She dreaded the probing questions from Mary; the inquisitive looks from the nieces and nephews; the inevitable lecture from her eldest brother, Aaron, who would undoubtedly remind her of her foolishness. Aaron's favorite pastime was cataloging Kate's faults, just to make sure she didn't forget what they were. According to Aaron, Kate was vain, proud, impetuous, and unbelieving. After he saw her face, he could add foolish to the list. That would make him very happy.

"Hullo!" came a shout from outside.

"Cum *reu*," Mamma called back.

The door flew open as if met by a powerful gust of wind. A tall, beardless young man blew in, smiling widely and carrying a large package under his arm.

Uncommonly handsome, his white teeth contrasted with his dark brown hair and blue eyes. Kate stared in disbelief. Could this broad-shouldered visitor be the same boy she'd thumped over the head in the fifth grade? She'd gotten into such trouble that day. Surely someone with such goodly features was not her eleven-year-old nemesis, was he?

Kate self-consciously raised her hand to cover her mouth. She didn't want anyone seeing her in such a state.

"*Gute maiya*, Emma," the young man said, walking quickly toward Mamma and removing his hat. He halted in his path as his eyes landed on Kate, and his expression turned to one of surprise. With something akin to awe in his voice, he said, "The nightingale has returned."

Wishing she could throw a flour sack over her head, Kate tried to smile. "There is no need to call me that. My brother would say it is gross vanity."

"Kate Weaver, you have a stunning voice, but the judges will never notice you if you don't sing with more power. Relax your tongue and stop trying to control the sound, honey. You want to stand out."

"Only the most wicked among us called you 'Nightingale.' We knew you did not wish to be singled out in that way, and we were unkind to tease you." The young man studied her face. "You are the same," he said, "except grown older."

He stared at her unashamedly while she resisted the urge to bury her face in her hands. Kate recognized admiration in his eyes and felt puzzled. Didn't he see the ugly purple and blue surrounding her eye or the cherry-sized bulge that used to be her lip?

Mamma disturbed him from his trance. "Will you eat something, Nathaniel?"

He looked at Mamma, and it seemed to take a moment for her words to register. "No, denki. I must get back to the workshop. *Mamm* asked that I bring this by." He held out the package to Mamma. "It is a tobacco poultice for the bruising. I thought it was for Solomon, but now I see…" His voice trailed off, and for the first time since he came, his smile disappeared.

"Do not worry, Nathaniel. Kate has had some trouble, but she is not made of eggshells."

Nathaniel nodded, doubt still plying the corners of his mouth.

"Tell your mother denki," Mamma said, taking his package. "She is always a kind friend."

Nathaniel examined Kate again. What was he looking for? Without a word he came closer and put his calloused hand to her face. Stunned, Kate sat perfectly still as he caressed her cheek with his thumb. "You need a comfrey paste for the lip," he said, his eyes riveted to hers. "And a different kind of poultice for the eye. How is the pain?"

Kate cleared her throat. "There is… It stings a little."

"My mother…will…know…what…," he said, seeming to lose his train of thought with each word.

He pulled his hand away suddenly and put on the smile he came in with. "I will come by later with more from my mother," he said. "And drink some rose hip tea," he added on his way out. "I will bring that too."

They watched him leave as quickly as he had come. Mamma clicked her tongue. "Even if the house burned down around him, that boy couldn't keep his eyes from you, Katie."

Kate groaned. "Oh, Mamma, I am so embarrassed. I've tried very hard to despise him ever since he kissed me. I think I was fourteen before I stopped sticking my tongue out at him every time he looked my way."

"I never understood why you disliked him so much after that kiss," Mamma said.

Kate played with the ties of her kapp. "The other girls made fun of me for weeks, and the boys sniggered every time Nathaniel came within spitting distance. I felt humiliated."

Both mother and daughter burst into peals of laughter. "Poor boy," Mamma said, wiping tears from her eyes. "It would throw his heart to the pigs if he knew."

Kate thought of his good-natured expression and handsome features. "Mamma, he has changed so much since I last saw him!"

"You remember Nathaniel King as *lang* and gangly, all arms and legs. As a teenager, his feet arrived at church service five minutes before he did. He's filled out nicely, wouldn't you say, leibe? With the arms of a carpenter."

Kate could only nod her agreement.

Chuckling, Mamma went back to tending her bacon. "You have been gone two years, and before you even left home, he spent several months as an apprentice to an uncle in Ohio. He has not seen you for like as not three years yet." She took her skillet off the cook stove. "If you like, I will invite him to dinner."

Kate grinned. "Will you wait until my lip grows smaller? If he wants to try more kissing, I need to be ready."

Mamma chuckled and shook her head. "Leibe, do not tease me. You will only raise my hopes."

Chapter Three

An hour before suppertime, *Dat* appeared in the threshold of the kitchen, where Kate and Mamma were finishing the snitz pies. He took off his muddy boots, hung up his hat and jacket, and washed his hands and face before giving Kate a serious look and beckoning her to follow him. After dusting off her hands on a towel, Kate reluctantly joined her father in the front room.

He motioned for her to sit on the overstuffed sofa facing the window then pulled up a chair almost knee-to-knee with her. Out the window, the sun peeked bravely through the clouds as water left over from the rainstorm dripped off the eaves of the house.

"Now, Katie," he said, shaking his finger in her direction. "Mamma insisted I stay away today so I would have a chance to calm down before speaking with you. I have paced the orchards all day, and now," he paused and raised his voice, "I have not calmed down. I missed my dinner, and I am hungry. It is no use trying to calm down. Tell me what has happened to you."

Kate lowered her eyes. "It will not make you happy."

"Leibe, nothing you could tell me about getting a black eye will make me happy," he said. "When my daughter comes home battered and bruised, believe me, I am ready to be made miserable." Folding his arms across his chest, he looked at her sternly.

"Oh, Dat," she said, a sob parting her lips. The tears flowed so quickly she did not have time to push them back.

Dat patted Kate awkwardly on the head. "There, there, liebe. No need to cry about it."

"I am sorry to bring upset to the house."

"Maybe now you will never want to leave."

Kate sniffed and wiped her eyes. "I do not know yet."

"I see," her father said. "They do this to you, and you want to return?"

"One man, Dat. They are not all like him."

"Too many are."

The room darkened as the clouds drifted over the sun. Kate sat up straight. "My friend, Maria, you remember. I wrote about her."

"You give her singing lessons."

"Jah. The father of her baby, he drank too much one night and came to hurt her and the baby, and I stood between them."

Dat shook his head. "Why must you do things like this, leibe?"

"You would have done the same."

"Jah, but that doesn't mean I want you to," he said.

Kate smiled. "I follow your example in all things."

"Was your friend harmed?" Dat asked.

"He broke her arm. The baby was not hurt."

"Did you call the police?"

"Yes. They took him to the hospital."

Her father raised an eyebrow.

"I am sorry," Kate said, the words tumbling out of her mouth. "I must tell you. I wanted to hurt him. I *tried* to hurt him."

Dat frowned. "Jah, Lord Jesus said to turn your cheek."

She lowered her head. She would do almost anything but make her father ashamed of her.

Dat patted her hand. "But He also said he who offends one of his little ones—it is better if a millstone is hung around his neck and he is thrown into the sea. Perhaps by sending this man to the hospital, you saved him from a worse fate."

Kate frowned. "Perhaps."

"What's done is done. You will hear no else about it from me. You have not been baptized yet," Dat said, with an emphasis on the *yet*. "But you still belong to this community, Katie, for as long as you choose. You are one of our daughters and will find love with us, not condemnation."

"Jah, I know. When I went away to school, I know everyone tried to understand and not to judge. Except Aaron. He did not understand."

"Your brother has only concern for you in his heart," Dat insisted.

"Very deep down, I think."

Dat smiled. "We all must learn what we must learn. Even Aaron." He scooted his chair away from her then fixed his eyes steadily on Kate. "If you go back to the academy, you will stay away from this man?"

Kate nodded. "I promise, Dat. I promise."

Dat slapped his knees. "*Gute*. Then let's eat."

Chapter Four

At suppertime, they came flocking to the Weaver home like chickens to the cornmeal pan. Kate's younger brothers, home from the dairy, plus her four older married siblings with their children, blew through the door at almost exactly the same time for supper. Elmer had set out early this morning to spread the word among the family that Katie had returned, and they were all to come to supper. Only Kate's younger sister, Hannah, who lived in Ohio with her new husband, was missing.

Mamma and Dat Weaver had nine children. Three sons, three daughters, then three sons. A perfect nine-patch quilt, Mamma always said. Kate sat smack in the middle of the bunch. Three brothers older, three younger. One sister older, one younger.

Kate's older brothers, Aaron, Zebulon, and Ike were each married with young children. Aaron, who lived next door, had five sons, and Kate knew how difficult it was for him to be humble about his two sets of twins. But if anyone was proud of his humility, it was Aaron.

Watching him walk into the house, Kate thought of her younger years and Aaron's almost daily criticism of her manners, her pride, and her thoughts, which, according to Aaron, were very wicked indeed. When, as a little girl, Kate would sneak out behind the barn and sing at the top of her lungs to an imaginary, adoring audience, Aaron had somehow always managed to find her and give her an abrupt slap across the back of her neck. In those days, Dat chastised Aaron almost weekly for faultfinding, but Aaron must have felt it his calling to pass judgment on his sister.

Kate frowned to herself. She mustn't think of Aaron so harshly.

Perhaps she truly had a sinful heart and God was trying to send her a message through her brother.

Aaron and his wife, Ada, marched into the house arm in arm, paying no heed to their unruly sons, who bounded in after them. It was as if the boys weren't even related.

Ada's eyes grew as big as half dollars. Her rosebud lips parted in shock. "Kate! Elmer told us it was bad, but I had no idea how awful."

Aaron merely frowned when he laid eyes on Kate. He granted her a cursory pat as he examined her bruised face. Kate braced herself for Aaron's displeasure, but Zeb and Anna arrived, and Aaron was swept aside as they hugged Kate affectionately.

Zeb took Kate's chin in his hand. "Poor girl. Does it hurt?"

Kate nodded.

Anna, Zeb's wife, took Kate's hand. "I missed you something wonderful. You are staying for a few days?"

"At least until September, Lord willing."

Anna hugged her again. "Gute. We'll see you often, then. We should make a quilt together."

"I would like that," Kate said.

Ike appeared at the door and threw out his arms. "Just look at you! Having to fight off those Englisch boys, are you?" He enfolded her in a rib-crushing embrace. "Remember when I fell out of the hayloft and broke my nose? I have never been in that much pain, ever."

"I remember," Kate said. "Your face was so swollen, I thought there was a stranger in our house for weeks."

"I had two black eyes to go with it."

Zeb punched Ike playfully in the shoulder. "And I can't say the new nose did anything gute for your looks."

Ike promptly took off after his brother. They ran around the kitchen like two teenagers, trying to catch each other, until Mamma scolded them to stop fighting before they broke something.

Kate squealed with delight when Mary's husband, Moses, carried in the new baby, and she snatched the little one from his father's arms the minute they crossed the threshold. Mary, Kate's older sister, followed close behind.

Cuddling the sweet-smelling bundle close to her heart, Kate stroked the silky, black peach fuzz on the top of his head and caressed his little fingers. "Mary, he is a beautiful buplie. His skin is so soft."

"Jah, he is perfect," Mary said. "He will be a fine man for his dat." Then she caught sight of Kate's battered features. "Oh no. I should have brought my arnica ointment. What have you done for the bruising?"

"Nathaniel King brought a poultice this morning, and he is bringing some other things later."

Mary touched Kate's lip. "I'm telling you now not to bother with a tobacco poultice. A comfrey compress is the only thing that will take care of those bruises."

Two long tables stood in the kitchen, one where the grandchildren sat and the other for the adults. Mamma, Kate, and Mary set all the food on the adult table and the young ones brought their plates to their mothers to be filled. Kate knew that, at nineteen years old, Elmer was not happy about sitting at the children's table, but he endured it good-naturedly. Twins Ben and Joe, at four years younger, didn't care where they sat as long as they were supplied with plenty of food.

Naturally, the attention at supper centered on Kate. Dat enlightened the family about her injuries, briefly repeating what she had told him. Already uncomfortable with the way Aaron looked at her, Kate was glad Dat had spared her the embarrassment of telling the tale herself.

"And now we will talk no more of it," Dat said, focusing a stern eye on Aaron. "What's done is done. Our Kate is home."

A knock at the back door interrupted Dat's lecture. Mamma jumped from her chair and opened the door to a little boy no bigger than a peanut.

"Well, bless my soul, if it isn't Daniel Herschberger," Mamma said, ushering the boy inside as she did every other visitor to the Weaver home. "What can we do for you, Danny?"

Daniel looked around the overflowing table and suddenly became shy. He sidled next to Mamma and nibbled on his fingernail.

"Where's your dat?" Zeb asked.

"He's with Lolly," Danny squeaked.

"Your cow?" Dat said.

Danny nodded. "Jah. Dat is wondering if you could help with the calf."

"Too stubborn to come without a fight, is she?" Dat said, smiling. Even though poor Dat had taken only two bites of his supper, he was more than willing to help at a moment's notice. He quickly rose from the table and lifted his coat from the hook. "Lead the way, Danny," he said as he opened the door and followed the boy into the chilly spring evening. He left a full plate of food and took his empty stomach.

It seemed as if Aaron had been eagerly awaiting Dat's departure so he could deliver a much-needed lecture to his disobedient sister. "This is what comes of seeking the world, Katie," he said. "The Englisch are ungodly and violent. You belong here in the community."

Anna, Zeb's wife, looked uncomfortably at Aaron and promptly changed the subject. "Tell us what you have learned at school, Kate. You are so brave to go to such a big place all by yourself."

Dear Anna. So considerate of people's feelings—noticing what others would not.

"It has been very difficult in some ways, especially at first," Kate said. "I am still so far behind the other students. Luckily, the academy emphasizes performance rather than academics, so someone with my background isn't completely lost."

Aaron's wife, Ada, sat next to her husband, her nose turned up ever so slightly. "And what have you learned in your fancy new school?" she said.

Kate ignored the petulance in Ada's tone. "I have heard such beautiful music that sends my heart to God," she said, glancing in Aaron's direction instead. Then she turned her attention to Anna. "There are oratorios that soar to the high ceiling of the cathedral and operas that would make you weep."

"Life is full of enough sorrows. What need have we to go looking for them in the theater?" Zeb said.

"Because of the stories they teach. They reveal evil and good so you may learn the difference and love the good. They show compassion and cruelty so you may choose the good way. The stories can point you to God."

Aaron shook his head. The others at the table hung onto every word she said, some uncertain, others enthralled.

Kate put down her fork and folded her hands in her lap. "Our opera workshop just performed an opera about a girl, Angelica, who lives as a nun in a convent because her family has rejected her."

"She is Catholic?" Ada said.

"Yes, and when she was young and unmarried, she gave birth to a boy, and her family took him from her and never allowed her to visit."

"What happens to her?" Mary said.

"When she learns her son is dead, she takes her own life. It is very, very sad."

There was a long pause at the table. "And when it is all done," Zeb said, "how does it bring you to God?"

"Angelica," Kate stuttered, "longs for acceptance from her family. But they are unforgiving. In the opera, you see the pain her family has caused her. You ache for their forgiveness, for Angelica. And you say to yourself—Who must I forgive today? Who is in pain and needs my love?"

Mamma wiped a tear from her cheek. "Jah, we all must ask God every day."

The spell broke when Ike's five-year-old son, Elias, came to the table with plate in hand, asking for more potatoes. No one was eager to return to the subject of Kate's schooling, especially Kate. Ike asked Zeb about the corn he was planting this year, and the conversation moved safely to other topics. Kate had neglected to mention that she sang the role of Angelica, and every performance she could not keep the tears from flowing when the little boy ran into her arms to greet Angelica in heaven.

Better not to tell. Better that Aaron and Ada not have one more reason to chastise her. Kate scolded herself again for being so petty. Why did she feel threatened by Aaron and Ada? They loved her and only had her best interests at heart. Didn't they?

With supper nearly over, Aaron, who must have thought it a great burden to remain quiet, started in on Kate again. And since he was the eldest, no one but Dat would tell him to hold his tongue. To make matters worse, Ada's father was the bishop of two districts, and this seemed to make Aaron believe he held some sort of authority over his siblings.

"Are you home for good this time, Katie?" he asked.

"I don't know."

"You will never get a husband if you keep going away," Aaron said.

"You don't know what you're saying, Aaron," Zeb said. "Kate is very pretty. The boys take to her like bees to honey. We older brothers could never keep them away before."

"But now is different," Aaron said. "I've heard talk."

Mamma lifted her head. "What talk have you heard about my madle?"

Aaron waved his fork in Kate's direction. "The longer she stays away, the more influence the world has over her. She will find it too hard to pull back and be baptized. Who will want to marry her?"

Ada nodded, all too eager to share the gossip. "To be honest, I am surprised she chose to return to us at all. They say Kate is worldly. And too old."

"That is idle talk," Mary said. "Kate is only twenty-two years yet."

"Jah," Aaron said. "Exactly. Her *rumschpringe* has gone on for six years. Most boys and girls choose baptism after two or, at most, three years. People start to wonder whether she will join the Church at all."

"Let them wonder," said Ike.

"The boys want Plain girls," Aaron said, putting a stop to any disagreement. "Not the worldly, vain sort. There might be a widower to take a fancy to her, if he's not picky. But a man who wants to be the bishop or a minister someday will not come near her."

A dull ache settled in Kate's stomach. Could Aaron be right? Most of the boys who had once offered to drive her home after Sunday-night singings and youth gatherings were married or courting.

A knock at the back door interrupted the conversation. "Who now?" Mamma said as she rose. She opened the door and then threw out her arms in welcome. "Look who is here," she exclaimed as she pulled a smiling Nathaniel King into the room.

Kate's heart did a single somersault before settling into a rapid thudding in her chest. Remembering how he was once the boy with cooties who'd kissed her on the playground, she felt her face get hot. Remembering the feel of his hand on her cheek earlier in the day, she felt her face get even hotter.

"Ach, I am sorry to interrupt," Nathaniel said, removing his hat and still grinning widely. "I thought supper would be over."

"Do not be uneasy, Nathaniel," Mamma said. "With all the goings-on today, we started supper almost an hour late."

"I brought some tea and ointment for Kate," Nathaniel said. Looking at her, he seemed to flush as red as Kate imagined herself to be. "How are you feeling?"

Kate brought her hand to her cheek self-consciously. "I am better."

Mamma pulled Nathaniel farther into the kitchen and removed the sack slung over his shoulder. "Cum, cum. You must have some snitz pie with us. It is from the last of the dried apples. You'd think with fifty acres of apple trees I would have dried more fruit last fall."

"No, denki. I do not want to pester you."

"You don't like my snitz pie?" Mamma said with a pout and a twinkle in her eye.

"Jah, of course, Emma. You are the best cook in Wisconsin," Nathaniel said.

"Then cum, sit," Mamma insisted, pulling another chair up to the already crowded table and directing Nathaniel to it. Sheepishly, Nathaniel slipped into the chair at the corner of the table across from Kate, crammed nicely next to Zeb and Anna.

In unison, Kate, Mary, and Mamma went to the long counter to cut and serve the pie. Kate gave her mother a meaningful look and pointed silently to her lip. Mamma only giggled and plopped a dollop of whipped cream onto one of the pie slices.

Once they served the pie, Mary, Mamma, and Kate sat down again to eat. Kate's return to the table seemed to remind Aaron of his duty to call her to repentance. And Nathaniel's presence did not deter him.

"Nathaniel," Aaron said, "you are of marriageable age. What do you seek in a worthy wife?"

Never losing that enchanting smile, Nathaniel said, "Do you know someone you want me to meet?"

Kate pulled her eyes from him and stared faithfully at the piece of pie in front of her. Why did Aaron have to stir things up?

"I have been telling Kate that a man does not want a wife who flirts with the temptations of the world," Aaron said.

Ada fixed her gaze on Nathaniel as if he were the only person at the table. "My sister Sarah would never dream of turning her back on our ways. She is nothing but completely faithful."

Embarrassed that Nathaniel should be witness to such a kerfuffle,

Kate tried to defend herself and put the matter to rest. "You know that I have always tried to understand and follow God's will."

"You cannot just do what you want and call it God's will," Aaron said. "Every time you go back to Milwaukee, you pull yourself further and further from us. Soon you will think we are too plain, and you will look to the world for your salvation. It is not the way, Kate."

Kate fell silent and let Aaron sermonize to his heart's content. She dared a look at Nathaniel. He ate his snitz pie, but the smile had disappeared from his face.

Aaron was just getting started. "'Wherefore come out from among them, and be ye separate.' That is our way. 'Touch not the unclean thing; and I will receive you.'"

"You are quick to judge, Aaron," Ike said. "Kate knows all that. She is not yet baptized. She is searching. That is what rumschpringe is for."

"And when will she be baptized?" Aaron asked. "The rumschpringe cannot go on indefinitely. It is high time she makes her covenant to the Church and God."

Kate could feel the discomfort growing. Mary and Mamma kept glancing at each other in dismay. And Anna, while never taking her eyes off her plate, seemed genuinely distressed.

Ike and Aaron continued to trade Scriptures and debate Kate's readiness for baptism, but Kate hardly listened. Instead, she ate her pie, intensely aware of Nathaniel sitting a few feet from her. As Aaron continued to preach, Ike's boy, Elias, came to the table wanting a cup of water. Nathaniel grabbed the pitcher, took Elias's empty cup, and set it on the table. "Say when," he instructed.

When the cup was half full, Elias said, "That is all, denki." Nathaniel kept pouring.

"Stop," Elias said a little louder. Still Nathaniel poured water into his cup.

The giggles bubbled from Elias throat. "Stop!" he repeated, almost yelling but not loud enough to interrupt *Onkel* Aaron.

Nathaniel smiled mischievously. "You didn't say 'when.'"

Just as the water reached the lip of the cup, Elias screamed, "When!"

The noise stalled Aaron for a second, but he simply glanced Elias's way and went right on talking.

Nathaniel set the pitcher on the table, and Elias laughed with glee. Taking it carefully by the handle, Elias sucked some water from the brimming cup and slowly carried it back to his chair. Passing two of his cousins, he showed them his cup. "I didn't say 'when,'" he said, beaming. "I didn't say 'when.'"

After the children finished with their dessert, they took turns at the sink washing their dishes and then clomped up the steep stairs to play. Without a word, Mary's three-year-old daughter, Sadie, came close to Nathaniel and held out her arms to him. Nathaniel bent over and slipped Sadie onto his lap. Sitting on her perch like she were the most important person in the world, Sadie patted Nathaniel's face and played with one of his ears.

Giddy, one of Aaron's little boys, sidled up beside Nathaniel and patted his leg. Nathaniel steadied Sadie with one arm, and then, making a fist, he gently squeezed Giddy's nose between his index and middle knuckles. He pulled his hand away and put his thumb between his fingers where Giddy's nose had been.

"I've got your nose," Nathaniel said.

Giddy opened his mouth as wide as a fish's and felt his face.

Nathaniel touched his thumb to Giddy's nose and opened his hand. "Don't worry, now. I put it back."

Kate grinned at little Giddy's puzzled expression. He lifted his arms to Nathaniel, who scooped up the boy and sat him next to Sadie in his lap.

"Look how sweet," Mary whispered. But Kate was already charmed by the sight.

As Sadie traced her small fingers around Nathaniel's palm, his eyes caught Kate's. She smiled and then looked away, embarrassed to have been caught staring.

Aaron then spoke directly to her, and she couldn't very well ignore him. "I always knew, Katie, that your vanity would be your stumbling block. You have a beautiful voice to sing praises to God, but you are proud. You want to show off. This is false pride. Am I not right, Zeb?"

Zeb shook his head. "You weary us with too much talking."

Aaron grunted and pushed his plate away. "You know I am right. If Katie will do as I say, she will walk with the Lord in heaven. Humble yourself, Katie, and quit these foolish, worldly ways." Sensing the tension in the room, he wound down. "I only say this because I am your brother and I am concerned for your salvation," he murmured resentfully.

Nathaniel lifted the two children off his lap and set them on their feet. He stood and looked Aaron squarely in the eye. "I have learned much from you this evening, Aaron," he said stiffly. "I can tell you have spent a great deal of time perfecting your doctrine. But I trust that Kate will follow God's way and not Aaron's way."

Aaron stared at Nathaniel in surprise. "Of course," he sputtered. "I do not follow my own way. Only God's."

Kate's heart all but burst with gratitude. She nodded a silent thank-you to Nathaniel. He smiled back.

"May we all do so," Ike said.

"I will go now," Nathaniel said, addressing Mamma. "Thank you for the pie. Manna from heaven could not have tasted better."

Mamma stood and wiped her hands on her apron. "Ach, no flattery. You tempt me to be prideful."

Elmer sat at the otherwise-empty children's table, eating his third piece of pie. "Good-bye, Nathaniel," he said. "Come see us again."

Donning his hat, Nathaniel looked once more in Kate's direction. "I will, Lord willing. No doubt about it."

* * * * *

Nathaniel bounded off the Weavers' front porch so light he thought he might fly home. Someone called his name, and he turned to see Aaron standing with both hands on the railing, staring at him.

"You like my sister?" Aaron said, more an accusation than a question.

"Why do you ask?" Nathaniel said.

"Do not hope for much. When September comes, she will go back to the school. Just wait and see if she doesn't."

"Then I have almost five months to change her mind."

Chapter Five

"I can't believe I let you talk me into this, Elmer," Kate said as her brother guided the buggy into place behind what seemed like a hundred buggies parked in the lane.

Elmer secured the reins and straightened his bow tie. "How else are you going to find a husband if you don't go to youth group?"

"The girls are so much younger," Kate protested, "and many of the boys too. I feel like an old mule among the colts."

Elmer made a face. "You have the strangest notions." He jumped from the buggy and came to the other side to help Kate down. "There are many boys and girls your age. Don't think you will stand out. You are just another girl come to the *singeon*, like everybody else."

Even at three years younger, her brother was often more sensible than Kate in the Amish ways. At the academy, Kate was accustomed to fighting for the attention of the instructors, making sure they noticed her above all other students. But the Plain People frowned on uniqueness and self-promotion. Individuals were discouraged from attracting attention. That is why, after much pondering and prayer, Kate had decided to leave home for the academy. In an Amish community, her voice would never be heard.

Kate adjusted her kapp while Elmer threw her shawl over her shoulders.

"The cousins might be here," Elmer added, draping his arm around Kate's shoulder. "Don't worry. It will be fun."

She saw the warmth in his eyes and tucked herself under his arm. "I'll stick with you. You are all the entertainment I need."

"I want to take Ellie Zook home tonight. Can you find another ride?"

Kate pushed away from Elmer. "I thought you were going to watch out for me."

"Why would I want to hang around you? You look like someone who gets in a lot of fights."

Kate cuffed her brother on the shoulder.

Almost two weeks had passed since her homecoming, and her lip had gradually shrunk to its normal size. The black around her eye had faded to a light yellow and would be barely noticeable in the dim light of the Yoders' barn.

Word of her violent encounter had spread throughout the community like a stiff breeze spreading dandelion seeds. Kate's first days home were filled with a variety of visitors who stopped by with pies or breads or embroidered hankies to help Kate feel better. The Plain People sought always to be compassionate. Two or three of the families were bound to say unkind things out of Kate's hearing, but most people avoided gossip and tried to be charitable.

John Yoder's barn was the largest in the district, perfect for singings and wedding parties. Young people in buggies arrived from every direction, the boys in vibrantly colored cotton shirts with black bow ties and suspenders and the girls in dazzling white kapps and black aprons. The floor was swept clean and the lanterns turned up their brightest.

As she ambled into the barn with her brother, Kate studied the hopeful faces of the wide-eyed teenage girls and the nervous, stoic young men. She recognized many of them but knew that few close friends would be there. Kate's two best friends from the one-room school were now married with families of their own.

Elmer scanned the eager faces. "Ah, there he is," he said. "Wait here, Katie. I will be back."

Elmer strode away, leaving Kate standing in the middle of the barn all by herself. As she surveyed her surroundings, she became aware of many of the boys staring at her. She put her hand to her forehead. Was the fading bruise around her eye that noticeable?

Looking to retreat to an inconspicuous corner, Kate noticed Sarah Schwartz, the bishop's daughter and Aaron's sister-in-law, standing with some friends. Sarah, a tall, pretty girl of nineteen, had never been un-neighborly to Kate, but neither had she gone out of her way to be a friend. Kate caught her eye, and Sarah acknowledged her with a plastered smile before she whispered something to her companions and they turned and walked in the opposite direction.

"Kate!" Two girls, wide-eyed and beaming, practically tackled her in their excitement.

Kate gave both of them pecks on the cheek. "I hoped I'd see you tonight."

Cousin Miriam Bontrager wrapped her arm around Kate's neck and studied her face. "I don't see no bruises. Well, I guess a little around the eye. I'm sorry I haven't come earlier to visit you. Two little brothers had the flu, and I needed to help Mamm."

The other cousin, Rebecca Miller, tucked an errant lock of hair under her kapp. "I wanted to see you something awful, but *Fater* said the buggy could not be spared. But Mamm practically begs me to go to the gatherings, so she let me come."

"Is your mamm still feeling poorly, Rebecca?" Kate said.

"She is taking some new medication that might help."

"And are you still working for Mrs. Johnson?"

Rebecca nodded. "She is grumpy as ever, but she sleeps most of the day."

Miriam leaned forward like she had a big secret. "Rebecca got a cell phone."

Rebecca shrugged her shoulders. "I am in rumschpringe."

"Do you have anyone to call?" Kate asked.

Rebecca smiled but lowered her eyes. "A few people. Mamm's not happy, but I can pay for it." She lifted her chin. "Besides, Joe Bieler bought a car. His parents are fit to be tied, but then parents will always find something to worry about."

Kate sighed. She knew a little of giving her parents something to worry about. "And you, Miriam. Are you and Ephraim engaged yet?"

Miriam stifled a giggle. "We promised ourselves to each other like as not five years ago."

"Miriam Bontrager," Rebecca scolded. "Does your dat know?"

"Of course he knows. Ephraim is the minister's son. Dat loves the idea."

Rebecca winked at Kate. Miriam, like Aaron and Ada, thought that a relationship to one of the elders lent her added importance. Or maybe it was just Miriam's dat who felt that way. Miriam and Ephraim had seemed destined for each other long before the lot fell to Ephraim's dat to be minister.

"Will there be a wedding this November?" Kate said.

"No, I'm eighteen yet. Hopefully next year."

"What about you, Rebecca?" Kate said. "Any interesting boys?"

Rebecca grimaced. "Who wants a husband?"

Elmer returned as suddenly as he had departed, with Nathaniel King following close behind. Nathaniel greeted Kate warmly, wearing the wide smile that almost seemed to be a permanent part of his face. Her cousins exchanged significant looks and backed away slightly. Kate was surprised by how overjoyed, how lightheaded, she felt upon seeing Nathaniel again.

In two years, none of the young men in Milwaukee *ferhoodled* Kate like Nathaniel had managed to do in the last two weeks. Many college boys sought girls who would trade their virtue like candy. Kate was perfectly aware of what went on between Englisch boys and girls. The girls willingly tarnished their honor for what they thought was love. But what they got from those boys was counterfeit affection. Nathaniel stood in stark contrast to what she had seen of the world.

"You look gute," Nathaniel said. "No bruises left. No swelling on the lip."

"Denki," Kate said. "Do you know my cousins, Miriam Bontrager and Rebecca Miller?"

Nathaniel vigorously shook hands with both cousins. "Jah, of course."

Rebecca grabbed Miriam's elbow and tugged her away. "We will talk to you after, Kate."

Elmer nodded to Nathaniel and then, for no reason at all, sauntered after the cousins.

Nathaniel nodded back then turned to Kate. "Your smile just about knocks me down every time I see it. Better than you sticking your tongue out every time you laid eyes on me."

Kate felt her face flush. "For a girl of eleven years old, that kiss was a grievous offense, Nathaniel King. Anna and Linda would not play with me for days because they said you gave me cooties."

"You did sock me a good one," he said, chuckling and rubbing his jaw as if still feeling the blow.

"You deserved worse."

Nathaniel stroked the stubble on his chin seemingly deep in thought. "I paid dearly for my transgression. You do not know how painful it was to be out of your good graces."

She would have truly felt bad about how she had behaved, except she could tell he was teasing. "Gute. Then you have learned your lesson."

"Jah, I have. I will never kiss you on the playground again."

Kate studied his face suspiciously. He sounded like he had every intention of trying it again—somewhere else.

"I am glad you have come," Nathaniel said. "Elmer claims he had to drag you out of the house. Do you not like the singings anymore?"

"Oh, jah, I love to sing. I just feel I am too old."

Nathaniel threw back his head and laughed. "I saw the eyes turn to you when you walked in, Kate Weaver. Your ripe old age does not seem to discourage anyone."

Kate had started to make an adamant denial of that nonsense when John Yoder climbed on a chair and called the gathering to prayer. Following the blessing, John invited everyone to sit at three long tables. Those who did not fit at the tables squeezed next to each other on bales of hay. Somehow Nathaniel managed to sit directly across from Kate at the table.

Everyone opened their prayer books and the enthusiastic singing began. Some songs were sung in unison, some enhanced with beautiful harmonies. Kate's soul floated to the top of the barn with the heavenly sounds. It didn't matter the circumstance, she loved to sing. She could be standing all alone on the stage singing an aria or here, in a barn among the Plain People, breathing in the spirit of the surrounding voices, each so different yet united in purpose.

One zealous young man started a baritone rendition of "The Puppy Parable." Everybody laughed then joined in for song after song from primary school.

Ever smiling, Nathaniel glanced occasionally at Kate and moved his lips, but Kate could tell he was not producing any sound. She raised an eyebrow, but he simply grinned and pretended to sing louder.

When the young people had their fill of singing, the Yoders passed out popcorn and dried fruit with lemonade to drink.

"Kate Weaver." A tall, stocky young man strode purposefully toward her, two dimples sinking into his cheeks as he smiled.

"Do I know you?" Kate asked, looking at the eager fellow in amusement.

"Caster Dan Zinck," the young man said. "I'm visiting from Ohio with the Beachys. I asked one of the local boys about your name."

"What part?" Kate said. "My sister Hannah Coblentz lives in Holmes County. Millersburg."

"I'm from Scio. Real small place. Don't get over to Millersburg much."

"How long will you be staying?" Kate asked.

"Clear through till harvest time," he said. "That's why I was wondering if you would like to—"

Before he could finish, Elmer and his buddy Jake practically sprinted to Caster Dan's side. Each placed a hand on one of Dan's shoulders. "Dan," Elmer said, "Elias wants to tell you all about the new water pump he rigged up for his dat."

Dan tried to be accommodating. "Jah," he stammered. "I would like to hear all about it. But first," he turned to Kate, "I would like to ask Kate if—"

Jake tugged at Dan's elbow. "Cum, Elias must leave soon. And you will learn something to take back to Ohio."

Dan looked at Kate helplessly as Jake pulled him away. "But I wanted to… Won't I see Elias tomorrow?"

They were already fifteen feet across the barn. "You need to meet my sister," Kate heard Jake insist as he coaxed Dan away from her.

Kate looked in puzzlement at her brother. "Elmer, what—?"

"He doesn't know."

"Doesn't know what?"

Taking Kate's elbow, Elmer gently pulled her aside. "Dan doesn't know that someone else is going to ask to drive you home."

Trying to ignore her fluttering heart, Kate studied her brother's face. "Who are you speaking of?"

"There is not a man in the district but would give a good report of him. He is always the first to jump in when a field wants plowing or a buggy needs repair. A gute man who deserves to be happy. We want him to have his chance with you."

The barn suddenly got very warm. "Ach, you are teasing me," she said quietly.

Elmer frowned at her. "Do I look like I am teasing?"

Kate did not reply.

"Just wait. But don't tell him I said anything. He would be embarrassed if he knew we conspired to bring you together."

Elmer walked away, and Kate put a cold hand to her warm cheek. She spied Nathaniel leaning against a wood beam, talking to three or four boys. She caught his eye when he lifted his head. His smile grew wider, if that was possible, as he stared at her, and his wintry eyes burned intensely. The blatant attention made her feel shy and giddy at the same time.

Soon other boys and girls pulled Kate's attention from Nathaniel. Some were strangers, but others were friends from families in the community. Kate visited and laughed until late.

Then the singing was over and, rational or not, Kate could not quell the disappointment that Nathaniel King had not asked to drive her home. She should have been satisfied. Much better not to encourage any young man, so unsure was she about whether she would be here come autumn. She could not be so unfeeling to anyone, especially Nathaniel.

Searching for Elmer in the crowd, she noticed a girl in a navy-blue dress sitting in the corner, her face buried in her hands. Quickly, Kate went to her and put an arm around the girl's shoulder.

The girl looked at Kate and dabbed her eyes with her apron. "Elmer's sister," she said, sitting up straight.

"And I think you must be Lizzie Troyer's youngest daughter."

"Jah," the girl said. "My name is Mandie."

"What is the matter, Mandie?" Kate said. "Can I help you?"

Mandie sniffed. "This is my first singing. I tried to be modest and demure like Mamma said, but Fran and Winnie say I am a flirt. Now they are off with boys and Micah is taking Ruth home and doesn't want me pestering him. I don't have a ride home because my brother has to have the buggy all to himself." Mandie wiped her eyes. "I dreamed it would be a most glorious evening, and now I will never marry because boys think I am a flirt. And I have to walk home all by myself in the dark."

"I am sure you are not a flirt, Mandie," Kate assured her. "We all have big dreams when we grow old enough for the gatherings. Before my first singing, I was so nervous I threw up all over my mamma's kitchen floor."

Mandie looked horrified.

"I've been to many youth gatherings," Kate said. "Most nights I have gone home with one of my brothers. Maybe you won't meet the right boy for many years. I am twenty-two years and still have not met a suitable boyfriend."

This news did not cheer Mandie. "And you're so lovely," she said. "If a pretty maid like you cannot find a husband, then there is no hope for me."

Kate laughed. "Cum, I will ask my brother to take both of us home. Or if he has invited a girl to ride with him and doesn't want us interfering, I will walk you home. I am not afraid of the dark."

"You are ever so kind," Mandie said. "My sisters always said so."

Before they could take one step toward the door, Kate saw him. Tall and muscular with coffee-colored hair and frosty blue eyes, Nathaniel made his way toward her.

He smiled at Mandie. "Hullo, I am Nathaniel King."

"Jah," Mandie stuttered nervously. "We all know who you are."

"Kate, you are flushed," he said, concern in his voice. "Do you want me to take you out to the fresh air? It would not be good for you to get sick just as you are feeling better."

"No, denki, I am gute." She fell silent, suddenly too nervous to say anything else.

Nathaniel cleared his throat and forged ahead. "Do you have a ride home tonight? Elmer says he cannot take you."

Kate thought her knees might give out at any minute. "No, I don't."

"Do you want to come with me?"

"That would make me very happy," she said, remembering to breathe. But then the concerto playing in her head went flat. "Oh, dear. I cannot go. I promised Mandie I would walk her home."

"I can take Mandie home too," Nathaniel said.

"Oh, thank you," Mandie said. "I won't make a sound, I promise."

"You do not mind?" Kate asked.

Nathaniel leaned close. "I would drive the entire grade school to Lancaster if I could sit next to you in the buggy."

Chapter Six

Mandie did not draw breath from the time she settled into Nathaniel's buggy until she entered the door of her white clapboard house. Sitting behind Nathaniel and Kate for the ride home, their passenger related story after story of her insensitive sisters, rebellious brother, and stern father. The sheer rapidity of her speech combined with Mandie's colorful vocabulary proved truly astounding.

Amused and occasionally shocked by what came out of the girl's mouth, Kate and Nathaniel frequently glanced at each other and tried to keep from bursting into laughter. Mandie would begin a story only to diverge from her subject to tell three more stories that related to the first story because the first story couldn't possibly be understood without knowing the other three or four stories that should have come first if she were thinking straight. Kate finally stopped listening altogether and simply nodded her head as if she were paying attention.

When Nathaniel reentered the buggy after walking Mandie to her door, he said, "That girl will marry someone who plans on being away from home often." They both laughed, exhausting everything they had bottled up on the ride to Mandie's house.

Nathaniel continued chuckling as he prodded the horse into a slow walk down the road. "Now," he said, "we will take our time."

The goose bumps took Kate by surprise. She wrapped her arms around herself.

"You are cold," Nathaniel said. After stopping the horse, he reached over and lifted a quilt from the back of the buggy, gently wrapping the colorful blanket around Kate's shoulders. Her skin tingled as his thumb accidentally brushed against her cheek.

"Is that better?" he asked.

Kate nodded, unable to meet his eyes.

A cool breeze skipped through the flowering trees along the lane, and the sliver of a moon peeked over the roof of Mandie's barn.

Nathaniel breathed in the scent of cherry and apple blossoms. "It was a gute time, jah? I have not been to a singing in more than two years."

"And yet you did not do so much singing."

Nathaniel chuckled. "No, I would rather listen to you sing. When you sing, the angels bid me closer to God."

"I cannot boast of myself," Kate said, glad that Nathaniel seemed to grasp what she had been trying to make Aaron understand. "My talent is not my own but one the Lord God has lent me. I fear if I bury it in the ground I am a slothful servant."

Nathaniel studied her face.

"I want to use the voice God has given me for His glory. That is the reason I went away to school—to learn how the Lord wants me to use this gift."

"But you have not found your answer?"

"No," Kate said, her voice breaking. "I have tried to do His will, but I can't help but think I have displeased Him."

"Surely not," Nathaniel insisted.

"Then perhaps He has given up on me."

Nathaniel shook his head slowly and hesitated before he spoke. "I don't believe God gives up on anybody. He didn't give up on me."

"On you?"

"Jah, I was a hard case." Nathaniel's mouth twitched into a half smile. "The day after my baptism five years ago, my dat had his stroke. I could not understand how the Lord God would allow that to happen after I had pledged my life to Him. I did not talk to God for days, so angry I was. I believed God had abandoned our family. Mamm and I still must do almost everything for Dat. He cannot walk or talk or feed himself."

"Jah, I am sorry."

"The day we brought Dat home from the hospital, Deacon Miller came to help me build a ramp for the wheelchair. My soul was so bitter, I could barely hide my hostility. The deacon saw what others had not and assured me that God had not forgotten me. 'Nathaniel, your heart is ready for God when you are in your darkest hour,' he said. 'Who shall separate us from the love of Christ? shall tribulation, or distress, or persecution, or famine, or nakedness, or peril, or sword?' I don't know why, but it was as if I heard that Scripture for the first time. That night, I asked God to help me see His love more clearly, even to see how my pain was evidence of that love."

Nathaniel wrapped the reins around his hand. "Grief is a stern teacher, but I am confident I could not have learned some lessons in any other way. For that, I am grateful. Grateful to God for loving me enough to stretch me and push me and crush me, to refine me in the furnace of affliction, to force me to stretch my faith beyond what I could see.

"God loves me more than I can possibly comprehend. He watches over me. He watches over all of us. But if the way were easy, how could we grow into who He wants us to be? How could our faith become unshakable?" He glanced at Kate then shook his head. "I am doing too much talking."

Kate tried not to let the tears slip down her cheek. "Not at all. What you say is very wise. I believe you, Nathaniel. I believe that you believe it."

"The blessed apostle Peter never wondered if walking on water was too hard. He jumped right over the side of the boat. Only when he took his eyes off Lord Jesus did he sink."

"But why will God not speak to me?"

Nathaniel shook his head. "I think when God is silent, He wants us to prove in our hearts that we are willing to follow Him no matter the cost. If all answers were crystal-clear, how could we show our devotion to Him?"

"There is a song I learned at the academy," Kate said.

"Sing it to me."

"Ach, no. It is a sin."

"Is it a sin for the sparrow to chirp in her nest? I will allow no wickedness in my buggy, you can be sure. I want to hear the song."

Hesitantly, Kate opened her mouth. She had never felt so nervous singing for anyone in her life. "I believe in the sun even when it is not shining; I believe in love even when feeling it not; I believe in God even when God is silent."

The breeze subsided as her voice floated into the sky, and even the night birds seemed to be listening.

She looked at Nathaniel. His eyes were closed and the reins had loosened in his fingers. Breathing deeply, he slowly opened his eyes. "Jah, I fear I sin by taking so much pleasure in your singing."

"I told you I should not sing."

"Kate," he said, "God will make known to you how He wants you to use this gift." He placed one hand lightly over hers. Kate held her breath. In one piercing look, he seemed to comprehend her deepest fears. "I do not know when, but I know you will find your answer, Lord willing. 'Rest in the Lord, and wait patiently for him.'"

Kate felt the truth of his words in the deepest part of her heart. Their eyes locked, and the profound silence between them seemed to draw her heart overwhelmingly close to his.

Withdrawing her hand, Kate tried to lighten the mood. "In the meantime, my brother is appalled that my rumschpringe has lasted six years and I keep returning to that worldly academy to seek fame and fortune."

The intimate moment gone, Nathaniel seemed to snap back to his happy-go-lucky self. "I can think of worse things to do during rumschpringe," he said. "Some boys buy cars or get in with a wild group of friends, and some girls get into trouble with the Englisch boys."

"Jah, I suppose you are right," Kate said. "What of your rumschpringe? Did you get into trouble?"

Nathaniel laughed. "I like to think I did not behave as foolishly as some. No, I knew very young that the *Ordnung* was the way God wanted me to live. I spent my rumschpringe reading."

"Reading?"

"Jah, three whole years of book after book, hiding them from my dat."

"What kind of books?"

"Science books, histories, medical journals. He didn't approve of some of my reading material. He didn't especially like my choice of novels, either."

"What novels?"

"Ach, whatever the librarian recommended. Dostoyevsky almost scared me off reading altogether. Hard to understand and very gloomy. *The Count of Monte Cristo* was exciting but made me sad to think how people could be so cruel to each other. My dat hated the horror ones. I read one where a shark ate something like five people, and I couldn't sleep for three nights after finishing it." He shook his head with a twinkle in his eyes. "But I am talking too much again. You will start to call me Mandie."

Kate laughed. "Only behind your back."

He silently gazed at her then lifted his hand as if he were going to touch her face. Then he seemed to think better of it and patted her awkwardly on the top of her kapp.

Tightening up on the reins, he said, "Will you allow me to see you again on Tuesday? I would rather not wait for the next gathering."

"Jah," Kate said. "That would make me very happy."

Kate's heart soared to the moon and crashed to the earth at the same time. Nathaniel was without a doubt the most appealing, most pleasing man she had ever met. How happy she would be to have him as her boyfriend. But realistically she knew she should not be so careless with her attentions. If she went back to Milwaukee, would it break his heart? Would it break hers?

Chapter Seven

Kate made sure the ribbons of her bonnet were tied tightly under her chin and broke into a full sprint down the long lane to the mailbox. Hungry for news from her friends and professors in the outside world, her favorite daily activity was checking the mail.

The cavernous metal box stood on a reinforced fence post facing the road, begging for letters. Many years ago Dat had come home with the thing, so proud that he had found it for a deeply discounted price at Weber's Market. The children used to tease their dat that their postal box could hold a set of triplets if the mailman one day felt inclined to deliver some.

Today, in its lonely interior, the mailbox held a single letter with a familiar return address. Finally, her first letter from Maria since arriving home three weeks ago. Kate ripped it open.

Dear Kate,

How are you? I'm sorry I didn't write sooner. I hope you are feeling better. You sound good in your letter. I am glad you are happy at home. My arm is okay.

The doctor says six more weeks in the cast. Alex crawls all over now, and I am on my toes all the time keeping up with him with only one arm. Yesterday Alex crawled so fast that he bumped into the table leg and got very angry. He just puts his head down and goes. He is so cute and we are much better without Jared coming over to bother us.

> *But this is the bad news. Jared is still in a coma. I've been to the hospital three times, but the doctors won't tell me anything because I'm not family.*
>
> *Try not to freak out. This is not your fault.*
>
> *Jared's mother keeps calling me. On Monday she came to my apartment and wanted to see Alex. I told her no. I was afraid she would take him. She said she is Alex's grandmamma so she has a right to take him.*
>
> *I wish you were here to tell me what to do. Mama is in Chicago, and I can't go there without losing my job. I will wait to hear from you.*
>
> *Maria*

Kate sagged against the fence post and clutched the letter to her heart. The morning after the horrible encounter, she had been so terrified and confused that she'd hopped on the first bus to Apple Lake.

Jared in a coma? How could that be? Guilt wrapped tentacles around her throat. She knew she had hurt him badly.

He'd stormed into the apartment, kicking the door open with those big boots he always wore. Kate could still remember the screaming. Some of it must have been her own.

"Don't think you can break up with me! I'll kill you first!"

It only took two blows from his bony fist to send Maria to the floor, where he would have kicked her to death if Kate hadn't hurled a book at his head. Swearing, he closed in on Kate and grabbed her by the neck.

Even two hundred miles and three weeks away from that terrible night, Kate put a hand to her throat and relived the panic of slow suffocation. Struggling fiercely to free herself, she had been seconds away from passing out when Maria attacked Jared from behind and he turned his rage on her. And so it went on for what felt like an eternity, when in reality it could only have been a minute or two as the two girls tried to fight off the violent drunk who was a good half foot taller than either of them. At one point he lunged toward the screaming baby, but Kate had flailed her arms wildly, sometimes hitting her target, and backed him away.

Knowing how ashamed her people might be if they found out, Kate still did not hold back. In one frenzied surge of terror, she threw herself into Jared with all her might, knocking him off his feet. His whole body went slack as he slammed his head into the corner of the kitchen counter. He slumped to the floor, and she landed on top of him, dazed and spent. As soon as she got her wits about her she jumped away, but he didn't move or open his eyes. Blood had slowly pooled on the floor around his head.

Kate studied the letter again as her chest heaved up and down, and she began to shiver uncontrollably. Would Jared die? She had never even considered the possibility. Was this God's punishment for her wickedness?

He commanded nonviolence from His People—even for self-defense. Nonresistance was Article Fourteen of the Confession of Faith. Better to die than to lift a hand against an enemy. She bowed her head and silently begged God to spare Jared Adams's life. Begged Him with every thought, every breath, every bit of strength she possessed, to make the man whole again, to not lay this thing to her charge. How could she ever live with herself or her community if she had blood on her hands?

Aaron is right. I am wicked.

She didn't know how long she stood there pleading with God, tears watering her despair, before four words came to her mind.

"Thy will be done."

The crux of everything. As the Lord wills, so will be. This idea, which permeated the very heart of the Amish way of life, sunk irrevocably into Kate's own heart. She had been seeking her own desires. She must put all her trust in the Lord.

Thinking back to that night and her split-second decisions, Kate knew that she would not have acted differently. She wouldn't have run away while Maria and the baby were in danger. Who was she to question whether it was the Lord's will to put her at Maria's apartment that night or to give her the strength to fight a drunken brute so he would not kill someone?

Lord willing, Jared would live. As the Lord wills, so will be.

"Be still, and know that I am God."

Kate dried her eyes, folded the letter, and slid it back into the envelope. She felt like a piece of taffy, pulled in two directions and stretched impossibly thin. Should she go back to Milwaukee to be with Maria? Should she stay here and uncover her destiny?

The answer glowed brightly in her mind. God had placed her here, and here she would stay until He nudged her another way.

Maria had slipped a photograph of Alex between the folds of the letter. On the back she had written, "He has your eyes." Kate smiled through her tears. She and Maria used to joke that Kate spent so much time caring for Alex that she was his second mother.

"Kate, are you all right?"

Kate turned around. Ada and her sister, Sarah, gawked at her from the other side of the fence. One of the disadvantages of having her older brother and his family live next door was that few things in the Weaver household were safe from Ada's keen eye. Kate wiped her face and nodded. "Hello, Ada. Hello, Sarah."

Ada looked at the letter in Kate's hand. "Bad news?"

"Just a letter from a friend in Milwaukee."

Ada clucked her tongue. "You miss that place right much, don't you? Some girls are suited for that type of thing."

Kate didn't answer.

Ada reached out and straightened a crease in Kate's apron. "You are looking healthier, Kate. Relaxation has worked wonders for your complexion."

"Denki," Kate said, doing her best to keep from frowning. She marveled that Ada could make a compliment sound like an insult. Jah, Kate's relaxation today had consisted of milking the cows, planting peas, mopping the floor, and baking four loaves of bread.

"Sarah came to help me get my spring cleaning caught after," Ada said. "You will watch my boys while we work, won't you?"

"I'm sorry, Ada. Mamma went to visit Aunt Erla, and I promised her I would finish piecing the quilt."

"I can't see how it is any trouble for you to tend to my boys while you quilt. There are always grandchildren running around over there. I am not well. My health prevents me from keeping up with those boys all day like you and Mamm can."

"Oh, jah, little boys can sure be a handful."

"It will be all right, Ada," said her sister. "I'll keep an eye on the boys and help *redd* up at the same time. We wouldn't want to interfere with Kate's plans. I will stay until we are done, even if it's late. I promise. We'll make do," Sarah said, a sigh of forbearance escaping her lips.

"We will do no such thing," Ada protested. "I'm sending those boys over, Kate."

Kate tightened her fingers around her letter, reducing it to a crinkly ball.

"You can work on the quilt while you are tending. If it's not too late, Sarah will drop by after cleaning and help with your quilt. She's as good a quilter as our mamm ever was. Just the other day Nathaniel King saw a quilt Sarah made for Luther and was amazed at how tiny and even her stitches are."

"Oh, stop, Ada," Sarah said, fixing her eyes on Kate.

"Stick me with a pin if I'm lying. Nathaniel has said more than once what a good homemaker you are, Sarah. It's no secret he admires your skills." She turned to Kate. "The skills a good Amish wife needs."

Biting her tongue on a tart reply, Kate smiled and turned her face toward home. "Sarah is wonderful gute with a needle. That stitching she did for your wedding was exquisite. I know it's wrong, but I have always envied your ability to make tiny stitches," Kate said. "My fingers are too thick. Good milking hands, Elmer says."

Sarah giggled. "They are not too thick."

"They are gute strong hands too, because when Elmer insults me like that, he usually gets punched."

"Jah, I have hit my brothers a time or two when they act ugly," Sarah said.

"I do not suppose you'll need to know how to quilt at the academy. So it's just as well you aren't very good at it," Ada said.

"Just as well," Kate said. She turned and walked quickly down the lane toward the house, saying, "Send the boys over. I will teach them some songs to pass the time."

Kate took one moment to enjoy the look on Ada's face before turning her back and striding toward the house.

I shouldn't have said that. Time to go home and repent right-quick.

Chapter Eight

Nathaniel ran his hand tenderly along the unfinished block of walnut, one of the most expensive pieces of wood he had ever purchased. Closing his eyes, he breathed in the earthy scent of wood fresh from the lumber mill. This was a special piece, one he would take great care in shaping.

The small room in which he stood served as his private workshop, where he made cradles, tables, and other furniture for family and friends. The larger rooms next door housed his cabinet business, employing a dozen men and taking in more orders every month. Amish workmanship was highly sought after by the Englisch, and Nathaniel was glad for it. The more business he attracted, the more men he could employ—men working to keep their farms and homes, and care for their families.

Meticulously, he made the measurements, looked at his drawings, and checked the measurements again, determined that not one mistake, not one imperfection would mar his efforts. Even at the risk of being proud, Nathaniel wanted this work to be his finest ever. For her.

The door opened behind him, and he turned around to see Mamm, hands on her hips, surveying the room. "You have not worked here for a long time," she said.

"Jah, I have been occupied with the business. And Dat," he said, putting down his pencil and smiling at his mother. "Did the baby come along well?"

"Feet first, kicking all the way. A fighting, fit, gute son for the Yoders.

But if I had known the child was wrong-side down, I would have sent Rosanna to the hospital. Too much can go wrong in such a delivery."

"You are a good midwife, Mamm. The mothers trust your skill."

His mother approached his worktable and touched the block of wood on top. "Walnut. Very expensive. What are you making?"

"A rocking chair."

"Who is it for?"

Nathaniel hesitated. "I think I will give it to my future wife, if the Lord God sees fit to grant me one."

"Oh, my son," Mamm said, coming near and placing her hand on his shoulder, "it is no mystery who you took home from the singing on Sunday. But only *I* know why you haven't been to one in more than two years."

"I suppose you do," Nathaniel said, reluctant to hear what else he knew she would say.

"Kate Weaver has wings on her feet. She will not be here come autumn time." Mamm cradled his chin in her hand. "Why do you want to break your heart again?"

"She never even knew me before, Mamm. This time is different."

"Is it?"

"For two years I have waited for the day when she would return. Now that she is here, can you blame me for hoping?"

His mother ran her thumb over his cheek. "I would never blame you. You deserve everything the Almighty blesses you with. I blame her. What happens when she flies off to Milwaukee and never returns?"

"It will be some consolation knowing I wore myself out trying to win her."

"Will it? When your dreams lie on the floor like a pile of wood shavings, will you be glad you gave your heart to her?"

Nathaniel stood and pulled his mother into an embrace. "I cannot give up chasing after happiness simply because there might be pain down the road. For the joy of having her as my wife, I am willing to do this. I know the risk, Mamm. I want to take it."

Mamm pulled away from him and wiped her eyes. "And what of her life out of our community? The women are whispering about almost nothing else. How much trouble did she get into there? What kind of a girl is she, really? She is not one of us."

Nathaniel gave his mamm a sharp look. "Who is talking about almost nothing else? Gossip is a sin, Mamm."

Mamm lowered her eyes. "You are right. Not everyone is talking. But my sister says—"

"Why do you listen to the tongue-wagging?" Nathaniel said, sitting and ostensibly studying his drawings.

"You know very well you could have your pick of any Amish girl in Wisconsin. And there is not one mother in the district who would not want you as a son-in-law."

Nathaniel chuckled. "Now you exaggerate."

Mamm did not give up. "Oh, Nathaniel, are you blind? Kate Weaver has tasted the pleasures of the world and will never be content with a simple life."

"I have already told you," Nathaniel said mildly, "I know the risk." Without looking at her, he caught his mother's hand and squeezed it lovingly. "Please do not worry, Mamm."

"For as long as I am your mother and you are my only child, I will worry and hope and pray for you. Do not ask the impossible."

Nathaniel nodded. "Then I ask you to let me choose my own path."

Mamm's expression changed, and she walked slowly around the table and took a closer look at Nathaniel's wood. "You are a gifted carpenter. It will be a beautiful rocker. I hope the girl you make it for is worthy of such fine work."

"She is. More than you know."

"I hope so," Mamm said. "With all my heart." After giving him one solemn look, she walked to the door of the workshop. "I'm going to read to Dat for a few minutes. Then will you put him to bed?"

"Jah, I will be right in." Nathaniel laid his hand on the piece of wood and looked up at his mother. "I love you, *mei mutter*."

"I love you, too, Nathaniel."

Mamm closed the door, and nothing but the hissing of the propane lamp interrupted the silence. The stillness amplified Nathaniel's thoughts. He was fully aware that his heart galloped far ahead. What if Kate had succumbed to the temptations of the outside world? How well did he know her, really? Was she still the girl he fell in love with, or did he only think he loved her?

No, Nathaniel could not bring himself to believe that Kate was anything but the lovely, virtuous girl he had dreamed about for so many months. A simple change of location on her part could not change the person she was. In such a place as Milwaukee, she had experiences Nathaniel probably couldn't even imagine, but he was certain deep in his soul that Kate had not cheapened herself in any way.

He carried his piece of wood to the saw table and began, carefully, to cut it to the size he needed.

Greater concerns tormented Nathaniel. His chance of failure was great. What if Kate chose another young man? Even though she was considered somewhat of an outsider, her beauty and kindness won over even the most hardened skeptic. The proof was blatantly evident at the gathering, where boys surrounded her all night. With so many eligible young men, Nathaniel was unsure of his ability to win Kate's heart. But he could only be the person the Lord God intended him to be. If Kate couldn't love him for the man he was, then he couldn't see sharing a life with her.

His worst fear was that Kate would decide to return to the academy, leave the community, and be lost to him forever. The very thought of such a possibility threatened to drag him down into deep despair. His hopes had skyrocketed on the day of Kate's return, but, as his mother warned him, he might be as worthless as a pile of wood chips come autumn. In spite of everything, he was determined to pursue a life with Kate Weaver until she chose differently.

But what if God chose differently?

Chapter Nine

"No one has ever taken me to the dairy on a date before," Kate said. She sat under an ancient willow tree with Nathaniel, a small bag of cheese curds cradled in her lap. Even in mid-May, it was nice enough to sit outside. The lawn in front of the dairy store was starting to green up from winter dormancy, with plenty of room for tourists or locals to picnic. A footbridge straddled a small stream meandering through the grass, and more than one willow grew along its banks.

Nathaniel stretched out his long legs. "What? None of your Englisch boyfriends were clever enough to plan an outing to the dairy?"

Kate tapped her finger to her temple. "Let's see. Since I can count the number of Englisch boyfriends I had on zero fingers, the answer is no. Just when did you develop this passion for cheese making?"

"I have always had a fascination for mold."

Kate laughed then offered him her bag of curds. "These were worth the entire trip. My newly discovered favorite food: jalapeño cheese curds."

Nathaniel made a face. "No, thanks. I feel like I am chewing rubber."

Kate plastered him with an indignant eye. "I never would have let you buy these if I had known. I cannot eat the whole bag."

"You are doing a gute job." Nathaniel chuckled as Kate cuffed him on the shoulder.

Kate motioned toward the gift shop attached to Eicher's Dairy. "We are the only Amish folk here," she said. "The tourists are gute business."

"Jah, I think the sign attracts them."

Kate read the large billboard standing above the dairy entrance. "'Eicher's Dairy. Monroe County's only authentic, organic Amish dairy. Always smooth, always creamy.'"

"It is wonderful-gute how many adjectives you can pack into one advertisement," Nathaniel said.

Kate kept reading. "'Milk, cheese, curds, cider, venison jerky, and quilts.' Cider from the Weavers' apples, I'll have you know."

"Jah, of course. I don't eat anything but Weaver apples." Nathaniel rolled onto his stomach, propped his chin in his hand, and gazed at Kate until his piercing eyes compelled her to look away. "Can I show you something?" he said.

"Of course," Kate said, glad to be able to reply with some semblance of composure. What was it about Nathaniel's stare that knocked her breathless and sent her head spinning into a jumble of random thoughts?

Nathaniel jumped to his feet and jogged in the direction of his buggy. Kate smiled at his boundless enthusiasm.

He returned carrying what looked like a small wooden box. When he came closer, Kate could see it was a miniature house complete with windows and a tiny front door. Without a word but grinning from ear to ear, he laid the house in her lap and sank next to her on the grass.

"Oy, anyhow!" Kate ran her fingers along the individually crafted shingles on the detailed roof and peeked inside the shuttered windows.

"Look at this," she said, as she swung the door open and shut on its little hinges.

"It's a birdhouse," he said. "There is an opening in the back so the birds don't have to learn how to open the door to get in, and there's a ledge to keep out the squirrels too."

Kate stroked the smooth walls and grooved shutters. "I have never seen anything so beautiful," she whispered.

Nathaniel beamed. "I thought you could hang it on one of the fence posts down your lane. With a good sturdy foundation, you can see it out the kitchen window."

Kate breathed in sharply. "*Oh, sis yusht!* Nathaniel. I cannot accept this. How many hours it must have taken you to make!"

Nathaniel's shoulders slumped, and he looked like a farmer whose crops were destroyed by hail. "You do not want it?"

"I like being with you just to be with you. Not because you bring me something."

His concern melted into a smile. "You like being with me?"

"Jah, certainly."

He contemplated that notion for a moment. "That is the nicest thing I have ever heard."

"Ever?"

"Certainly in the last ten years."

"Gute, then you understand you don't have to bring me gifts."

"But the first present I tried to give you went horribly wrong. I am trying to make up for it."

"And what present was that?"

"The kiss, of course. I liked you, so I naturally thought you must like me and were hoping for a kiss. But instead, you slugged me."

Kate nodded her head in satisfaction. "You deserved it. That was the worst moment of my life. At least in my eleven-year-old life."

Nathaniel grimaced. "The worst moment of your life. I have to live with that on my conscience." He picked up a pebble from the ground and rolled it around in his palm, his eyes glued to his hand. "Especially since it was the best moment of mine."

Kate giggled. "The best? Poor boy. You have led a very boring life."

He grinned. "Unfortunate but true. And, ach, how I have regretted it since."

"Of course you regret it. I hit you very hard."

He sat up and studied her face. "I regret that my actions hurt and embarrassed you. I would do anything to change that."

"I was eleven, Nathaniel. Exactly half my lifetime ago. I think I can move past it now, don't you?"

"You did allow me to bring you to Eicher's Dairy today. This is progress. Perhaps next week I will try taking you to Burger King." Nathaniel's eyes flickered with mischief, and he scattered grass on Kate's shoulder. "There has been a gross misunderstanding, though. I made this birdhouse for your mamm. You would not refuse a gift for your mamm, would you?"

Kate couldn't suppress a smile. "You are a rascal, Nathaniel King, and jah, my mamm would love a birdhouse." She put a hand up to halt his rejoicings. "But don't give her any more gifts, either, unless you are ready for a stern scolding."

Chapter Ten

Kate ambled down the road, her basket hanging casually over her arm as she hummed "O Mio Babbino." Dat couldn't spare the buggy, so she was forced to walk the five miles to the Millers' house. Not that she minded. The crisp spring afternoon provided perfect weather for a stroll, and the long walk gave her plenty of time to be alone with her jumbled thoughts.

After "O Mio" she favored the fence posts with the "Queen of the Night" aria. The energetic tune inspired her to skip along the pavement. With every stanza, the sound got bigger and the dancing became livelier. "The Doll Song" was accompanied by hand waving and toe tapping that put Kate completely out of breath.

That must have been why she didn't hear the buggy come up behind her.

"Kate Weaver, what do you think you are about?"

Kate turned to see a buggy stopped in the middle of the road with two women staring curiously from the front seat.

Grinning, Edna Miller held tightly to the reins of her horse and leaned out of the buggy like a tree bent in the wind. "You better climb in here before someone sees you wildly flailing about, liebe. Someone besides me and my sister. We don't count, do we, Naomi?"

Naomi and her legendary sour disposition sat next to her sister with her arms folded and a prominent frown plastered on her face. "I think we count for plenty," she said.

"Denki," Kate said as she began to climb into the buggy.

"*Nae*, nae, sit in front," Edna said. "The back is loaded with Luke's stuff. That man is the worst pack rat I ever knew."

Kate squeezed into the front seat next to Naomi, who didn't seem to want to scoot over one bit for an unwelcome guest. Good thing all three of them were on the skinny side. Edna urged the horse forward.

"You are very kind to offer me a ride," Kate said. "I was actually coming to your house."

"My house? I am honored," Edna said. "But it is such a long walk—especially if you dance all the way."

"Acting awfully wild, if you ask me," Naomi said, sniffing the air as if expecting to pick up the scent of sin.

"Don't be rude, Naomi." Edna eyed Kate and smiled. "We're coming from my daughter Lizzie's house. The new baby isn't taking well to the nursing, and you should see Lizzie's timid husband. As helpless as a kitten in a canal."

"Oh, that is too bad," Kate said, trying to ignore the hostility oozing from Naomi as she stared unabashedly at Kate.

Edna glanced at her sister and sighed. "Lizzie will get the hang of it. That first little buplie is always so hard to nurse. "

Kate swallowed hard. "How is Lizzie feeling after the new baby?"

"Ach, poorly to be sure. The midwife said it was a hard delivery. Lizzie probably should have been in a hospital, but she's a little afraid of them. And she wanted to have her first baby at home. But with Naomi taking care of her, she'll be fit as a fiddle in no time. Naomi has a healer's touch. If she would show a cheery disposition once in a while, she wouldn't scare off so many patients."

Naomi leaned her elbow on her knee and pinned Kate with an accusatory stare. "It is high time you stopped all this nonsense."

Edna sighed again, louder. "Naomi, please."

"'Resist the devil, and he will flee from you,'" Naomi said.

Edna nudged her sister with her elbow. "Do you remember how we talked about sticking our nose into other people's business?"

Naomi snorted. "I'm simply saying what everybody is thinking."

Edna prodded the horse to go faster. "Naomi, Kate is a good girl. Shame on you for prying. Let's talk about something less distressing, like the dysentery epidemic in Africa."

Stifling a smile, Kate tucked a loose lock of hair under her kapp. "Nae, Edna, it is all right. I know what people must be thinking about me. But that is why we have rumschpringe—so young people can decide for themselves."

Naomi folded her arms and harrumphed. "It is shameful when children use the rumschpringe as an excuse for gross wickedness."

Kate found the courage to put her arm around Naomi, who looked at her as if she were a creature from another planet. "My Amish faith and my desire to sing have struggled with each other for many years. I want to know God's will for my life. If I want an answer, I have to do my part to get one. 'Faith without works is dead.'"

Naomi shrugged Kate's arm from her shoulders. "I can tell you right now: God wants you to be baptized."

"How do you know?" Kate said.

"Because He wants everyone to be baptized."

Edna clicked her tongue in indignation. "Naomi, do not presume to counsel the Almighty. You do not know."

"Here is where God has placed her. She should not seek to leave her place."

"Maybe the Almighty placed her here to struggle," Edna said. "He gave her a beautiful voice, didn't He?"

"But where does the wickedness end with that sort of life?" Naomi pressed a finger into Kate's arm. "I will tell you. It ends in your destruction."

The buggy jerked to a halt, and Edna breathed a sigh of relief. "To your house already, Naomi. Denki for coming with me."

Kate practically leaped out of the buggy. Naomi scooted over and slid slowly to the ground, grunting and panting as she went. When she steadied herself on her own two feet, she shook her finger in Kate's face. "Mark my words. The path you are on leads to nowhere but hell, young lady."

"Good-bye, Naomi. I'll be here at seven tomorrow morning," Edna chirped.

Kate climbed back into the buggy and Edna snapped the reins before Kate could even plant herself firmly in the seat. As they drove away, they watched Naomi hobble to her front door in her orthopedic shoes.

"I hope you will forgive Naomi," Edna said. "She tells it how she sees it, and sometimes she doesn't wear her glasses."

Kate managed a half smile. "You might not believe this, but all opinions are welcome. My dat would say that the ones that make me uncomfortable are the ones I should pay most attention to."

"Most young people are not mature enough to see the truth in that." Edna winked at Kate. "Naomi often has sensible opinions, but the way she delivers them chases away all but the most humble."

The *clip-clop* of the horse's hooves changed to a muffled crunching as they turned from the paved street to the gravel road that led to Edna's house.

"What's in the basket?" Edna asked.

"I brought you a loaf of bread and a jar of apple butter," Kate said, lifting the cloth draped over her basket.

"Bread and a visit. This really is an honor."

"I need some advice."

"Ah, shall I take you back to Naomi's? She hands out advice like trees hand out leaves in the fall."

Kate grinned and shook her head. "Maybe some other time."

"You come to counsel with Luke?"

"Nae, I want *your* advice."

"Me? I am not qualified to give advice to anyone," Edna said. "I am a simple Amish housewife who knows how to get my laundry clean, milk my cows, and cook a filling meal. Your mamma can do all of those things better than I."

"But you left the community once. During rumschpringe."

Edna nodded and pursed her lips. "I suppose I did."

"And you are the bishop's wife."

"Ach, what do I know as the bishop's wife? Luke does the ministering. I tend the house." She waved her hand dismissively. "Besides, I am not *your* bishop's wife."

"Bishop Schwartz is my sister-in-law Ada's father. It seems strange to go to him."

"Perhaps."

"I want to know why you left Apple Lake and why you came back. Or is it rude to ask something so personal?"

"Nae, but I do not talk about it much. It was such a long time ago. But Luke loves to tell the story."

"He does?"

"Oh, jah, he puffs out his chest and struts around because I chose him over a very handsome Englischer."

Kate pictured Luke Miller. A fine, gute man, but not handsome. His bushy eyebrows dominated his round face, and his cheeks were pockmarked with the scars of teenage acne.

"Todd Bryson was a sight. Curly golden hair and blue, blue eyes. I loved him—as much as an eighteen-year-old girl can know about love. He asked me to go to Chicago with him and a group of friends to live and find jobs."

"And you went."

"Your vision can cloud over when you are in love. I did not think of my family or my future. I wanted to be with him." She pinned Kate with a stern eye. "But I want you to know, I did not do anything to shame myself. I lived with some of the other girls. And he in an apartment of boys."

"How long were you there?"

"Not long. Luke came storming into town about three months later and gave me an ultimatum. 'I will wait no longer for you, Edna Schrock. There's three other girls back home if you'll not have me.'"

"What did you say?"

"I yelled at him. He yelled at me. We made so much noise, the upstairs neighbors pounded on the ceiling. And then he kissed me right on the mouth and I thought I'd died and gone to heaven. I packed up my things and came home with him, and we haven't ever once yelled at each other since we were married."

"One kiss changed your mind?" Kate said.

"Nae, that was more like the icing on the cake. About two minutes after I got to Chicago, I realized what I had left behind. The exciting world outside of Apple Lake wasn't all that exciting. It was loud and rude and frantic." Edna regarded Kate with a perceptive eye. "You know what I am talking about."

Kate nodded.

Edna patted Kate's arm. "The Plain life is simple and slow, but it is not for everyone. The way we live requires great sacrifice. We sacrifice the self to find God. 'He that loveth his life shall lose it; and he that hateth his life in this world shall keep it unto life eternal.'"

"It is so different from where I have been the last two years," Kate said. "Selfishness there is encouraged. My professor scolded me once for letting someone else in line ahead of me during an audition."

"Jah, I can imagine."

"But the Amish way isn't the only choice that requires sacrifice. I love to sing, but if I choose the academy, I will be separated from my family. It will never be what it was."

"I do not know what to say to you, Kate, except that my family is the most important thing in the world to me. That is what I learned those few weeks in Chicago. I could never give up my family." Edna studied Kate out of the corner of her eyes. "Then again, I cannot carry a tune in a bucket. So I never faced your dilemma."

"Will I go to hell?" Kate said quietly. That seemed to be Naomi's opinion.

"Oh, sis yusht! What an idea! If you choose to follow your music, then believe in God and live a good life. I cannot believe you will go to hell. But decide now how it will be. If you leave after you are baptized and have made your pledge to God, that is another story. But before? Of course not."

Kate hadn't realized how tense she was until she looked down at the balled-up fists in her lap. She relaxed her shoulders and took a deep breath. "That is what I wanted to know."

Edna was thoughtful for a minute. "You say you need experiences."

"Jah."

"Then come with me tomorrow to the rehabilitation center. Naomi and I volunteer there once a week."

"I don't think Naomi will welcome my presence."

"Ach, that girl has had a bee in her bonnet since nineteen-seventy-three. Don't mind her."

"Then I would love to come with you."

"Gute. I will pick you up at seven-ten. And don't be late. Tardiness puts Naomi in a bad mood. And you don't want to see her in a bad mood."

Kate laughed. Edna could summon mirth from a funeral gathering.

Chapter Eleven

Dear Kate,

So, an interesting Amish guy? Is he hot? I will miss you desperately if you decide to be baptized, but knowing your disposition, you would be very happy there.

Jared's condition deteriorated this week. I am so frightened and upset. They still won't let me see him, and his mother is demanding more time with Alex. How can I keep Jared's mother away from my baby? I have never had the forgiving heart you possess. I hate his whole family. But I think of you and try to be kind. It hasn't worked so far, but I am trying.

If you come back to school in September, you're welcome to live with me. My brother says he will pick you up and bring you to Milwaukee anytime you want. I think he has a crush on you.

Maria

Kate folded her letter and stuffed it into her apron pocket. But she brooded over its contents while she browsed the rows of quilts. She looked up as an Englisch couple in Bermuda shorts and sunglasses crossed the threshold of Martha Mullet's quilt shop.

"Take a look, Vivian," said the man as he removed his floppy hat. "If you can't find a quilt in here, you are the most persnickety person in the world."

Kate moved away from the new customers, losing herself deeper among the dozens of quilts hung in neat rows around the shop. There were a fair amount of quilt shops in Apple Lake—many Plain folk had stores attached to their homes or on their property—but none were as large or well-stocked as Martha's. She carried quilts made by local Amish as well as inventory from as far away as Pennsylvania and Ontario. Her store sat in the heart of downtown Apple Lake—if four street corners could be classified as downtown—and attracted a plentiful tourist business.

"Can I help you find something, Kate?" Martha adjusted a lopsided quilt on the hanger and glanced at the customers who had just entered her shop. "Before the crowds get heavy?"

"Denki. Anna and I are making a baby quilt, and I am looking for ideas."

Martha pointed to the back corner of the store. "Any of our designs would make a nice baby quilt, but our smaller ones are over there if you want to take a look. I got a new pattern from my cousin in Lancaster that is a variation of the log cabin. So cute. Let me know if you need anything—although the afternoon rush is about to start and you might not be able to find me before nightfall."

Kate smiled. "I will manage."

Martha bustled over to the awestruck customers standing in the center of the shop. "Can I help you find a quilt?"

Kate strolled up and down the rows of quilts, her eyes feasting on the vibrant colors. She marveled at the intricate appliqué designs, each so unique and so skillfully crafted. Appliqué was completely beyond Kate's abilities. Just like she had told Sarah Schwartz—gute milking hands but unfit for quilting.

What *was* she good at? She liked to garden and can and even do laundry. But what was she good at?

The answer was obvious. She was good at singing. And in this community, they couldn't care less. Sometimes she felt about as small as an ant on a watermelon.

Her mouth twitched upward at the sight of a bright pink and green watermelon appliqued on a nearby quilt. Not always that small. During her visit to the rehabilitation center with Edna and Naomi, she sang opera songs to several patients, Amish and others, and got nothing but sincere gratitude in return. One elderly woman told Kate her singing took the pain away and asked her to hurry back. Was this how she should be using her talents?

No matter what Aaron or Ada or anyone else believed about her motives, she yearned to know the mind of Heavenly Father concerning her life. When she peeled away the layers of her choices, His will lay at the heart of it all. She would do anything God asked of her. That intense yearning was the reason Nathaniel said she would surely get an answer. "'If any of you lack wisdom, let him ask of God, that giveth to all men liberally, and upbraideth not, and it shall be given him,'" he had repeated to her on more than one occasion.

Running her hand over a charming pink-and-purple quilt on one of the tables, Kate decided it would be the perfect pattern. Not too difficult but quite beautiful. She lifted it from the pile and found a place to sit on a small wooden chair tucked between two rows of plump quilts. The pattern was a series of butterflies cleverly sewn from a combination of squares and triangles. Kate smiled. She could stitch straight lines with proficiency. Matching corners was another story, but Anna could see to those details.

"Titus put my sewing machine into good shape again. Gute thing, because the girls need new school dresses for the fall."

Two ladies—Kate couldn't tell whom—wandered down the row behind her. She listened to their friendly chatter as she drew the butterfly pattern into her notebook. She didn't really pay attention to what they said until she heard her name.

"Our church is at Weavers', Lord willing. They have a nice big room for it."

"Weavers'? Have you seen Kate Weaver since her return? They say she had a time of it in Milwaukee. Someone beat her up."

Kate held her breath and clutched her hands together to keep from trembling.

"Oh, Lisa, she looked something terrible. And she is such a pretty girl too. Her dat was fit to be tied."

"Seeing as how she probably bears the guilt of it. He should have put his foot down when she wanted to go off to that academy," said Lisa. "My Adam never would have stood for it."

"What choice did Solomon have? He could not very well lock her in the house if she set her heart on going. Oh, look at this one. A double wedding ring."

Kate slunk down in her chair for fear of being seen.

"That girl always had a rebellious spirit, Diann. Even in primary school I could see it—wanted to show off her talent and put herself above others simply because she could sing. Too vain for her own good."

Kate bit her lip as a growing ache throbbed in her chest.

"She was proud of her talent." A quilt swished close to Kate's head. "But is there one among us who has not been guilty of pride? Kate is young. She will learn."

"I reckon she learned plenty at that academy," Lisa said. "Ada told me she came back worldly and headstrong." She lowered her voice. "Her dat must stiffen his spine and do what needs to be done to rein her in."

"Poor Emma, to have such a daughter."

"Miriam says the girl loves the world too much to be content with the Plain life. It is better that she leave us than stay and influence the young people."

Kate realized whom she was overhearing. Miriam was Nathaniel King's mother, and Lisa Fisher was Miriam's sister.

"But has anyone tried to help her? Bring her back to the love of Christ?" Diann said.

"It would do no good to try," Lisa said. "She has already dug her hole deep enough. Unfortunately, my nephew has caught her eye, but we pray that will come to nothing. All Miriam can hope is that Kate will stay away from him."

Kate held her breath as she heard the two women move away. She had to flee before the sob that wanted to escape her lips gave her away. She slung the butterfly quilt over the chair and bolted for the door, making sure to keep her head low so that no one would catch a glimpse of her face before she managed to make her exit.

How could people say such things about her parents—two of the kindest, most charitable people in the world? Kate had never known Dat to raise his voice in anger or to rule his children with force or fear. His hurt was tangible when Kate left home for the academy, but he had never upbraided or pressured her. He gave her wings in hopes that she would fly back to him of her own accord.

My dat is five times the father of any man in this community, she wanted to scream. They should be ashamed to speak of him so.

Kate hurried outside and ducked into the narrow alley between buildings before tears soaked her cheeks and the hurt bubbled over into loud sobs from her lips. Did everyone talk about her like this, clicking their tongues and shaking their heads in resignation, as if Kate were some lost cause beyond help or redemption? Did they all wish, like Miriam, that Kate would go back to Milwaukee and leave them alone, never again to disturb their peace?

She leaned her back against the side of the shop and let her head fall back until it rested on the wall behind her. Would her absence be the best thing for everyone? Would anyone miss her if she were gone?

A soft voice intruded into her thoughts. "In that position, your tears run straight into your ears. Then your hearing gets all sloshy." The words were teasing, playful, but when Nathaniel King said them, they felt like a caress against her skin.

She stood up straight and quickly wiped away any evidence that she had been crying. A futile gesture, since he had already seen her, but one that made her feel more presentable.

He came to her and laid a gentle hand on her shoulder. Eyes brimming with concern, he studied her face. He lifted his hand, hesitated for a moment, then took his thumb and wiped a single tear from her cheek. "Oh, Kate," was all he said.

The compassion in his voice ambushed her and the tears flowed anew, unchecked down her cheeks. Maybe there was one person in Apple Lake who would miss her if she were gone.

"Quilt shops aren't usually a touching experience for me," he said, "but take me into a lumberyard among the two-by-fours and freshly cut planks and I weep like a baby. The new wood smell always gets me right here." He tapped his chest with his fist.

Kate laughed through her tears. "I think it was the bear-claw pattern on that quilt hanging in the window that inspired me. I could never look at a burgundy red without having a deeply emotional experience."

"Here," Nathaniel said, putting his hand into his pocket. He pulled out a crisp white handkerchief and handed it to Kate. "I carry this with me wherever I go."

"It comes in handy," Kate said, sniffing and mopping up the moisture from her face.

"And not just for wiping faces. You can use it for a bandage and tourniquet if you cut off your finger with a circular saw. Or if you stuff one end of it into your hat, it hangs down to prevent sunburn." He motioned with his hands how to stuff it into a hat. "And if you are an old lady, you can use it to wave to people who are leaving on trips. My *grandmammi* wouldn't be caught dead waving at someone without her hanky. She insisted on the handkerchief method. I think it used to be one of the original Confessions of Faith."

"You truly need nothing else in your pocket to be perfectly happy," Kate said, feeling steadily better.

Grinning, Nathaniel stuck his hand into his pocket again. "Well, not entirely true." He withdrew his fist and showed Kate. "Without fail, I carry four things in this pocket. The handkerchief, in case I encounter a pretty girl crying in the street; breath mints, in case I want to talk to that pretty girl; a pocketknife, because I might want to clean my fingernails; and my travel-sized measuring tape, because you never know when you're going to want to measure something."

"Like the quilts in Martha's shop," Kate said.

"Or the wheels on that buggy over there," Nathaniel said, pointing in the direction of the street.

"Or how big that tree is."

Nathaniel nodded. "Or how big my neck is. That always impresses the girls."

Giggling, Kate wadded the handkerchief in her fist and leaned against the wall. "And how many girls have asked to measure your neck?"

"Ach, too many to count."

Nathaniel leaned closer to Kate and placed his hand on the wall twelve inches above her head. His smile, which had faded when he first encountered her, returned with full force, sending Kate's senses reeling. "I love it when you laugh," he said.

Suddenly shy, Kate lowered her eyes. "Nathaniel King, do not embarrass me."

They both heard someone clear her throat and looked up to see Nathaniel's aunt Lisa and another woman staring at them.

Kate stiffened.

Nathaniel immediately removed his hand from the wall but kept the dazzling smile constant on his lips. "Hello, Aunt Lisa, Diann. Do you know Kate Weaver?"

Lisa glanced at Kate then back at Nathaniel. "A single man who has been baptized, such as yourself, must watch himself carefully. You cannot flit about the town doing whatever you want, seeing whoever you want."

Nathaniel seemed genuinely puzzled at such an onslaught, but his smile stayed put. "Denki, I will live by that advice."

"Gute," said Lisa. "Now you can walk me home."

When Nathaniel hesitated, she said, "Cum, cum. I need your arm to support me."

"But Lisa," said Diann, "we came in your buggy."

Lisa shot Diann a look. "I can fetch it later."

Diann squinted her eyes and wrinkled her nose. "Now that is plain silly." She nudged Lisa with an elbow. "Leave your nephew to his private conversation and drive us home. I've got laundry yet to look after."

Lisa relented. "Very well," she said. She peered at Nathaniel, obviously trying to sear a hole into his forehead. "Mark my words." She shook her finger at him. "Mark my words."

Both women continued down the street and were soon out of sight.

Nathaniel held out his hand. "Could I borrow that hanky?"

Kate handed him the slightly damp piece of cloth.

He waved the handkerchief in the air like a flag. "I surrender, Aunt Lisa. I surrender." Smiling at Kate, he folded the handkerchief and put it back in his pocket. "Very gute. We have found a new use for the handkerchief. Oh, wait. Do you still need it?"

"Nae," Kate said. "Unless you want to take me into a grocery store. Lettuce always makes me teary."

"I will not take you to any distressing places," Nathaniel said. "But would you care for a short outing to my farm? It is only a fifteen-minute walk across the fields."

The thought of an encounter with Nathaniel's mamm coupled with the memory of all she'd heard in the quilt shop stomped on her momentary happiness and, try as she might, she found it impossible to hold back new tears.

Nathaniel's troubled expression reemerged. "I hate to see you like this." He softly brushed another tear from her face. "Tell me what I can do."

"Ach, it is nothing. A long walk will do me very much gute, I think."

"And you can water the fields as we go. The farmers will be grateful." He grinned and winked at her. "There is the smile I've been so eager for."

Kate sniffed. "Do you think we could avoid seeing your mamm today? I look like I've been crying."

Nathaniel nodded thoughtfully. "We don't have to go into the house. I want to show you something in the barn."

"Absolutely not, Nathaniel King. Every time you say you want to show me something, you give me a gift. I will not stand for it," she said, smiling to herself at his crestfallen expression.

He spread his hands to show he had nothing to hide. "Why are you so suspicious?"

"Because I know you too well."

He didn't reply but casually took her hand and led her out of the alleyway. The unexpected gesture unnerved her.

As soon as they were to the street, however, he released his grip. "I will not hold your hand in public." His eyes twinkled with mischief. "Like Aunt Lisa said, I must watch myself."

It was a pleasantly warm walk to the Kings' property. With the sunlight soaking through Kate's black bonnet, she almost felt like herself again. She picked up a stick and tapped each fence post along the lane.

"I heard from my professor yesterday," she said. "I got the highest rating ever by an academy student at the Padlow vocal competition."

Nathaniel looked at her out of the corner of his eye and gave her a belated smile. "Congratulations. But I am not surprised. I've always known you were very, very gute."

"I do not mean to brag." She shook her head. "I suppose I am bragging, but you and Elmer are the only two who care about my singing. I like to share the good news with someone."

She could see the muscles of his jaw tighten but the smile stayed in place. "I want you to share—everything. Otherwise, half of yourself would be a stranger to me."

They ducked into the cool barn and let their eyes adjust to the dimness. Kate's fears of meeting up with Nathaniel's mamm lessened. The barn sat almost a quarter mile from the house.

"We only have one cow," he said. "And three horses." He walked to the corner and tapped on the buggy standing there. "And a special buggy for Dat and his wheelchair. We don't take it out often, except for church."

"Where is your workshop?"

"Attached to the house. Dat built the barn out here because Mamm didn't want to be bothered with the flies."

"Or the smell, probably," Kate said, gazing at the bales of hay stacked neatly against one wall.

"Cum," said Nathaniel, barely able to contain his excitement. "Will you allow me to show you something?"

Kate groaned. "Ach. Very well, even though my better judgment tells me you are up to no good."

He motioned for her to follow and led her to an unused stall. Among the soft mounds of hay sat a black-and-white cat surrounded by seven kittens—two jet-black and five black-and-white mixes.

Forgetting her troubles, Kate squealed in delight and knelt down for a better look. "Can I hold them?" she asked.

"Jah, of course. They are ready to leave their mother. She does not mind."

Choosing one of the solid black ones, she picked it up and nuzzled it against her cheek. The kitten mewed quietly. "Oh, it is so soft. Look at his tiny nose and tiny paws."

Almost forgetting Nathaniel was there, Kate fussed over the kittens, holding and petting them one at a time, giving them temporary names, and talking to them as if she were carrying on a conversation with one of her brothers. She sat cross-legged and let all seven of them crawl around her lap.

"Aren't you sweet," she said, picking up the other black one, the smallest of the litter. "Are your brothers and sisters nice to you? You tell them to be nice or Auntie Kate will scold them."

Nathaniel, who was standing with his elbows draped over the stall door, chuckled in amusement. "You should be their mother. They don't get this much attention from her."

Kate stifled a grin. "Quit your teasing, Nathaniel King, or I will have to scold you too."

Nathaniel left his perch and squatted next to Kate.

Welcoming his closeness, she laid a hand on his arm. "Denki for bringing me here today. This is just what I needed."

His eyes held a tenderness Kate had not seen before. "Do you like them?" he asked, almost in a whisper.

"I love them."

"Gute. Which one do you want?"

"You want to give me one?"

"Jah. They are weaned now."

Kate snapped her head up to glare at Nathaniel then plopped the kitten next to its mother. "Wait a minute. You almost tricked me."

Nathaniel shrugged innocently. "Trick you?"

"You promised no more gifts."

"This isn't really a gift. I have to find a good home for each of these kittens. You would be doing me a favor by taking one off my hands."

Kate didn't for a minute believe his story about needing to get rid of the kittens, and her practical side told her she should stand her ground. But kittens loved unconditionally and never gossiped or chastised someone for being too worldly. And she didn't really want to resist

Nathaniel's enchanting smile or the way he looked at her like she was the only person in the world. Was it the warm tone of his voice that sent chills down her spine? Surrender seemed her only option.

"You are so thoughtful, Nathaniel. I would be very happy for a kitten."

He gazed at the kittens for a long while then looked away and stared out the high window. "Denki, Nightingale," he whispered. "Denki."

Chapter Twelve

Kate cuddled the furry black kitten in one hand while pouring fresh milk with the other. The kitten mewed and fussed until Kate set the tiny animal on the floor. She stroked her finger lightly over the kitten's head while it lapped up its breakfast from one of Mamma's cereal bowls.

"And what do you think you have there?" Mamma said as she came into the kitchen.

Kate gave her mother a half smile. "It is a gift, Mamma."

"A gift! Another gift from that boy I am not supposed to know about? If he wants to be secretive about his courting, he should think better about bringing you a present every time he comes."

"They are not just for me, Mamma, or I would never have accepted them," Kate said. "They are for all the family."

Mamma laughed. "Ach, does that young man think I just fell off the turnip truck? Soon I will have to move out of the house to make room for all the gifts that aren't really yours." Mamma bustled over to the kitten and bent down to run her hand over its soft fur. "Did you tell him I am not keen on animals in the house?"

"I did not have the heart. He was so excited to give it to me."

"You do not have the heart to ever disappoint him, I think," Mamma said. When Kate did not reply, she added, "She will be a very beautiful cat."

"I can keep her in my room," Kate said.

"For a few more weeks, until she is old enough to look after herself. Then she stays in the barn with Rollie and the cows," Mamma insisted.

"What will I tell Nathaniel?"

Laughing, Mamma stopped her ears with her hands. "Ach, do not say his name! How are you supposed to court in secret if your mother knows so much? It is lucky that you did not betray his last name. Still, you have gotten my curiosity up. Now every time I meet a 'Nathaniel' I will look at him and wonder if he is your boyfriend."

Kate joined in the laughter. "Oh, Mamma. The secret courting happened in Grandmammi's day, not now. But when you see my mystery boyfriend, perhaps you should tell him you will soon be living in the barn to make room for all his gifts."

"I could never scold the poor boy. He could not be more altogether-turned-every-which-way in love with you. He has enough to worry about." Mamma's cheerful expression faded, and she grasped Kate's hand. "If you leave us, leibe, you will let him down softly?"

Unable to speak with the boulder-sized lump clogging her throat, Kate nodded.

"Jah, I know my Katie." Mamma gave her hand a squeeze. "Will you separate the cream and make the butter before you mop?"

"Jah, of course."

Mamma smiled weakly, picked up the compost bucket, and hurried out the back door.

Kate couldn't help but feel a slight twinge of resentment that Mamma felt concern for Nathaniel King's feelings and seemed to disregard Kate's. But she immediately regretted that unworthy sentiment. Of course her family cared about Nathaniel. He was one of the community. Kate felt more like an outsider every day.

She playfully fondled the kitten's ears, feeling renewed gratitude for Nathaniel's gift. She would be a beautiful cat, as Mamma said.

"He's taking a great risk, you know." Kate snapped her head up and saw Elmer, arms folded, leaning against the doorframe.

"Don't sneak up on me like that," she said. "You shaved ten years off my life."

"I was just standing here. It's not my fault you never notice me. The kitten saw me."

Kate rolled her eyes.

"The big question is, did Mamma see the kitten?" Elmer said.

"Jah. She's been banished to the barn as soon as she is old enough."

Elmer knelt next to Kate and rubbed the kitten's head. "It's too bad you had to come to the one house in Apple Lake that does not welcome furry creatures. Mamma is very hostile about cat hair."

"She is pretty, though, isn't she?"

"A gift from Nathaniel?" Elmer said.

"Jah. How did you know?"

"That is probably the dumbest question you have ever asked, and I've heard some dumb ones."

Kate cuffed Elmer on the shoulder before he could scoot away from her.

"You can't keep anything from me. I'm your brother. And smart. Too smart to be fooled."

"And humble."

"Jah," Elmer said. "Humility is my best quality."

Kate lifted the kitten into her arms and nuzzled it against her cheek. "A kitten is a practical gift. Nathaniel has a gute head on his shoulders, you know."

Elmer scratched his head. "If that is true, why is he taking such a chance with you?"

"What nonsense are you spouting?"

"Just in case you haven't noticed, Nathaniel is well-liked and highly respected. He cares for his dat, and he employs eleven or twelve men in his business. He's the first to help solve problems with windmills and propane tanks or rebuild after a fire."

"Jah, of course people regard him highly. He is a gute man. I know that."

"He has made it perfectly clear how he feels about you," Elmer said. "To everyone. When it comes to Kate Weaver, we all know right where he stands, even though no one is sure how you feel about Nathaniel. He doesn't hold anything back or try to be anything less than honest about his intentions."

Kate lowered her head and looked at the floor. "Jah, I know. It is one of the things I love about him. But you cannot blame me for that."

"No, of course not. I don't. But, Kate, if you reject him, the entire community will know, and they will pity him. They might treat him with uncommon kindness, but he will still feel their pity. And such a man as Nathaniel surely would dislike being pitied by anyone."

Kate couldn't meet Elmer's eyes. She handed him the kitten then stood and pulled an empty pitcher out of the cupboard. "If you tell me this to make me feel worse, it's working."

"Don't go along your merry way, searching to discover yourself, and forget that Nathaniel has feelings too."

"Do you really believe me to be that uncaring?"

"No, but I see that other things pull at you besides Nathaniel King."

Kate lifted the spigot jar, full of last night's milking, from the icebox. "You are my little brother, Elmer. What do you know?"

"I was the only member of our family who came to your farewell recital, remember? Everyone else thought it would be improper. With all the applause, you smiled so wide I could count all your teeth. I know you took three extra bows at the end of your performance. I know you love to sing. That would be hard enough to leave behind. But you also like the attention from people who admire your talent."

Instead of responding, Kate opened the spigot and let the milk drain into the pitcher. She closed the spigot when nothing was left in the jar but the cream from the top. "Do you think I'm wicked, Elmer?"

"Aaron and Ada believe they are qualified to judge such things," Elmer said. "But not me. Last week at the dairy, Matthew Eicher told me I had a head of cheese."

Kate couldn't help but chuckle. "I have always believed that."

Elmer laughed too. "No, no. I mean a head *for* cheese. He said the batches I make are especially good, and from now on, he wants me to supervise making the cheddar. I would never tell this to anyone but you, but I am tempted to be proud. Someone sees that I am good at something, and I am glad for it. Is it wrong to feel that way? Is it wrong to feel satisfied that I have done a job well and maybe brought in more business for the dairy? I do not know. Is it wrong for Aaron to plant the most beautiful, best-tended garden in the community? Does he take pride in his work?"

"Of course not."

"But is he tempted? And what about Mamma? She is a very good cook, but no one other than Nathaniel has ever praised her for her skill. Does that make her sad?" Elmer put the kitten by her bowl of milk and unfolded himself from the ground. "Here," he said. "Let me help you."

Kate handed him the churn and he nimbly turned the crank on the top of the glass jar that rotated the blades inside, which would eventually transform the heavy cream into butter.

Elmer glanced at Kate. "I think about you a great deal. When you are gone to the academy, I wonder if you are happy. Wonder if the attention brings you what you are looking for. I don't have any answers, but I know a little bit how you feel."

"I truly want to do God's will. You believe that, don't you?"

"I do not believe. I know."

"Going off to school two years ago, I was sure that I had chosen the right direction for my life. I wanted to sing. And I am afraid that my own desires shout so loudly, I won't be able to hear the will of God when He speaks to me. This talent I have, the talent God has given me, can open so many doors for me. No one in the community but Nathaniel knows anything of my success at the academy. I've already attracted the attention of the people at the Met National Council auditions."

"Is that important?"

"It is a feather in my cap, to be sure. I've won two singing competitions this year, and my vocal coach, Dr. Sumsion, she says I could be a big star someday."

"I can guess what she thinks of the Plain life," Elmer said.

Kate heard Dr. Sumsion's voice in her head. *"Go back to that Amish town, and what will you become? An Amish farmer's wife, never knowing how far you could have gone with your voice."*

"My own people know nothing of what I have accomplished in this other world. And, jah, I know it is the grossest pride to wish they knew, to want my family to be pleased. But none of you really care."

Elmer momentarily paused the cranking. "It brings you much pain."

Kate fell silent. She had already trusted Elmer with too much information. She did not want him to think badly of her. And he didn't know the half of it. Only days before she left Milwaukee, she had auditioned for *Romeo et Juliette*, the student opera, and was waiting to hear if she got the title role. Who in her family would want to hear that piece of news?

"I'm sorry," he said.

To most people, Kate's choice would be easy. Who would not jump at the chance of celebrity and riches? But Kate had grown up in a place where, until recently, she felt love permeating the very atmosphere. How much acceptance did Kate feel from the other girls competing for roles? Or the judges and critics who analyzed every sound that came out of her mouth? The world of auditions, competitions, and self-promotion could be very cold.

Even after the most stunning performances, majestic concert halls were left empty and dark. Would that be her fate? She might live her life being admired but not loved—her fans not caring about her as a person as much as they cared about her as a celebrity.

At school she convinced herself that she could still visit her family, could still be a part of them. After all, as long as she was not baptized, they would be allowed to see her. Shunning only took place after a baptized member went astray. But she knew she was only fooling herself. A music career such as the one she wanted would take her to the coast or, more likely, to Europe, and she would not see Mamm and Dat for months or years at a time. They certainly would not travel to visit her and never dream of actually seeing her perform. When she could come back for a rare visit, they would welcome her, but she would be a guest and not one of them. She would be a stranger in her own home, an interloper in the Amish community she loved so dearly. Only now was she beginning to see the stark reality. Her family would be lost to her forever.

Elmer looked at her doubtfully. "I shouldn't say this. I know it's unfair, but..." He looked down at the churn in his hands. "Please stay, Kate. You have no idea how happy I've been since you came back. Remember how we used to sit out on the porch and talk until Mamm scolded us to get to bed?"

"Or we'd hide from Aaron, and I'd sing to you?"

"Or make faces at each other during services?" He frowned. "Kate, if I lose you, I'll be devastated." He stared at her, his eyes full of emotion.

Kate felt a tear slip down her cheek. "I am sorry about all this."

"Now here I've made you cry, when all I wanted was to make you feel guilty."

They laughed, and Elmer handed her the churn. "I've got to get to the dairy. While I am gone, think on this. Some of the blessed apostles were nothing but humble fishermen—and the Lord Jesus, a carpenter. They did not need to be famous. Perhaps you do not need fame either." He took his hat from the stand and opened the door. "Tell Joe and Ben that if they are not at the dairy in ten minutes, I will make them do the mucking out."

Wrinkling her nose, Kate took up the churning.

Despite all her struggles, she took comfort in the thought that Elmer trusted her motives. So did Nathaniel. That was all the reassurance she needed.

Chapter Thirteen

Kate opened the front door to see Nathaniel standing there with his permanent smile. He always sent her heart racing.

"Ready?" he said.

"Jah, denki for the ride."

She, Nathaniel, and Nathaniel's mamm were taking a trip to La Crosse with an Englisch friend Nathaniel had met through his cabinet business. By buggy the ride would certainly be a long trek, but by car the trip took less than an hour.

Nathaniel let her lead the way to the car and opened the door for her.

"It is fortunate that your need to travel to La Crosse happened at the same time as my plan to visit a vendor in the city," Nathaniel said.

Kate inwardly vowed to be more careful about what she told Nathaniel. She had mentioned that she needed to go to La Crosse, and in less than a day, he had the entire trip arranged. She smiled at his readiness to do anything for her, and she would never willfully take advantage of his abundant kindness. But once the words were spoken, the trip to La Crosse became inevitable. Nathaniel would hear no objections.

Kate climbed into the backseat with sheer dread. A ride to La Crosse sitting next to Nathaniel's mamm—who, on good authority, did not approve of Kate—didn't seem like a pleasant way to spend the morning.

Nathaniel's mother, Miriam, was as reserved as Nathaniel was cheerful. Kate remembered Miriam from her childhood as the woman who brought over foul-tasting concoctions when Kate or one of her siblings fell sick. Mamma would insist that Kate drink every last drop of the mixture that tasted like dandelion juice and rancid milk blended together.

"Gute maiya, Miriam," Kate said, hoping she sounded sufficiently humble and deliriously chipper.

Nathaniel's mamm nodded and forced a half smile.

Kate busied herself fastening the seat belt. "Thank you very much for driving us, Dr. Delange."

"No problem," said the doctor. "I've got to go in to the college for a few hours, so it's no trouble at all."

Kate settled into her seat and glanced at Miriam out of the corner of her eye. Miriam seemed determined not to speak, and Kate nearly resolved to remain silent. If she did not say anything, Miriam would not be able to find fault with anything that came out of her mouth. But she soon thought better of it. Nathaniel glanced back at the two of them anxiously, and Kate knew it was her responsibility to break the ice.

"Nathaniel tells me you delivered a baby this week," Kate said with forced enthusiasm.

"Jah, Ervin Stoltzfus's boy."

"How much did he weigh?"

"Seven pounds," Miriam said, looking out the window.

Kate persisted. "What did they name him?"

"Ervin Junior."

Nathaniel craned his neck to look at his mamm as if to prompt her into a friendlier conversation. "He is the first boy after five girls."

"Oh, what a nice blessing for them," Kate said. "I am sure they were mighty proud to have a boy yet."

Miriam propped her elbow on the arm wrapped around her waist and looked at Kate. "There is nothing wrong with a girl baby."

"Oh no, of course not, but after five girls, a boy would be a nice surprise." She glanced at Miriam for any kind of response. She didn't get one. "My sister-in-law Ada has five boys. I know she would look on a baby girl as a true blessing."

Miriam said nothing—simply went back to staring out the window. Getting Miriam to say more than three words at a time proved much like pulling teeth.

Nathaniel cleared his throat. "Tell Kate about the Miller twins, Mamm."

"She does not want to hear about the Miller twins."

"Oh, jah, I would love to."

Miriam turned herself so she could look at Kate straight on. "I want to hear of your time at the academy."

The heat traveled up Kate's face.

"How do you pay for tuition?"

"The professor got me a job at a bakery in the mornings, and I taught voice lessons in the afternoon to kids from some local high schools. Plus I was awarded two grants, one scholarship, and a student loan."

"You're rich," Dr. Delange said from the driver's seat.

"Were you in any plays?" Miriam persisted.

"Operas. And concerts."

"How did they have you dress? Like as not, you weren't in Amish clothes," Miriam said.

"For both operas, I dressed as a nun. Once a French nun and once an Italian nun."

Miriam's eyes narrowed. "Surely you did not always perform as a nun."

Nathaniel glanced uncomfortably at his mother then fixed his eyes on Kate.

"Nae," Kate said. "For auditions or recitals I borrowed formal dresses from my professor or one of the other girls at the academy."

Miriam turned to face forward, as if she were finished with the conversation. "Huh," she grunted. "I never cotton to such vanity."

She folded her arms, leaned her head against the window, and closed her eyes, blocking any further attempts at conversation. The gesture did not escape Nathaniel's notice. His attempt at a reassuring smile came out more like a wince, and he tried persistently to include Kate in his conversation about fly-fishing for the rest of the trip.

The doctor dropped them off on a central street corner in La Crosse in the rising heat. Kate pulled a slip of paper from her pocket and got her bearings.

"Do you know where you are going, Kate?" Nathaniel said.

"Jah. Directions to the music shop are clear enough."

"We will come with you. Then we can go to the distributor and Mamm's stops after."

Kate shook her head. "I know you are pressed for time. I will go and meet you here at noon."

"Are you sure?"

"After strolling down Kilbourn Avenue in Milwaukee, I can walk anywhere by myself."

Nathaniel grew a concerned look. "Is that a dangerous place?"

She smiled. "I've never encountered any sort of trouble on the streets of Milwaukee. I'll be fine."

"I know you will." Nathaniel gave her one last glance before taking his mother by the arm and disappearing down the street.

Kate wandered the other way, directions in hand, looking for the little music store Dr. Sumsion instructed her to find. Her professor had asked Kate in her last letter to buy the music to an obscure little opera by Chabrier. Ach, Kate detested singing French. Her German came out flawlessly with its forceful consonants and powerful vowels, but her French? Kate's diction was atrocious, and she had to concentrate faithfully to keep whole phrases from sounding like she had a stuffy nose. But Dr. Sumsion insisted that Kate needed the practice during the long summer absence, and the song would leave Kate breathless, literally, when she rehearsed it.

Dr. Sumsion had either forgotten or chosen to ignore the fact that Kate had no access to a piano in Apple Lake, nor would she be fortunate enough to locate an accompanist among her Amish neighbors. At least she could look it over and become familiar with the passages before she returned to Milwaukee. *If* she returned.

Kate,

Enclosed is a list of songs I want you to learn for the Felsted competition. You are a sure contender to win the whole thing this year. Don't underestimate the importance of preparing while you are at home. Do your vocalises every day and become familiar with the pieces.

Dr. Matthews thinks I am pushing you too hard, but I told him that you of anyone are capable of incredible things when you put your mind to it. The people in Apple Lake have no idea what an amazing talent they have living in their midst.

Sincerely, we miss you terribly and want you to come back. Don't stay away too long. You'll want to be back in plenty of time for school in September.

Much affection, Dr. Sumsion

The tugging and pulling on Kate's heart intensified with every letter from Milwaukee, whether from Maria or her professor or one of her other friends. They truly loved her there. But then she thought of Elmer and Mamma and Dat. She loved them like her own soul. Could she turn her back on them and the world she grew up in?

Kate could not have been more than four blocks from where the Englisch doctor had dropped them off when her directions sent her around a corner and down a narrow street with run-down buildings and unkempt lots. It seemed unlikely she would find a music store down this street, no matter how out-of-the-way it was. Halfway down the street, Kate stopped and examined her paper. Apparently she had taken a wrong turn, and an uneasy feeling crawled up her spine. She snapped her head to the left as a noise caught her attention. Three men, perhaps slightly younger than she, stood in the narrow space between two buildings, smoking cigarettes and staring in her direction.

Her heart beat faster, and she scolded herself for being so skittish. She'd heard too many horror stories while living in Milwaukee. Surely she had nothing to fear in a small place like La Crosse.

"Hey, Amish girl!" one hollered. "You wanna smoke?"

The three exploded with laughter, and Kate thought it the wisest choice to ignore them and walk away. A boy with a bottle of beer in his hand called to her. "Amish girl, he offered you a smoke."

Lowering her head, Kate quickened her pace and kept walking. The boy suddenly appeared in front of her, blocking her path on the sidewalk.

"Hey, look, guys! It's a *pretty* Amish girl."

"Aw, leave her alone, Mark," said his friend.

Mark studied Kate's face with bloodshot eyes and a look she'd seen a time or two at the academy. "I thought all Amish girls was ugly as sin." He stepped closer. Kate could smell the drink on his breath.

He reached out a hand to touch her, and she stepped back, lifting her head and squaring her shoulders. "Please let me pass," she said, mixing her confident tone with disdain. She hoped that if she sounded unafraid, the boy would think better of picking on her.

His expression flared with anger. "There's an Amish girl at the store who won't even look at me. Or talk to me."

Kate's heart beat in her throat. Could she walk away and hope he gave up? She moved to her left and took a quick step before Mark grabbed her arm and pulled her back.

Her mind raced through ideas for escape. *How did Maria avoid a slap from her boyfriend when he was drunk and angry?* But thinking of Maria brought back all the emotion associated with that horrible night.

Stop it, Jared! She hasn't done anything to you! Get away from the baby!

At that moment, the memory of the terror was so palpable Kate could barely stand. "Let go of me. Leave me alone." Even helpless as she was in Mark's grasp, the notion came to her that she didn't want to hurt this young man the way she had hurt Jared. Too frequently in her dreams she saw Jared's ashen face as the paramedics lifted him onto the gurney—and the blood soaking the bandage around his head. That night, with Maria and the baby in trouble, desperation had transformed Kate into someone she didn't recognize. And she never wanted to be that person again.

She turned her face away so his foul breath wouldn't make her sick.

The other man came up behind her and snatched her wrist roughly. Pain traveled up her arm.

"Please, let me go," Kate begged, as she pulled as hard as she could to free herself from both men.

Kate heard a roar behind her as a large hand forcefully shoved Mark away from her and back five feet. In relief, Kate looked up to see Nathaniel, eyes ablaze, daring the second man to come closer. He released Kate's wrist and bolted down the street with a speed Kate would not have believed possible.

Nathaniel then turned and advanced on Mark. Kate didn't know what he was planning to do, but she didn't want to find out. She touched his arm before he could move any closer to the much-smaller man and gently nudged Nathaniel toward her. The gesture accomplished what she wanted it to. Nathaniel's rage evaporated as he shifted his attention to her and cradled her face in his hands. The compassion in his eyes calmed her pounding heart considerably. She lifted her hand to her cheek. It was wet. She must have been crying.

"Are you all right?" he asked.

Kate nodded. Not hurt. More shaken up than anything.

The boy in the alleyway disappeared, but Mark scowled and unwisely rushed at Nathaniel, his fists raised and flailing. Without hesitation, Nathaniel turned and punched Mark squarely in the mouth. The powerful blow sent Mark to the ground, sprawled unconscious on his backside.

Panting heavily, Nathaniel looked at his fist as if his hand had acted of its own accord. A look of horror spread across his face.

"Kate," he murmured, "what have I done?

Chapter Fourteen

The deliveries of cakes and cookies and Yankee Bean Soup started up again as soon as the community learned of the incident. That Kate had been forced to endure such an attack made her the recipient of much sympathy.

Dat went without dinner again the next day before calming down enough to hear the story, not just from Kate but from Nathaniel as well. With his middle daughter getting into all sorts of scrapes lately, he insisted his nerves were frayed and he was wasting away to nothing. He thanked Nathaniel for looking out for his daughter and asked if he would consider a permanent position as Kate's guardian.

Elmer tried to stifle a grin when he heard about it. "Of course we must forgive him, but maybe we can take comfort that the boy felt a bit of God's wrath through Nathaniel." This response prompted a cry of shock from Mamma, who was appalled that Elmer harbored such vindictive thoughts. She promptly sent him out to shovel manure in the barn.

Ben and Joe looked at Nathaniel in wonderment but said nothing about the incident. If they expressed admiration for Nathaniel's actions, Aaron might accuse them of a interest in violence.

Aaron, who came over to the house too often, laid the blame entirely at Kate's feet. "Kate, your worldliness has brought misfortune to more people than just yourself. Nathaniel was never in a lick of trouble until you returned home and dragged the innocent man down with your worldly ways. You should be ashamed of yourself. It is better that you leave him alone and return to Milwaukee. He should not be made to suffer for your stiffneckedness."

And Ada was not above repeating gossip. "I am telling you this for your own good, Kate. Many people think you are worldly and vain. If you would settle down and quit trying to upset the apple cart, things would be better for you."

Even as bad as Kate felt, Nathaniel was having a worse time of it. Distraught at what had happened to Kate and so ashamed of resorting to violence, he practically begged the police officer in La Crosse to put him in jail and throw away the key.

It hadn't taken more than a minute after Nathaniel laid Mark out flat before a police car rolled down the street and pulled next to the alleyway. A thin, balding officer, who seemed in no particular hurry to investigate, got out of his car and sauntered up the sidewalk.

"Officer Hansen. The neighbors called me," the police officer told them, gazing with apparent disinterest at Mark who, by then conscious, sat on the ground gingerly massaging his jawline. Mark must have had more than one brush with the law, because the officer didn't even bat an eye when he saw the young man.

"Is there some kind of trouble?" the officer said.

"We was just messing around," Mark said.

"We? What, you got multiple personalities now, Mark?"

Mark pointed indignantly at Nathaniel. "That guy hit me."

"Stop talking and let the lady tell me." Officer Hansen hooked his thumbs in his belt and turned to Kate. "Are you hurt, miss?"

"No," Kate said, still trying to catch her breath. "He blocked my way and then he and his friend grabbed my arm. They wouldn't let me go. Nathaniel pushed them away, and this boy tried to hit Nathaniel."

Officer Hansen studied Nathaniel. "What do you have to say?"

Nathaniel stood stunned and mortified. "He was scaring Kate, but I shouldn't have hit him. I take full responsibility."

"He probably broke my jaw," Mark protested.

"Then why are you still talking?" Officer Hansen said, glancing at Mark before turning back to Kate. "So would you like to press charges?"

Kate shook her head.

"Charges?" Mark said. "I'm the one who got smacked."

The officer glared at Mark. "Get your sorry hide out of here before I arrest your whole family."

Mark didn't have to be told twice. He took off down the street and didn't look back.

When Mark was out of sight, Officer Hansen put a hand on Nathaniel's shoulder. "Any man would have done what you did," he said.

Nathaniel lowered his head in despair. "Not the men in my community. We believe in peace. *I* believe in peace."

Officer Hansen frowned. "Even a good thing can be carried too far. Peace and nonviolence are nice ideals to hang your hat on, but sometimes, like it or not, they're not practical. Even a peaceful man must defend his loved ones from attack."

"That is not what I believe. Jesus chose not to resist but to give His life freely. We trust in God instead of our own power—instead of the arm of flesh. Even if my family were being attacked, the Lord's will is to overcome evil with good and hope for a better world in the kingdom of God."

"Should you have walked away and left this woman to the mercy of those punks?"

"No," said Nathaniel, "but I could have thrown myself in front of her and let them hurt me instead."

Kate's heart swelled at the kindness of this man, but she said nothing. She only looked into his tortured face and dearly wished she could ease his pain.

"Now that would have been real nice. Then I might have been arresting the kid for murder."

"I could have taken it," Nathaniel said. "'Resist not evil: but whosoever shall smite thee on thy right cheek, turn to him the other also.'"

"And I say you're a danged fool," said Officer Hansen—but he said it with a warmth in his voice before climbing into his squad car and driving away.

Kate sighed. This mess had occurred two days ago, but every gesture, every sound and smell were perfectly fresh in her mind: the alcohol on Mark's breath; the friend yelling at him from the alleyway; the pain when the other man clutched her wrist; and most haunting, the look on Nathaniel's face.

The family had retired earlier, but Kate did not follow them up the stairs to bed. Nathaniel had promised to visit her tonight, and she anxiously awaited his arrival, to discover what she could do, if anything, to comfort him. She had never seen him so utterly miserable, and Kate was painfully aware that Aaron was right. She had caused Nathaniel too much trouble.

The single kerosene lamp over the table cast long shadows at the corners of the room. Sitting in the kitchen, looking at recipe books without really seeing them, Kate heard a soft tap on the back door. She hurried to open it. Nathaniel stood dejectedly on the back steps.

He shuffled into the kitchen and took Kate by the shoulders. He moved his hands to her wrist and studied the ugly purple bruises there. "Oh, Kate," he said, emotion spilling out of his throat. "I am so sorry about what they did to you."

His compassion nearly reduced Kate to tears. She cleared her throat instead. "It is not bad, Nathaniel. It pains me to see you fret over this. I care more about how you are feeling."

He took her hand. "I have no concern for myself."

"You are very unhappy, Nathaniel. How can I help you?"

He paused and then walked to the sink, where he leaned both hands against the counter and looked as if he were trying to push the whole thing out the wall. With his back to her, he said, "To own the truth, Kate, I've never felt such despair. You can't help me."

Kate could not let him suffer alone. She went up behind him and put her hand on his shoulder. "Then I will share the despair with you," she said.

"I won't allow that."

"There's nothing you can do to stop me," she said. "I can't help but be sad when you are."

"Daily, I struggle to perfect my life, to be a better man each day than I was the day before. But you can never take the true measure of a man until you test his will. This was my test to prove to God that I am truly peaceful in my heart, that I will choose the way of nonresistance." He turned to face her. "And I failed. I am so very wicked."

"That is not true, Nathaniel."

"It is, because even though I regret using violence, I do not regret defending you. And I still feel retribution festering in my heart. When I saw him holding you with those dirty hands and I heard you screaming, I had to protect you."

"Do not condemn yourself for that. I don't. Neither does my family. Even Aaron doesn't think it is your fault. I am more than grateful to you. Ach, to think what could have happened if you had not heard the yelling." Her voice broke, and she could not speak for a moment. "If you felt drawn to find me, perhaps God led you. And if God's hand was in it, how could it be wrong?"

"It is wrong because God put me there to protect you without hurting anyone else. And I failed."

"Then I hate to ask what you think of me. I put a man in the hospital, Nathaniel." She couldn't bring herself to tell Nathaniel that Jared was still there. "I did much more than knock him to the ground."

"You had to protect yourself. And your friend."

"As you protected me. You should judge yourself with the same mercy you are so eager to offer me."

Silently, Nathaniel gazed at her. She stared back at him, trying to read every thought hidden behind those icy-blue eyes. Not a word passed between them.

Then, in an instant, Nathaniel surprised and thrilled her by taking her into his arms and holding her tenderly. "I hope this does not cause you distress, Kate," he whispered, "but...I love you."

Kate experienced the overwhelming feeling of flying, higher and faster as if there were no end to the sky. Closing her eyes, she buried her face in his chest. She couldn't answer him. He didn't seem to expect her to.

"I love you without reason. You compel me to feel better even though I have no right to feel better."

She savored his earthy smell, basked in his radiating warmth, before he broke the spell and nudged her away to arm's length. He smiled. "I must not compound my sin." Breathless and shaken, she knew exactly what he meant.

"Tomorrow I will meet with the elders and ask for forgiveness," he said. "But I don't know how I can ever hope to be made whole. My true character has been revealed, and I can't forgive myself for that."

"'He is faithful and just to forgive us our sins.' The Lord Jesus would not want you to carry a burden He has already carried for you."

He looked at her, his gaze steady and warm. "Why, in even the worst times, do you make me feel very, very glad to be alive?"

She blushed. "It is one of the great mysteries, to be sure."

At arm's length, he caressed her cheek with his thumb while studying her face. A thousand tiny threads of fire passed through her body.

Suddenly he withdrew his hand and reached for the doorknob like a lifeline. "This courting business will be the death of me," he said. He shot one last glance in her direction and bolted out the door.

Kate later lay in her bed, fighting off sleep as it crept over her. She wanted a few more minutes to bask in Nathaniel's words.

"I love you, Kate. I love you without reason."

Had she ever felt so whole in her life—like every corner of her being was filled with the glowing embers of a cheery fire?

Nathaniel loved her. Next to her father, the best man she had ever known.

Why? He could have the love of any girl in Apple Lake. He wouldn't have needed to coax and agonize and slave for anyone else in the entire community. Why did he love her? Trying to answer that question made her head spin.

She *did* know that the uncertainty and effort made his love all the more precious. For a man like him to give his heart so freely to her was no common thing. She savored her part in something extraordinary and drifted off to sleep with a smile on her lips.

Chapter Fifteen

Nathaniel lightly tapped the baseball with the bat in the direction of little Amos, who picked up the ball and chased Nathaniel to first base. As the little boy reached out and tagged him, Nathaniel flopped to the ground in front of the base and grunted in mock agony.

"Ach, you got me, Amos," he moaned, as the boy jumped on top of him in a fit of giggles.

"I did not touch you that hard, Nathaniel," Amos said, grinning. "You do not have to fall down all the time."

"Falling down is part of the fun of the game," Nathaniel said, simultaneously tickling Amos, setting him on his feet, and then placing the hat back onto Amos's head.

Summer baseball after suppertime was an ongoing tradition for Nathaniel and the children. Young ones not yet in school and older children who managed to finish their chores gathered after the evening meal to play. For early June, the weather had finally turned warm enough to allow them to play outside without their lips turning blue.

Baseball was Nathaniel's favorite game, and some of the children were really getting good at it. His heart felt so light, he thought he might break into song right there on the field. But, no, he'd leave the singing to the only person he cared to hear, the delightful girl who had a greater claim on him than ever before. He thought his heart would burst out of his chest at the mere thought of Kate, the way it pounded until it ached with the pain and longing of not being with her. Was it too early to see Dat to bed?

He handed the ball to freckle-faced Johnny Herschberger. "I've got to go now. Thanks for letting me play."

"Did your mamm call you?" a boy named Thomas said.

"No, but look," Nathaniel said, pointing to the back of his house in the distance. "She's lit the lantern in the window. That means it's time for me to go home."

"But you are old," Thomas said. "Do you still have to obey your mamm?"

"Always honor your fater and your mutter, Thomas. Then you will live long on the earth."

Amos ran to Nathaniel from first base. "Hit one far!" he yelled.

"I must go now."

"Just one more?" Thomas said.

"Just one more! Just one more!" the children chanted as they gathered around Nathaniel and looked up expectantly.

Nathaniel gave in. "Who will pitch to me?"

"I will," Reddy volunteered.

"All right." Nathaniel sent three bigger boys out over the pasture fence and scooted the rest of the children behind him. He directed Reddy Samuel to pitch from farther back. "I don't want to hurt anybody," he said.

Samuel's first pitch came right down the middle of the plate, and Nathaniel put all his power into the swing. The ball careened off the bat with tremendous force, whizzed past the boys waiting to catch it in deep outfield, and flew over two fences before coming to rest just feet away from the Millers' back gate.

The children whooped and hollered and acted like the colossal hit was the most exciting thing that had happened to them in their entire lives.

"Did you see how far that went?" Amos yelled.

"That's the best one he ever did," Mary said.

The boys charged with fetching the baseball raced each other to retrieve it and then dashed back to the ball field, raising the ball like a trophy.

Nathaniel handed the bat to Thomas before saying, "I'll come tomorrow night if I can" and jogging home.

Smiling to himself, Nathaniel tapped his boots on the back step to clear away the dirt and went inside the house. After the refreshing evening air, the heat in the kitchen was stifling.

"Ach, Nathaniel, you stink to high heaven," said his mother when she got close.

"It's fresh air mixed with hard-earned sweat," he said sweetly as he chased Mamm around the room trying to catch her for a hug.

Mamm moved away from him and protested loudly. "You smell like Dat used to when he came in from the fields at night, especially in the spring. I wouldn't let him near me until he sponged off his whole body."

"I better go clean up, then," Nathaniel said cheerfully, "or I'll never get a wife."

"Maybe would you put Dat to bed first?"

"Jah, Dat first, bath second, finding a wife third," he said.

Someone knocked on the back door. "Speaking of finding a wife," Mamm said, smiling at a private joke.

Nathaniel opened the door to Ada Weaver and Sarah Schwartz. They both smiled coyly and batted their eyes in unison.

"Sarah, Ada, come in, come in," Mamm said, trying to act surprised but not fooling Nathaniel. "What brings you here so late?"

Ada pushed Sarah in front of her. "This is the first time I could get away from those bothersome children. Ach, to have the life of any other woman, without five boys to vex me all day long." She marched into the house and put a basket on the table. "My very bones are tired." She arched her back and massaged her shoulders for a few moments. "Albert jumped off the wagon and bumped his head; then Giddy broke two jars of apricots all over my clean kitchen floor and Lee cut his foot on the glass. That's my life, one mess right after the other."

"Oh, poor Lee," Mamm said.

"I'm glad to have such a thoughtful sister as Sarah. She is always a great help to me," Ada said.

Sarah gave Nathaniel a demure smile. He thought she was very pretty. Not as lovely as Kate, of course, but better looking than most of the girls her age. But if she turned out to be anything like her sister in temperament, Nathaniel couldn't muster even the slightest interest in her despite his mamm's scheming. He hated to disappoint her, but Mamm's plots and ploys to involve him with other girls were pointless. Nothing could possibly take his attention from Kate.

Ada pulled a piece of fabric out of the basket. "I've come for some help with this quilt binding. It's so adorable when it's cut on the bias, and I don't quite understand how to do that."

"Oh, that's easy," Mamm said. "I'll draw out the cuts on some paper." Mamm went to the drawer and pulled out paper along with the scissors and tape. "Nathaniel, why don't you show Sarah the cradle you are building for Mary's baby while I do this?"

"Let me show her another time, Mamm. I've got to get Dat down to bed yet."

"That can wait a few minutes."

Nathaniel didn't want to hurt Sarah's feelings since he knew why she had come, but he did want to nip everybody's hopes in the bud. "Another time, Mamm. I want to get to Kate's before it's too late."

Nathaniel caught the crestfallen look on his mother's face and saw Ada's irritation. But Sarah had turned her face away, so her expression, if there was one, was hidden.

"Very well," Mamm said in surrender, but Nathaniel could see her quickly formulating another plan.

Without waiting to discover what the plan was, Nathaniel tromped into the bedroom to take care of Dat.

* * * * *

Dat sat in his room in the wheelchair, gazing out the window. Mamm had bathed him earlier, and his hair was still damp.

"You see our game?" Nathaniel said, pushing his dat to the side of the bed.

His dat replied with a barely audible grunt.

"Jah, you taught me everything I know."

Nathaniel knelt down and removed Dat's slippers, replacing them with a fleecy pair of socks. Dat seemed unusually agitated, nodding his head back and forth and letting out the drawn-out moan he used when things were out of sorts. Nathaniel sat on the bed and stroked his dat's hand and hummed a familiar tune. He only sang for his dat.

The effect was almost immediate. Dat calmed down and glued his eyes to Nathaniel's face.

"You should hear Kate sing," Nathaniel said. "You would feel like you had bathed in the waters of Bethesda. Kate has the most beautiful voice. She says the Met people are interested in hearing her sing. The Met is an opera company in New York. Kate says they are very important. I am so proud of her." He tried to ignore the yawning pit in his stomach.

The subtle change in Dat's expression did not escape Nathaniel's notice. "Okay, I am not especially excited that the Met people want to hear Kate sing," Nathaniel said wryly, "but I am attempting to be supportive of Kate's choices."

The nagging doubt knocked his confidence down a notch as he pulled back the covers and lifted Dat into bed. "Is the pillow gute?"

Nathaniel moved the wheelchair to the wall and pulled up a chair. "There is a girl in the kitchen Mamm wants me to marry."

Dat moved his eyes upward.

"Jah, she means well, but I love Kate. Mamm will not accept that." Nathaniel took his father's hand. "I want you to meet Kate, but I am afraid to bring her home. She senses the hostility from Mamm. I wish Mamm would try to understand."

Dat slowly nodded, and Nathaniel could almost hear his voice. "As the Lord wills," Dat would have said.

Nathaniel smiled sadly as he watched Dat settle onto his pillow. With his slowly wasting body, he seemed to disappear beneath the covers. "As the Lord wills," Nathaniel said as he picked up the Bible from the table next to the bed and began reading quietly.

"'I am the resurrection, and the life. He who believeth in me, though he were dead, yet shall he live.'"

While he read, he stroked Dat's head until the older man fell asleep.

When Dat's breathing became steady and relaxed, Nathaniel stood up, placed the Bible back on the table, and gave his father a light kiss on the forehead.

* * * * *

After cleaning up, Nathaniel went into the kitchen to tell Mamm goodbye before heading to Kate's. He hoped he had taken long enough that Sarah and Ada had given up waiting and gone home.

No such luck.

They sat at the table with Mamm, intently studying the paper she folded and unfolded in her hand.

Mamm jumped up and quickly poured four cups of coffee. "Sit, sit, and have some coffee before you go," she said. "Running after girls can wait a few minutes. I feel I don't see you ever."

Nathaniel tried to act agreeable to his mother's request. He loved Mamm dearly, but the extra time spent with Dat and the fact that he hadn't seen Kate for three days had heightened his anticipation of seeing her until the yearning hung about him like the smell of a potent herbal tea. His need to be close to Kate threatened to overwhelm every other part of his life. He had no desire to spend one more minute humoring Mamm in her yearning to marry him off to Sarah Schwartz, the bishop's daughter. But there was more involved than his wishes.

Suppressing his irritation, Nathaniel pulled up a chair next to Mamm and as far away from Sarah as possible. Though he wouldn't have stayed merely to satisfy Mamm in regards to Sarah, his instincts told him that Mamm could sense that she was no longer the most important person in his life—that in a way, she was losing him, probably had already lost him, and she needed the reassurance of his love more than ever.

Mamm handed him a large slab of white bread with a jar of jelly and a knife. He didn't protest, just spread a healthy dollop of jelly onto the bread and started eating. Like Dat, Mamm seemed restless. Nathaniel would make her unhappy if he appeared to be in a hurry.

"The bread is wonderful-gute," he said between mouthfuls.

"Sarah made it," Mamm said.

"It is very, very gute, Sarah."

Ada studied Nathaniel's face while Sarah smiled but avoided his eyes. "She made it for you," Ada said.

"For me?"

"I...feel bad about the trouble in La Crosse," Sarah said.

"Jah," Ada added. "Most people are feeling sorry for Kate, but it can't be all pies and cakes for you, either."

"You are very kind, Sarah, to make the bread, but it does not matter about me," Nathaniel said, placing his half-eaten slice on the table.

"Of course it matters!" Ada insisted. "Kate dragged you into her troubles. We all saw how you suffered. Rumschpringe or no rum-schpringe, had Aaron been Kate's father, he would have given her the strap the day she started all this nonsense with that voice teacher. He would never have allowed the GED books or the graduation test. Nothing. Aaron has said many times that Solomon coddles her, gives in to her. He makes it too easy for her to break with our ways."

Nathaniel placed his cup on the table and slowly wiped his hands on the napkin. "I will give thanks to the Lord tonight that I did not have such a father as Aaron," he said quietly. "Cruelty should never be a substitute for good parenting."

Ada widened her eyes, and she couldn't have looked more horrified if he had slapped her.

Mamm thumped her fabric on the table. "Nathaniel, there is no need to be so sharp. Ada is only expressing an opinion."

Nathaniel folded his arms and frowned at Ada. "I apologize. I do not mean to be rude."

Sarah tried to pretend there was nothing out of the ordinary. "I think we know how to do the binding now, don't you, Ada?"

Ada nodded curtly and quickly gathered fabric and paper into her basket.

Mamm's eyes darted from Nathaniel to Ada. "You will come back if you have any questions?"

"Jah," Sarah said. "I think we can manage."

The sisters finished collecting things from the table, said their good-byes, and hurriedly slipped out the back door.

A disheartened sigh escaped from Mamm's lips. "You didn't have to ruin a pleasant conversation."

"Pleasant for whom?"

"Ada goes rattling her tongue too much, but she doesn't mean anything by it."

"Is that what you call it, rattling her tongue? I will not sit by and let her say such things. God does not rule by force, but with persuasion and love. Regardless of what they think of Kate, Aaron and Ada have a warped perception of God's dealings with His children."

"She was referring very specifically to Kate, and you took offense for the whole world."

"I took offense for Kate since you will not."

"Why should I?"

"Mamm, how can I make you understand what a gute and worthy girl Kate is?"

"Worthy? Because of her and what happened in La Crosse, you walked around this house so sad I feared you wouldn't recover."

"I recovered, Mamm. You did not need to worry."

"It need never have happened. Life flowed so much more smoothly before she came back."

"It breaks my heart to hear you talk that way, Mamm. It is true that I sank very low. But that cannot be Kate's doing. Only my own." Nathaniel fixed his gaze on his mother. "I am glad for what happened. The despair prepared my heart for the lesson God wanted to teach me. How could I understand my weaknesses if my strength had not been tested? How would I have known what I needed to learn?"

Mamm shook her head. "You are so very wise, my son. Like your father. You see so much gute in people that I cannot."

"I see the gute in Kate that you will not."

"I will not apologize for how I feel. The more time you spend with her, the more I worry that this will end badly for you. She has given you no promise, no sign that she will be here in September. You offer her everything and expect nothing in return and spend hours in your shop crafting that rocker she may never use. The time has come for her to make a choice. If she loves you, she should get off the fence and quit playing a game with your life."

Nathaniel exhaled slowly. In his less charitable moments, such thoughts had crossed his mind. He had to admit that what was happening between Kate and him did sometimes seem like a futile chase. Did he appear like a stray cat, following after Kate for any morsel of food she might throw him? And did he care if that's how everyone saw him, when being with Kate left him so deliriously happy? Was he a fool to stay on such a roller-coaster ride?

He cleared his throat and tried to sound matter-of-fact. "You can't talk me out of loving her."

Mamm lifted her chin slightly as she stood and cleared the cups from the table. "You love her?" she said, not looking at him.

"Jah."

Mamm was quiet. All that could be heard was the tinkling of the cups in the sink as she washed them. "Then may the good Lord bless you."

* * * * *

The fine sandpaper glided along the arm of the rocker like ice skates on a glassy lake. Kate would never get even the tiniest sliver from the rocker Nathaniel was making. Once he finished the first armrest, Nathaniel started sanding the other one, painstakingly shaping the piece of wood with finer and finer grains of sandpaper. After running his hand back and forth across the surface, he smoothed it and smoothed it again, caressing the beautiful wood until it almost shone.

Though always a detailed craftsman, Nathaniel had never spent more time or care on a piece of furniture before. He would see to it that every joint fit perfectly, every piece lined up flawlessly, and every surface felt as silky as Kate's soft cheek against his calloused hands.

The meticulous work kept his mind off his doubts and his worst fears. What if Kate would never use his rocker?

What if she rejected his gift?

Chapter Sixteen

"We'd sure have a lot more peace and quiet around here if you'd stop that whistling," Luke Miller said, holding his drill aloft like a torch. Luke, bishop of one of the districts in Apple Lake, was a short man with bushy eyebrows and a thick beard that made up for the disappearing hair on top.

The ten men in Nathaniel's workshop were busily putting together an order for a customer in La Crosse. A cacophony of tools powered by the drive shaft echoed off the high aluminum ceiling along with Nathaniel's whistling.

"Ach, was I doing it again? Sorry," Nathaniel said.

"It would be bearable if you could carry a tune."

The men within earshot laughed at Luke's grumbling.

Nathaniel chuckled and shuffled through the invoices that constituted this month's orders. "The windows are open and the diesel engine drowns out my music. Why are you complaining?"

"You're so blamed cheerful all the time. Makes a man want to tear his hair out," Luke said.

"If you had any." Zeke Kauffman, Nathaniel's oldest employee, laughed and clapped Luke on the shoulder.

"You're a grump, Luke," said Calvin. "Nathaniel's trying to balance out your sour disposition."

"His whistling makes me sourer."

"Have some patience with the poor kid, Luke," Zeke said. "She's a mighty pretty girl."

"Then why doesn't he marry her and give us all some peace?"

"I am working on it," Nathaniel said.

"If you ask me," Luke said, "she is the one working on you."

Calvin glanced uneasily at Nathaniel. "Nobody asked you, Luke." He pulled out a handkerchief, wiped his brow, and found something on the other side of the workshop that needed his attention.

Without looking up, Nathaniel slowly replaced the papers in their correct order and hung the clipboard on the peg. "I'll try to curb the whistling."

Zeke furrowed his brow and put a hand on Nathaniel's shoulder. "Luke doesn't mean any harm when he spouts nonsense like that."

"I see what I see," Luke said. "She bats those long eyelashes and Nathaniel comes running."

Adam Zook and Marvin Mast came through, carrying a stack of finished cabinet doors between them. Luke pointed at Adam. "You go to the singings. How does Nathaniel behave?"

Walking backward, Adam looked behind him to see where he was going. "He don't sing, that's for sure."

Panting with exertion, Adam and Marvin propped their load on the saw table. "We don't see much of him when Kate is around," Marvin said. "He circles her like the sun."

"Or like a whiny puppy," Luke said.

Adam looked at the ground. "I won't say a word against it. Nathaniel knows what he is doing."

He nudged Marvin and they picked up the wood and headed to the varnish drying room, muttering softly to each other.

Nathaniel pried his eyes from Adam and looked from Luke to Zeke. "Am I doing something wrong?"

"No one would fault you for anything," Zeke said.

"You are a fine, handsome boy," Luke said. "Of course she welcomes your attention. And you make it no secret that you fancy her. What we all want to know is, does she fancy you? You have placed yourself at her beck and call, but do you ever sense that you are her second choice?"

Nathaniel looked away and massaged his forehead. It was easier to pretend that everything with Kate was going according to plan. "Jah, I feel that way some days," he said.

"And you follow her like a puppy yet. We all see it."

Nathaniel looked around his workshop, sure he would see all eyes upon him. No one but Luke and Zeke paid him any heed. "Is that what they think?"

"Some," Zeke said. "You should guard yourself more carefully, or you will look like a fool when she leaves in September."

Nathaniel's heart sank to his shoes. He threw up his arms in resignation. "What can I do? I cannot be anything less than honest with my feelings. In private or in public."

"The world is alluring to our young people," Luke said, sounding like a bishop now. "Some think the Plain life dull compared to what is out there." Luke sat on Nathaniel's gray metal desk, arms folded, one foot resting on the floor. "My Edna ran off to Chicago with an Englischer during the rumschpringe. Told me she was confused and asked me to wait for her. He was a handsome boy, that Englischer."

"Yet she chose you in the end," Nathaniel said.

"I was not content to leave her in Chicago. If she was to reject me, she would do it once and for all."

"You were not so confident then as you sound now," Zeke said.

"I was confident that the Lord's will would be done," Luke said. He frowned. "But not confident she would choose me. I told her I would wait no longer and forced her hand. She loved me enough to surrender her life in Chicago."

Nathaniel closed his eyes. He was not so confident. Kate held all the control in the relationship. Did that make him less of a man? A slobbering puppy? And if he made demands on Kate when she was not ready, could he bear the thought of losing her because he'd pushed too hard?

Did she see him as a pleasant summer diversion before she went back to the academy in the fall? He wanted to believe in her sincerity, but wiser men than he made him doubt himself.

Could he be sure of anything?

Was it time to force Kate's hand?

* * * * *

Several hours later, Nathaniel strolled down the street toward his wagon with five two-by-fours draped across his shoulders.

Whistling.

He couldn't help it, and Luke Miller wasn't within earshot. His little trips to the lumber store were some of the few times he could tweet like a bird without being scolded. And why shouldn't he whistle when he thought of Kate?

Trouble was, he spent so much time thinking of her that he had little time to think of what to do about her.

He had parked his wagon in the vacant lot next to the Methodist church so it would be close to load the wood. Squinting against the bright white of the small church building, he saw two Englisch ladies standing motionless beneath one of the windows. Did they need help?

He moved closer until he heard the strains of heavenly singing floating from the open window. The singer released the notes with energy and passion as the melody went higher and higher, spinning out of the church like birds taking flight. Nathaniel would recognize that voice in his sleep.

He stepped deliberately until he joined the women under the window, being careful not to knock anyone with his long pieces of wood.

"Beautiful, isn't it?" whispered one of the women. "I've been standing here for twenty minutes."

"That accompanist is marvelous," the other woman said. "Is it Hilda?"

Her friend shrugged her shoulders.

Nathaniel listened intently to the technical pieces he couldn't begin to recognize. The music's difficulty surpassed anything ever sung at a simple gathering. The pianist kept up with Kate's enthusiasm, not missing a note for all Nathaniel could tell.

Kate had found someone to practice with her so that come September, she'd be ready for school again.

Ready to leave him.

Taking care with his load, which seemed heavier by the minute, Nathaniel nodded good day to the women and wandered down the street to his wagon.

He wasn't whistling anymore.

Chapter Seventeen

Dear Kate,

Jared's family is arguing about whether to take him off life support. His mom is hopeful for a recovery, but the doctors are not holding out much hope.

His mother accused me of luring her son to my apartment with the intention of hurting him. I know she is grieving for her son, and I will try to have compassion. She has come to my apartment late at night and screamed at me, so I moved in with Carlos for a few weeks. He is a good brother. Jared's mother doesn't know where Carlos lives.

Would I be selfish to say I miss you and hope for a visit soon? I need your calming influence in my life. You would know what to say to make Jared's mother feel better. I only make her angrier. Carlos says he will pick you up and bring you back when you are ready to come. He would do anything for you. Do not stay away too long.

Love, Maria

* * * * *

Kate and Nathaniel walked hand in hand around the edge of the pond, their way lit by the brilliantly white moon directly overhead. Kate no longer needed a shawl in the evenings. The late June weather had turned decidedly warm. With its remote location and heavy growth of birch trees, Barker's Pond was fast becoming their favorite spot when they wanted to be isolated from curious eyes.

Kate looked with wonder at the transformation of the scenery since spring. Branches grew lush with new leaves, birds seemed to occupy every tree in the woods, and wildflowers bloomed on the ground like stars in the sky. She marveled that she had been getting to know Nathaniel for fewer than three months and already he was the best and brightest thing in her life. How had she even been able to smile before knowing him?

"You are very quiet tonight," Nathaniel said, pulling her away from her muddled thoughts.

"I am? I'm sorry."

"Do not apologize. Are you feeling well?"

"Jah, no cause to worry about that. I suppose I'm thinking deep things," Kate said, trying to act more like herself. Two letters had arrived from Milwaukee today. Both equally as troubling, but for completely different reasons. The one from Maria made Kate fret more than ever.

I should be there with her, she thought.

The other letter had brought "good news" that would not be good news to Nathaniel. Should she tell him?

"Deep things, huh?" Nathaniel said.

"Sometimes anger bubbles to the surface. And a desire for retribution. For my friend Maria and the baby. Things are not going well for her in Milwaukee."

"Is her boyfriend bothering her again?" Nathaniel asked.

"No," said Kate, evading his eyes. Nathaniel knew most everything about that horrible night, but she was afraid he would be ashamed of her if he knew she had hurt Jared badly enough to put him in a coma. "Maria has other problems. I wonder if I should…"

"Be there with her?" Nathaniel finished her sentence.

Clearly reluctant to take the conversation where it was pulling them, Nathaniel cleared his throat and ambled along the edge of the pond. "The cinnamon rolls were wonderful-gute tonight," he said, patting his stomach. "I wish I had more of them."

"Nathaniel," Kate scolded, "you are lucky they didn't have to roll you out of that house." But looking at him out of the corner of her eyes, with his flat stomach and muscular chest, she couldn't imagine there was an ounce of fat on his entire body.

"I eat and eat and still I am so hungry. My stomach is like Jacob Newswenger's well, deep and empty." He bent over, scooped a pebble from the ground, and flung it into the pond. Kate watched as it skipped twice before disappearing into the water.

"How do you do that?" she asked.

"It's all in the wrist," Nathaniel said. "I will show you."

He instructed her on how to pick a good rock and explained the correct technique for making it skip across the water. To no avail, Kate tried lobbing rocks lightly at the surface. She tried a sideways casting technique. Finally she attempted to slap a pebble down in the shallowest part of the pond in hopes that it would bounce back at her. She was a lost cause. A complete waste of a throwing arm.

Nathaniel, unable to hide his amusement, laughed harder with every attempt. In exasperation she threw down all the rocks she held in her fist. Nathaniel picked one up and hurled it at the water, skipping it three times.

Kate turned up her nose. "Of course you can do it. You've got all those muscles and arms made of iron and massive shoulders and such. But who needs all that power when I can move the water with my voice?"

Nathaniel, smiling widely, looked at her with skepticism. "With your voice?"

"It's a well-known fact that sound vibrations can move objects."

He folded his arms across his chest. "All right, Miss Scientist. Show me."

Kate started with a comfortable high note, letting it spin out the top of her head and holding it for a few seconds before falling silent. Nathaniel studied the water attentively, watching for any sign of vibration. Nothing.

She tried again. This time she didn't mess around. She trilled a note toward the top of her range, something above a high C, and watched as the pond seemed determined to hold perfectly still.

Nathaniel chuckled quietly. Kate caught a laugh in her throat, took a deep breath, and let out an impossibly high note that surely only dogs and small woodland animals could hear. The water, heedless of her struggle, calmly held its ground, echoing only the reflection of the bright moon in its clear depths. Not even the tiniest bubble.

Now both Nathaniel and Kate laughed hysterically, Kate in turns trying to scream a ripple out of the water or moan a note low enough to create a wave.

"I promise," Kate said through her uncontrollable giggles, "I saw it done once with a crystal goblet." They laughed so hard that they had to hold each other up or risk falling on the muddy bank.

Someone came crashing through the trees to their left. Elmer and a tall, plump girl appeared from the undergrowth, gazing wide-eyed at Kate and Nathaniel.

"Kate," Elmer said, "what are you doing? We thought something was dying over here."

Surprised but still laughing, Kate took a small step away from Nathaniel. "We didn't expect to see anyone."

Elmer motioned toward the girl. "This is Priscilla Bender from La Crosse."

"I'm staying with my cousin," Priscilla said, gazing moony-eyed at Elmer.

Kate couldn't blame her. Elmer was quite a good-looking fellow.

"Why were you making all that noise?" Elmer said. "Were you preparing for your—what's the word, Kate? For the academy?"

Kate felt heat creep up the back of her neck. "Role," she said, almost under her breath.

"Jah, *role* in the opera."

Nathaniel released Kate's hand.

"You need practice," Elmer said. "You sounded like two badgers fighting."

"It was nothing," Kate said, still trying to gain her composure. "We were playing around."

"Ach, be quiet about it, then. And stay on this side of the pond. I'll take Priscilla to the far side."

"We promise not to trespass on your half," Kate said.

"Thanks," Elmer said dryly. "Come on, Priscilla." Elmer and Priscilla turned and walked back through the trees the way they had come.

Kate sensed a sudden change of mood from Nathaniel and, guessing his thoughts, resolved to put him at ease. "It is not anything I have agreed to. I might not even get the part. The professor wrote me a letter and said I am one of three girls being considered, that's all."

"An important role?" he said quietly.

"Yes, Juliette in *Romeo et Juliette*." She couldn't keep the excitement out of her voice. "Most girls would do anything for such a chance. It's a difficult role. To even be considered for it when I am so young is…" She lost her train of thought when she saw a shadow cross Nathaniel's face.

"This is a great honor for you," he said, his voice flat.

"Yes, Nathaniel. But this doesn't mean I am certain of going back. I am…it makes me excited to think…they like my voice."

He turned his back on her and looked out over the pond. "And when do you think you will be certain?"

"I—I am waiting upon the Lord. Like you said."

"Why wait? Why not go now and seize this great opportunity? Playing Juliette will bring you all the attention you could ever want."

His reaction made Kate suddenly dizzy, as if Aaron had come up behind her and slapped her upside the head. "You know it is not like that. I'm trying. I'm praying very hard to know."

He turned to look at her. "Are you? You tell me this, but I don't know what to think. All I see is that you are still firmly attached to the world. Aaron says you get two or three letters a week from Milwaukee. Ada and Mamm both recognize signs that I have missed."

Kate tried to purge her voice of resentment. "Jah, Ada and your mamm watch me very closely."

"I am tired of pretending to be happy for you when you tell me the Met wants to hear you sing or you might win another part. The truth is, I am not happy. When you talk of such things, you speak as if you have made up your mind. With every new opportunity back there, my hopes sink more. How can I stand it any longer?"

Kate touched Nathaniel's arm. "I never meant to make it sound that way."

Nathaniel took off his hat and ran his fingers through his hair. "When I'm with you, I feel as if I am soaring through the sky. As if I am standing on top of the highest mountain with the wind at my back. But when we are apart, the dread grabs my throat and won't let me breathe. I wonder, 'Is today the day she will cut my legs out from under me and send me crashing to the ground? Or will she stick a knife in my chest like her Englisch friends are so fond of doing to each other?' I have been a fool to love you when it is plain that you will leave me come autumn. I can't bear to be so high and so low at the same time."

Firmly, he took her shoulders. "Look at me, Kate. People are talking, laughing at me because I am a slobbering puppy when it comes to you. Either you choose me or you don't. Which is it? I must know."

Tears stung her eyes. "I don't know. You said you would be patient. I don't know."

Nathaniel scowled. "I cannot wait longer. I will not wait longer."

Kate, stunned into silence, could only stare at him and plead with her eyes.

Nathaniel deserved answers, but answers refused to come to her. She had spent so much time on her knees, they were black and blue. She had consulted with the bishop's wife and her parents and her siblings and faithfully studied the Bible looking for hidden wisdom on every page. She had turned everything in her life over to God, and the price of devotion climbed steeper and steeper. She didn't deserve the love of such a good man. What else would God require of her?

"Your silence speaks volumes, Kate." Nathaniel's breathing was labored, and he would not look at her. "It is over between us." He turned his back on her and moved in the direction Elmer had gone. "I will ask Elmer to take you home."

Without another word of explanation, he disappeared through the trees more swiftly than Kate could have imagined.

Chapter Eighteen

"Nathaniel, are you all right?"

Alphy Petersheim, already stooped with arthritis and age, didn't have to go much farther to peer under the kitchen cupboard where Nathaniel knelt clutching the back of his head.

"Jah, I am okay. Just clumsy," Nathaniel said.

"I heard you yell and thought maybe the pipe burst."

Nathaniel panted in an attempt to lessen the pain and pulled himself out from the cupboard. "I dropped the wrench on my thumb then sat up too quickly and forgot to mind the pipe."

He fingered the bleeding goose egg on the back of his head.

"Good gracious, boy. Must have hit hard. Nancy will fix you right up yet."

Alphy leaned heavily on his cane as he made the long trek to the bedroom to fetch his wife.

Nathaniel pulled a handkerchief from his pocket and dabbed the blood from his hair. Not too bad. He wouldn't need stitches. But, oh, sis yusht, it hurt. Almost as bad as his thumb, which throbbed forcefully and had already turned red.

Nancy bustled into the kitchen with a small first-aid kit. "For goodness sake, Nathaniel. What did you do to yourself?"

She ordered him to his feet and insisted he sit at the table. "Let's have a look." She gently parted his hair and examined the wound. "Doesn't seem fair that you came here to do a good deed and got repaid in pain."

"I am afraid I am not very sharp today," Nathaniel said.

Nancy nudged his chin in her grandmotherly way and looked into his eyes. "Oh, jah, sure enough you are coming down with something." She put the back of her hand to his forehead and clucked her tongue. "No fever, but I should have guessed you felt poorly. You didn't have nary a smile when you came in."

Nary a smile. Nathaniel hadn't smiled for four days. And whistling? Absolutely no whistling. Luke Miller must be happy as a clam.

"I will put some ointment on the head, but it is not deep. Let me see the thumb." She took his hand in hers. "As sure as rain you will lose the nail. Lance it with a needle when it fills with blood. Let me see if I have ibuprofen."

Nancy shuffled out of the kitchen. Nathaniel groaned and returned to his place under the sink to fix the clog for the Petersheims. He had almost finished when he'd hurt himself. Every task took a hundred times more concentration than usual, and with his head so full of Kate, concentration was well-nigh impossible.

His effort to clear his head proved useless. Kate, it seemed, was everywhere, even when she was absent. She had appeared at the auction two nights ago looking so beautiful that the sight of her made him ache. He had promptly run out and walked almost five miles before realizing he had left his buggy at the auction. What would he do when church services came around the following week? He contemplated joining the Methodists for worship so he wouldn't have to lay eyes on Kate at *gmay*.

His ultimatum hadn't exactly turned out as he thought it would, and he felt like a fool. He, who prided himself on being so open-minded and long-suffering, had melted under pressure.

In his haste, he had neglected to calculate the cost of his outburst. He couldn't eat or sleep or work. Even Luke Miller had noticed something amiss.

"Go home to bed," Luke admonished him yesterday. "You are useless in the shop."

Nathaniel tightened the last washer just as Nancy returned with the painkillers.

Do you have anything for this puncture wound in my chest? he wanted to ask. *Or something to cure "stupid"? I need that pill mighty bad.*

Chapter Nineteen

"Ouch!" Sadie squeaked and yanked her hand out of the middle of the raspberry bush.

"Watch the brambles, leibe," said Kate, "or you will come away with lots of scratches and no raspberries."

Sadie held up her finger to show her aunt. "I'm bweeding."

Kate pulled a hanky from her apron pocket. "Just a teeny bit." She dabbed Sadie's finger then put the hanky back in her pocket and kissed the injured pinky. "There now, all better."

Satisfied, Sadie picked up her pail and gingerly reached into the bush to retrieve a plump red berry. "This is for gute jam," she said grinning, her pain forgotten amid the prospect of homemade raspberry preserves.

Kate wiped the sweat from her forehead and surveyed the bushes, which were meticulously staked and tied in tidy rows. She and Mamma spent hours every week tending the family garden. For this early in the season, the canes already sagged with ripe fruit. The harvest promised to be good.

Sighing plaintively, Kate bent to her task and tried to focus on raspberries and freezer jam and aphids. Anything to keep the oppressive weight from squeezing the air right out of her.

Even with Sadie chattering beside her, Kate's mind involuntarily galloped directly to Nathaniel. It seemed as if a load of stones sat oppressively on her chest, which made thinking of him and breathing at the same time extremely difficult. Less than a week had passed since he'd told her he was done waiting, but it had seemed like a year.

Even though the memory of that night brought fresh pain every time Kate thought about it, she could not find it in her heart to blame Nathaniel. What right did she have to ask anything of him, especially his unquestioning devotion? She had pushed his patience to the limit with her uncertainty, and he had chosen to let her go. In her rational mind, she could not but agree with him.

Besides, how much better for him to break away from her now, before the pain of her leaving cut him down even further. She could not bear the thought of hurting him. How much worse would a separation have been in two months' time? This way was better for him. Better. Much better.

And still she grieved. If Nathaniel's actions had accomplished one thing, they had succeeded in helping her understand how much she cared for him and how much it hurt to lose him. *It is better this way,* she kept telling herself. *As the Lord will, so will be.*

"Hello, hello, hello," Sadie said.

"What is it, Sadie?" Kate said, with her head bent low over a bush.

Sadie giggled. "Hello, hello."

Kate looked up only to meet eyes with Nathaniel, who stood a few feet away from her, clutching a bouquet of wildflowers. Kate's heart refused to remain calm, pounding rebelliously in her chest.

Sadie had attached herself securely to Nathaniel's leg and seemed content to hold on forever. He patted Sadie on the head and looked at Kate. "I couldn't last a week."

His tan face almost glowed under the shade of his hat, and she found it impossible to look away from his icy-blue eyes. No smile graced his face today, but he was plenty handsome without one. And why did her knees go all shaky over the stubble on his chin? How in the world did a little stubble have such power over her?

"Nathaniel."

Her quiet acknowledgment seemed to be all he needed. "I'm sorry," he said, plunging headlong into an apology. "I'm sorry for everything I said. I'm sorry for making you cry and for leaving you there like that. This has been the most miserable six days of my entire life." He tried to take a step toward her, but Sadie still clung tightly to his leg. "I didn't sleep a wink, I ate less than I slept, and"—he held up his thumb to reveal a pitch-black nail—"I smashed my thumbnail because I was too distracted to hold tight to my wrench."

Unable to stir herself from this stupor, Kate remained still.

He tried to take another step with Sadie still hanging on and then bent down and whispered something to the little girl. He handed her the flowers, and she took them carefully and put them into Kate's hand.

"These are for your mother," Nathaniel said.

Kate couldn't keep from laughing, even though her eyes brimmed with tears. "Gute, because I would have had to refuse such a beautiful gift for myself." She brought the flowers to her nose and breathed in the sweet fragrance before she handed the bouquet back to Sadie. "Take the flowers to *Mammi* and ask her to put them in some water, please."

Sadie walked carefully to the house, her little legs moving as fast as she could go without disturbing the blooms in her hand. Kate and Nathaniel stood frozen, looking at each other.

"I don't blame you if you never want to talk to me again. I should have at least shown the courtesy of driving you home. There is no excuse for my behavior."

Kate shook her head. "That would have been a very uncomfortable ride. And very long. You were right, Nathaniel. How can I ask you to wait for me? It's unfair."

"You are not asking anything of me. I give it freely." His face was inches from hers. "Because I love you. Love is unselfish and kind and suffers long. It suffers long, Kate. I'm determined to learn patience."

Kate put a hand to her heart in an effort to slow its racing. She gazed at Nathaniel until a movement out of the corner of her eyes caught her attention. Peering at the house, she spied Mamma, Mary, and her sister-in-law Anna watching them. Each of Kate's relatives smiled from ear to ear, and though she could not hear them, Kate guessed they were clucking and giggling over her newly returned boyfriend.

Kate groaned in exasperation. "Come on, Nathaniel."

Nathaniel followed Kate around the side of the house.

"This should keep us safe from curious eyes," she said.

He moved close again, daring Kate to shy away from him. She held her ground until the twins and little Giddy came tearing around the side of the house, carrying rags and buckets. Kate stepped quickly away from Nathaniel to avoid the inevitable stares of her brothers and nephew.

As was to be expected, the surprised boys stopped dead in their tracks when they saw Kate and Nathaniel standing in the side yard as if a meeting in the middle of the day were as commonplace as rain in the springtime.

"What are you doing here?" Joe said, his adolescent voice squeaking like a rusty gate. He'd heard of the incident at the pond from Elmer and sounded ever so mildly hostile.

"I came to deliver something to your mamm," Nathaniel said, not missing a beat and ignoring the nudge Kate gave him with her elbow.

The twins stared at Nathaniel, then at Kate, then back at Nathaniel. They obviously concluded that Kate didn't look distressed or eager to leave Nathaniel's presence. Joe shrugged. "Don't let us disturb you, then. We're only doing all the chores around here while you two do important things like talk about the weather."

The boys turned their backs and ran to the carriage house, presumably to clean and oil the buggy.

"Come," Kate said, motioning for Nathaniel to follow her. "Let's go sit on the porch."

"Are you sure?" he said as they walked to the front of the house.

"They'll find a way to spy wherever we are." She sat on the bottom step. "I will sit and you can stand over there so you are not tempted to make a pest of yourself and get closer than is proper."

Nathaniel laughed and planted himself next to Kate. "Have you ever measured how far away 'proper' is? In inches, I mean."

She pushed him away and refused to let him sit. He was forced to stand on the flagstones resting his arm on the handrail.

"You haven't answered my question yet. Will you let me court you? Until the summer dies and my heart dies with it?" he said.

"Don't sound so hopeless. I might be here in the fall."

Delight spread all over his face, melting any resistance Kate might have felt. "That would be too wonderful even to hope for," he said.

"You are very noble to persevere," she said, "but if you are determined to stick with me, nothing could bring me more happiness. Although I feel utterly selfish for it."

"You are the most unselfish person I know," Nathaniel said. "That is why I am hoping you will forgive me. Will you? For losing my temper and hurting your feelings? I think I've done more repenting in the last two months than I've done in my entire life. How can I ever hope to be a gute man when I make a mistake at every turn?"

"I don't love you because you are perfect. I love you because you are passionate and lighthearted and you try too hard and get frustrated. I love you because God is first in your life and you won't settle for anything less."

"I know but—" Nathaniel stopped mid-sentence and eagerly sat next to her. "You...love me?"

"Jah, I believe I do," she said.

His smile could have blinded the sun.

"Don't make too much of it," she teased. "You *had* to know."

"No, I didn't!"

Relishing his nearness, she leaned her shoulder against his. "I wish I could think of something for your mamm. To make her like me."

"I'm sure my mamm likes you. She just takes a little time to warm up to people."

Kate didn't want to argue with him. After all, he hadn't been the one to hear Lisa Fisher's gossip.

"There is something you can do for my mamm."

"What?"

"She is having a quilting circle next week at our house. I know she needs help."

Kate gave Nathaniel an uncertain smile. He couldn't have chosen a less attractive activity. Miriam was sure to be seriously underwhelmed by Kate's lack of sewing skills. One more thing to add to her list of reasons for not wanting Kate to marry her son.

"You can bring Mary," Nathaniel said, when he saw her hesitation. "My mamm will be so pleased."

Kate swallowed the bitter taste in her mouth. If only she believed that were true. "There is one more thing," she said, as her mouth went dry. "I don't blame you if you change your mind right now, and we can pretend this conversation never happened."

"What is it?"

"I am singing in a concert in Madison tomorrow for the academy. Do you want to take back your apology?"

His eyes lost their sparkle for a split-second but then he smiled. "I told you I would learn to be patient. This is my first test."

Chapter Twenty

Kate stepped off the bus onto an unfamiliar street corner in Madison. Dr. Sumsion embraced her almost before her feet hit the ground. "Kate, you made it! I was beginning to think we'd have to cut all your songs."

"Sorry," Kate said. "The bus service from Apple Lake is not always reliable."

"Today of all days, I wish Amish people drove cars." Dr. Sumsion, a short, plump woman with salt-and-pepper hair and a no-nonsense smile, handed Kate a suit bag. "Go and change. Chelsea and the new student, Shannon, are in there already. And find a place to warm up. The concert starts in a half hour."

The hot summer sun reflected off the black pavement, and sweat trickled down Kate's neck before she even set off for the hill. She trudged up the slope hoping the borrowed formal would be sufficiently modest. She'd been very explicit in her last letter to Dr. Sumsion: *The dress must have sleeves.*

Dr. Sumsion called her back. "Kate, I added the Mozart back into the program. Ryan's ready to do it."

Dr. Sumsion had asked her to join a group of students from the academy for an outdoor concert at one of Madison's parks smack in the middle of her Amish summer. It was a long way to travel to perform five or six songs, but the wages paid for the trip and Kate sought as many experiences as possible in which she might be able to hear God's voice and understand His will. Faith without works was dead. Would He speak to her heart today? Kate smiled plaintively. The only person who seemed to speak to her heart was Nathaniel.

She glanced around as she made her way to the large white building at the corner of the park. Her heart pounded when she spied two young men standing directly in her path. Surprised at her own reaction, she still made a wide circle to avoid them. The encounter in La Crosse so many weeks ago had left her skittish. For a moment, she longed for the comfort of her own cozy home tucked among the apple trees.

After slipping through the side door, Kate let her eyes adjust to the dimness. Hearing voices, she walked to a lighted room at the end of the hall and stuck her head through the doorway.

Chelsea Webster sat in an overstuffed lounge chair drinking designer water while another girl paced around the room doing lip bubbles at increasingly high frequencies. Catching sight of Kate, the new girl almost choked. Then she tried to talk through her coughing spell.

"What...are you...wearing? Are you...a nun...a singing nun?"

"Shannon!" Chelsea said. She jumped up and pounded Shannon on the back with the heel of her hand.

"Chelsea...stop...you're making it worse," Shannon stammered.

A short dishwater blond, Chelsea was a year ahead of Kate in school and quite protective of her seniority. She'd made no secret of her displeasure when Kate won the role of Angelica last year and displaced Chelsea as Dr. Sumsion's favorite.

Chelsea handed Shannon a bottle of water and left her to wheeze on her own. She brought another bottle to Kate. "We thought you wouldn't make it. Shannon was going to attempt *La Traviata*. But right now she's in no condition to sing anything. I'll be your understudy, Shannon. Can I have 'O Luce'?"

Shannon took a swig of water. "No, thank you. I'll be fine."

Thin and tall, almost as tall as Elmer, and with a full head of thick auburn hair, Shannon wore a cobalt-blue knee-length formal that made the irises of her eyes striking.

"Sorry about that," she said. "Your clothes took me by surprise." Shannon tilted her head to one side. "What are you? I mean, is that a rude question? I don't want to be rude."

Kate shook her head. "I'm Amish."

"Wait a minute," Shannon said. "Harrison Ford was in that Amish movie."

"That movie is the only thing people know about us."

"Are Amish allowed to see movies?" Shannon said.

"We do a lot of things before baptism."

"Like go to the music arts academy?"

"Jah."

"But after baptism, the academy is forbidden, right?" Chelsea said.

"We give up the things of the world at baptism."

"Wow," Shannon said. "How long before you have to get baptized?"

"I do not have to be baptized. If I don't join the Church, then I will pursue a career in opera."

"But if you get baptized?"

"I will give up the singing," Kate said.

Chelsea and Shannon looked at each other.

"What will you choose?" Shannon said.

"I don't know. I am waiting for God."

They stood in silence until Shannon said, "You better get into your dress, Kate, or Dr. Sumsion will have a panic attack."

Kate went into the bathroom and took the dress from the suit bag. It was a beautiful, glossy, lime-green fabric with a fitted bodice and V-shaped waistline. It also had sleeves and a high neckline. *Thank you, Dr. Sumsion.*

After pulling the dress over her head, Kate looked in the mirror. Dressing up was one thing she loved about performing. She never felt as beautiful as when she floated onstage in a stunning formal. Gross vanity, as Ada and Nathaniel's mamm would both remind her.

Kate started her lip trills before she even walked out of the bathroom. She only had a few minutes to warm up.

"Did you know that Amish people don't use electricity or drive cars?" Shannon was saying as Kate returned through the door. "They only have to go to school until the eighth grade. And they don't worship in church buildings. They meet in everybody's houses." Shannon's eyes were fixed on her phone as she punched the screen rapidly.

Kate looked at Shannon in amusement. "Jah, I knew all that."

"Not you, Kate," Shannon said. "I'm trying to educate Chelsea."

Chelsea sat in the same lounge chair, applying another coat of black mascara. "Ten minutes ago you knew less about the Amish than I did."

Shannon pried her eyes from her phone long enough to glance at Kate. "Holy cow! Your hair is so long and pretty down like that. Chelsea, did you know that Amish women don't cut their hair?"

"Yes, Shannon, I know. I've been with Kate at school for two years. You've never even met her until this afternoon."

They heard the *clip* of Dr. Sumsion's heels down the hall before they ever saw her. She entered the room like a tornado and handed each of them a slip of paper. "Here is the order of the program. Get up and down as quickly as possible. Ryan and Brandon are waiting outside. Oh, Kate. That dress looks nice."

Dr. Sumsion took a deep breath as she pressed the top of her pen up and down, up and down. "Everything must be perfect today, girls. Singing outdoors is challenging because you tend to want to fill the space. Remember, you have microphones, so don't over-sing." She gave them a wan smile. "But knock 'em dead."

Kate took a sip of water as the butterflies began their frenzied flight in her stomach. She had never been able to decide whether she loved or hated that nervous feeling right before she stepped onto a stage.

The girls tried to keep pace with the professor as she led them down the hall to the outside door. "My water!" Chelsea squeaked. She ran back to the room and reemerged carrying two full bottles.

"Chelsea, you're going to have to run off the stage in the middle of your aria to go to the bathroom," Shannon said.

"Do you think they'll be able to hear me sing from the stalls? I could open a window."

The concert consisted of several well-known numbers from popular operas. Spectators sat on lawn chairs or blankets, and Kate and her fellow students took turns performing while accompanied by a piano, two violins, and a cello.

The final number, "Un Bel Di" from *Madame Butterfly*, was Kate's. As she always did when she performed, she pictured herself as Cio-Cio San, the ill-fated woman in the opera. The lyrics were in Italian, but she understood the meaning of every word. She envisioned the pitiful woman waiting patiently for a lover to return from the sea—a lover who ultimately forsakes her.

"I stay upon the edge of the hill and wait for a long time, but I do not grow weary of the long wait."

Instead of a handsome naval officer, Kate saw Nathaniel's face in her mind's eye. She pictured him sitting in solitude, crafting his wood with those sinewy arms and gentle hands. He raised his head, and she imagined the look of longing she had seen so many times before.

"I promise you this. Hold back your fears—I will wait with unshakable faith. I will wait."

Wait for what?

For me to rip his heart to shreds.

As the last strains of the violin faded mournfully, she put her hand to her wet cheek. She felt a suffocating ache for her family and home, for Nathaniel's arms and his heart. *I cannot bear to hurt you.*

After one breathless pause, the crowd erupted into applause and cheering. Had she ever experienced the profound emotion of that song before? Perhaps for the first time she knew what it meant to love someone so deeply that she wept for the possibilities—the bittersweet choices and the yearning for God.

Kate took her bow then left the stage. Ryan and Shannon pushed her back up the narrow steps for a second call. She bowed again, overwhelmed at the audience response and again as her feelings for Nathaniel saturated her senses like a cool summer cloudburst.

After another modest curtsy, Kate jumped down the steps and pulled Ryan, Shannon, and the others on stage with her. The five held hands and bowed together, and then each bowed again separately. Before the applause finally subsided, Chelsea bolted off the stage and made a beeline for the bathroom. Shannon laughed and winked at Kate.

When they exited the stage, Dr. Sumsion grabbed Kate's arm and pulled her aside. "A triumph, an absolute triumph," she said, squeezing her hand. "You all did the academy proud." She leaned closer to Kate's ear. "There is someone here to see you." She pulled Kate away from the gathering crowd of admirers toward a woman in her late thirties and an older man who stood apart from the throng and studied Kate.

Without even knowing who they were, Kate felt intimidated. The man wore a flawless gray suit and green silk tie with a matching handkerchief in his lapel pocket. The woman, in a peach jacket with a pencil skirt, dripped with importance—diamonds, her comfortably worn accessories.

"Kate, this is Jim Talbot, chairman of the academy foundation," Dr. Sumsion said, pushing Kate forward to shake hands with the couple. "And this is Nannette Parrish. She's new to the board and will be overseeing the production of *Romeo et Juliette* this fall."

Jim Talbot flashed impeccably white teeth to go with his impeccably tailored suit. "We understand you auditioned for the opera before the end of spring term, Kate. Dr. Dibble is adamant that you are the only voice worthy of Juliette. We wanted to hear you sing before making any casting decisions." He turned and nodded at Miss Parrish. "And I must say, we are impressed. This is a talented bunch of students, Dr. Sumsion."

Miss Parrish turned up her nose ever so slightly and folded her arms. "You are quite young to have the biggest role in the student opera. Young singers are seldom ready for the demands of a full-scale production. But we have made our decision, and the role is yours."

A pile of rocks settled in the pit of Kate's stomach. "Oh, thank you," she said, adding a lilt to her voice with some effort. "I am thrilled you think I am worthy of the role. This is a—a dream come true."

Dr. Sumsion wrapped her arms around Kate. "Oh, my dear, this is wonderful. You will be fabulous. There could never be a more beautiful Juliette."

Ryan and Shannon came up behind Mr. Talbot. He turned and greeted Ryan with a slug to the arm.

Ryan employed his best English accent. "Did you bring your smoked eel and caviar for a little soiree on the grass this evening, Miss Parrish?"

Miss Parrish eyed Ryan with studied apathy. "Lose some weight and you'll be the perfect Romeo. Stay fat, and we'll demote you to Friar Lawrence."

Ryan laughed and took a step back. "Ouch, that hurts. I'm not even a bass."

Mr. Talbot turned to leave. "We'll see you all there in a few weeks for start of term. Miss Weaver, congratulations. Make the most of your summer. By the end of November you might wish you'd never heard of the Milwaukee Music Academy."

Mr. Talbot walked away, and Miss Parrish fixed her eye on Ryan.

"I'm not kidding, Mr. French. Lay off the cheeseburgers, or Miss Weaver will be singing 'Ne Fuis Pas Encore' with someone else."

Dr. Sumsion ran after both of them for a parting word.

"Do you want me to drive the heel of my Jimmy Choo into her forehead?" Shannon said.

Ryan shrugged. "Nah, Nannette loves me. But Kate, did I hear right? Are they giving you Juliette?"

Kate managed a half smile and nodded. "I—I can't believe it. It is an amazing opportunity."

"That's fantastic! And I get to kiss you." Ryan pumped his fist in the air. "Provided I can lose enough weight to convince Nannette to cast me. Five pounds should do it."

Shannon silently searched Kate's face while the others gushed. Grabbing Kate's arm, she said, "Hey, guys, Kate and I are going to change."

She linked her arm with Kate's and led her up the hill. "Juliette. The role of your young lifetime." She stopped walking. "But you're not happy about it."

The rocks in Kate's stomach grew heavier, and her voice cracked. "I have been over this in my head too many times to count."

"I'm so sorry."

"Is God playing a game with me? Deliberately clouding the waters by enticing me with this role? I do not know what to think."

"I'd never second-guess God," Shannon said. "But maybe He is trying to help you by showing your choices so clearly. On one hand, your talent practically guarantees a fabulous singing career. On the other hand, you have your family, your faith, your way of life—"

"Nathaniel."

Shannon's jaw dropped. "Nathaniel? The plot thickens." She considered this new information. "A boyfriend?"

"Jah."

"He's who you were thinking about when you sang." She tightened her hold on Kate's arm. "No wonder that was the most moving performance of 'Un Bel Di' I've ever heard. Is he good-looking?"

Kate smiled in spite of herself. "Very good-looking. With a heart of gold."

"And you love him."

"Jah."

Shannon nodded. "So God is saying, 'Look, Kate. Here are your two clear, well-defined choices. Go for it.'"

Go for it.

"But what does God want me to do?"

"God wants you to be happy."

Kate thought about that for a minute. "Yes, He does."

Shannon grinned. "Not that I'd like to see Chelsea get Juliette. She's a prima donna, and Ryan can't stand her."

"Jah, they would be very happy to see each other die at the end."

Kate and Shannon walked up the hill arm in arm, Shannon chattering merrily about the latest opera website.

Kate nodded politely when necessary but didn't really pay attention. She sensed that she was enticingly close to an answer yet more confused than ever.

Chapter Twenty-One

With trepidation, Kate stood on porch of the Kings' small farmhouse. She hadn't been inside Nathaniel's home since she had come here for Sunday services over two years ago. And she had never associated Nathaniel with this home in which he grew up. She ran her palm along the silky-smooth porch railing sanded by a skillful carpenter's hands and saw Nathaniel with new eyes. Though small, everything about the front yard testified to the diligence of those who lived there. The short picket fence surrounding the perimeter was painted bright white, with no flaking paint to be seen. The meticulously trimmed bushes huddled close to the petunias, thick and vibrant against the ground. How did Nathaniel and his mamm manage it all by themselves?

Kate and her sister Mary were the last of the quilters to arrive. Before they had set foot from Mary's house, the baby had spit up all over his clean clothes and had to be stripped from head to toe and redressed before the sisters could harness the horse to the buggy and make their way to the quilting circle. Bouncing the baby on her hip, Mary opened the door for Kate, who held a basket of fabric in one arm and Sadie in the other.

Kate's heart sank as she scanned the group. Ada sat on the far side of the quilt with Sarah Schwartz, quilting feverishly and ignoring Kate's arrival. But they both pursed their lips and exchanged knowing glances when she entered the room.

"Kate and Mary. So good to see you," Edna Miller said, bobbing her needle over and under the fabric stretched onto frames. Dear Edna was a welcome sight. She always took people at face value and never gossiped. "Will we see you at the rehabilitation center tomorrow, Kate?"

"Nae. We are canning tomatoes starting early. But the week after for certain."

Several women already busily added the small, delicate stitches that Amish quilts were famous for. The quilt, a relatively simple Wild Goose Chase design, took up most of the space in the front room and dazzled Kate's eyes with its vibrant contrasts and moving patterns.

"Cum, cum, sit down," said Esther Yoder, scooting to make room on the bench on her side of the quilt. "As soon as this one's done, we've got to finish another for the Haiti auction. And even though Ada keeps telling us how fast Sarah is, we need many hands to get done."

"It is beautiful," Kate said. "Who put it together?"

"Miriam, of course," Edna said. "She's got an eye for the colors."

Macie Herschberger held out her arms. "Let me see the buplie, Mary. He is so chubby. Are you feeding him buttermilk?" The room tinkled with the laughter of busy women as Mary handed the baby to Macie.

In consternation, Kate noticed her heart racing unnecessarily fast. Ach, she knew why her throat dried up and her breathing got faster as she crossed the threshold of the Kings' house, and it wasn't because Ada seemed to take pleasure in badgering her. The powerful need to impress Nathaniel's mother would surely render Kate incapable of doing so.

Placing the basket of fabric on the sofa, Kate clasped her hands together to keep them from shaking. It was no secret that her son's attentions to Kate displeased Miriam. If Lisa Fisher's overheard conversation and Kate's trip into La Crosse hadn't been proof enough, Ada was always ready to supply Kate with the latest gossip.

According to Ada, Miriam considered Kate an outsider, a proud and worldly girl whom Miriam's son followed around like a puppy. Kate had heard it all, some of the rumors from Ada, some from cousin Rebecca, and the worst from Aaron, who didn't seem to consider listening to tittle-tattle about his own sister sinful. Nathaniel would be mortified if he knew that Kate had heard the gossip, which chiefly originated from his own mamm.

Nathaniel's mamm poked her head in from the kitchen. "Aw, Mary and her sister," she said, without making eye contact. "Some of the children are out back if you'd like to send your little one to play, Mary. I'll be right in. I'm just getting Hezekiah settled for a nap."

Miriam's scant acknowledgment of Kate confirmed Kate's suspicions. Why had she come?

To make Nathaniel happy, that was why. But either Nathaniel was completely blind to Miriam's dislike, or he suffered from an acute case of wishful thinking. Resisting the urge to leave the house and run clear to Milwaukee, Kate sat on the bench next to Esther and began studiously threading a needle.

Esther's small daughter, Susie, sat under the quilt and ran her fingers along the deep blue fabric on the underside.

"Susie Lynn, you're underfoot," said her mother. "Go outside with Sadie and run around."

Susie did as she was told and took Sadie by the hand, and soon Mary and Kate were free to sew without interruption.

The ladies took turns passing the baby. Eventually he landed on Beth Yoder's lap. "I'm eighty-four years old," she said. "The eyes are pretty near useless. Can't see well enough to thread a needle to save my life. I come to the quilting bees to visit and hold babies."

Kate smiled in her direction. Beth did both of her jobs well.

Soon Miriam joined the circle, and the girls and women stitched with a rapidity that would have put any sewing circle in the world to shame. And they talked at a pace that would have set any Amish husband's head to spinning. Despite her discomfort, Kate laughed out loud several times, completely entertained by the chatter of the good-hearted women surrounding her.

"Edna," Beth said, "Albert wasn't at gmay last Sunday. Have you got the flu at your house?"

Edna let out a loud guffaw. "That boy! He gets himself into more scrapes."

"I know exactly how you feel. My boys are nothing but trouble," Ada said, sighing loudly.

"What happened to Albert?" Mary said.

Edna pulled her needle through the top of the quilt. "Disobeyed his dat by coming home late one night and walked right into a skunk in Masts' pasture. Poor boy could hardly breathe from the stink."

"Oh no!"

"You can be sure I did not let him set one foot in my house. I burned his clothes and made him eat and sleep outside for a week."

Everyone laughed.

"I suppose he'll come home when he's told next time," Edna said with a wink.

"My boys won't do anything they're told," Ada said. "They will be the death of me." She looked around the room for sympathy. "But then, nobody knows how I suffer."

"Kate," Esther said, "tell us about your school. It has been too long since we have seen you."

"Some of us have been pining terribly for your return," Edna teased, obviously unaware that, to at least one woman in the room, it was no joke.

"Jah, our family is grateful to have her home," Mary said.

"Of course," Edna said. "But I am talking about a particularly handsome boy who has never taken an interest in any other girl in the whole community. *He* seems to be very glad you are back. Isn't that right, Miriam?" Some of the women giggled. Not everyone had heard the gossip. Others bent their heads more diligently over their needlework. Ada's frown could have sent the livestock running for cover.

Miriam did not reply. She seemed to be concentrating very hard on untangling a knot in her thread.

Kate squirmed. Edna, without guile or pretense, thought she was bringing up a subject that would give pleasure to both Kate and Miriam. But Kate would just as soon not discuss her relationship with Nathaniel in front of these women, especially his mother. From the cast of Miriam's complexion, she felt the same way.

Edna persisted. "My husband says that since you've come home, the boy hasn't stopped whistling. And my dear Luke has no patience for whistlers."

"I don't know what whistling has to do with anything," Ada said, trying to pick a fight where there wasn't one.

"I am simply pointing out that Kate comes back and my husband cannot get a thing done at Nathaniel's workshop because the boss is whistling all the time. I think Kate has made the boy very happy."

Words exploded out of Miriam's mouth. "Until September," she said. "He's only allowed to be happy until September when school starts. Isn't that right, Kate?"

Ada nodded her agreement.

Kate could have heard a quilting needle hit the floor. Half the women stopped their work to look at Kate. The other half stared at Miriam. "I—I hope he is happy, that he is happy always," Kate stammered softly. She glanced at Miriam, who returned her gaze with thinly veiled contempt.

All of a sudden, Miriam stood and tossed her thimble into the small box on top of the quilt. "Look how fast the time is moving. We've been working so hard that I have completely forgotten to get dinner," she said, as if she hadn't just silenced the room with her outburst.

"Nothing too hard," Esther said, trying for a carefree lilt to her voice.

"Edna brought bread and cheese," Miriam said. "I'll cut some vegetables and we'll be set." She headed into the kitchen.

With more courage than she had ever before been able to muster, Kate stood. "I'll help," she said to no one in particular. Mary gaped at her, eyes full of alarm. Kate nodded reassuringly and marched into the kitchen.

Miriam, her back to Kate, peeled a cucumber with dizzying speed. When she heard Kate come in, she glanced over her shoulder. The peeling slowed considerably and then started up again, double time.

Kate came within an inch of turning around and slinking back into the living room, which was still eerily quiet. Instead, she squared her shoulders and steeled herself for what was to come. She had no idea what to say, but she knew Nathaniel would want her to try.

For his sake, she would try.

"If you have another peeler, I will do carrots," Kate said.

"I don't have another peeler. I've never needed another peeler."

"Then shall I cut the cucumbers after you peel them?"

Miriam practically shoved the cucumber in Kate's hand. "Jah, fine."

Kate took the cucumber, retrieved a knife from the block, and started slicing. She stayed quiet long enough to formulate some kind of coherent sentence. What did Nathaniel's mamm want to hear?

"I do not wish to hurt Nathaniel," Kate said.

"It must be so nice to have a summertime boyfriend, glad as he can be to do anything and everything for you. My son might be taken in by your brilliant green eyes and pretty face, but I am not."

Still hearing nothing from the adjoining room, Kate laid down the knife and put her hand lightly on Miriam's shoulder. "Could we step outside for a moment?"

Miriam kept peeling. "I have nothing to say to you."

"Please, Miriam."

After what seemed like an eternity, Miriam laid her cucumber and peeler on the cupboard and tromped out the door, not bothering to see if Kate followed her. She walked past the children running wild in the backyard and made her way to a cherry tree a few hundred feet from the house. With arms tightly folded, she turned, stood, and glared as Kate caught up to her.

Struggling to emulate Nathaniel's humility, Kate tried to see his mamm with compassion. Miriam's only child, the one whom her life orbited around, no longer looked on Miriam as the center of his life. She had been replaced by a girl who, by all appearances, treated Nathaniel's affection lightly, like a worn article of clothing that could be easily tossed into the laundry bin.

Suddenly Kate's heart ached for this woman who had lost her husband so young and knew she might lose her son as well.

"Your son is deeply good," Kate said, not shying from Miriam's icy reception. "He is more wonderful than I deserve, I know. But he loves me. What would you have me do?"

"I want you to stay away from him."

Kate looked down at her feet and then lifted her head to study Miriam's face. "If God means for us to be together, the fault will be on your head if you separate us. Are you willing to live with the consequences of such a decision?"

Miriam flashed an expression of stubborn refusal. "How could the Almighty want you to be with my son?"

"Are you able to judge such things?"

Scowling, Miriam turned her face away. "Even if you stay here, you will both be miserable."

"Why do you say that?"

Instead of answering, Miriam pulled Kate to sit next to her on two overturned boxes that were waiting to be filled with cherries. Her demeanor softened somewhat as she studied Kate's face.

"I have never shared this with anyone, so I will thank you to keep it quiet. But Nathaniel's happiness is at stake, so I will risk it. To make you understand." She laced her fingers together. "I know what you struggle with, the two choices that war against each other in your head." She cleared her throat. "I see so much of myself in you. Too much."

"How so?"

Miriam pursed her lips, and Kate could tell she chose her words carefully. "I suppose I was a strange child. Full of woe, my pappa would say. I used to stare out the window and think, just sit and think, and try to make sense of all the thoughts that jumbled in my head like a swarm of bees. I felt the strap more than once for daydreaming. At fourteen, I begged Pappa to let me go to the Englisch school. I got the strap over and over for my wickedness, for wanting to escape the place where the Almighty had placed me."

Miriam turned her face from Kate. "I didn't care how many times Pappa punished me. I asked him again and again to let me go to school. My whole body ached with the desire to be a doctor. But Pappa would not allow it. It is not our way." Miriam exhaled forcefully. "Perhaps you think me deerich, a fanciful woman, but I know I could have done it. It is boastful to say, but I was the best student in the school. The smartest."

Kate laid a hand on Miriam's arm. Miriam pulled away.

"After I married, I fought hard against the resentment. It felt like my pappa had placed me in a box and nailed it shut. Hezekiah is a good man. He did not understand, but he could see I was suffocating. He gave me permission to learn from a local midwife. I didn't go to school, so the bishop was lenient about it. Being a midwife was not my dream, but it was something."

"Jah, that is something."

"But it doesn't matter. I was never happy with the lot the good Lord gave me. My resentment toward the church and my pappa, even Hezekiah, festered every day. I made my husband miserable."

"And you think I will make Nathaniel miserable in the same way?"

Miriam nodded. "Can you really be content to abandon your education, your one chance to escape, and live the simple life? And if you do, will you resent Nathaniel for keeping you here? Doing his laundry, cooking his meals, tending his children? How long before your home becomes a prison?"

Kate stood and stared at the green pasture in the distance without really seeing it. "I didn't know anyone else felt this way. I have been offered the biggest part in our opera this fall. I do not know if I can give that up."

"Nathaniel stands in your way. If you stay here, you will despise him. And if you leave, you will break his heart beyond repair." Kate turned to her, and Miriam lifted her chin in defiance. "I'm not going to let you do that."

"But are our dreams wicked? Why did the Lord God give you a brain if He didn't want you to use it? Why would He give me a voice only to bid me to keep silent?"

"You think I know the answer?" Miriam said.

"Why would He give me this love for Nathaniel if not to nurture it?"

Miriam had no reply.

"I am blessed with a father who understands, and I am not forced into anything. Nathaniel…" Kate's voice caught in her throat. "Bless his goodness! He tries not to pressure me to make a decision. You must have felt like a captive."

"Jah, and I despised my pappa for it."

"But aren't you doing the same thing when you try to force Nathaniel to want something he does not want?"

Miriam folded her arms and looked away.

Kate took a deep breath. "Every choice involves some kind of pain. Choosing one path means rejecting another along with everything down it. You cannot ever know for certain you would have been happier as a doctor. I do not pretend to have as much experience as you, but I believe you must stop looking back." She touched Miriam lightly on the shoulder. "That was Lot's wife's mistake."

"Don't you think I know that? I have paid dearly for my wickedness. God took my first four babies." She paused briefly then pressed on. "After Nathaniel, the doctor said I would never have another child. Then the Lord struck down my husband as punishment for my stiffneckedness. I bear the guilt for all of our misfortunes."

Stunned, Kate said, "Can you really believe the Lord God is so vindictive? That He waits for you to think a wicked thought or do a wicked deed so He can strike you down with His anger? I cannot trust in such a God. He wants us to be happy. I know He does." She risked a hand on Miriam's arm. "I am glad you never became a doctor. I wouldn't have known your son," she said. "And maybe you do not dislike me as much as you hoped you would?"

"How could I dislike you? I have been in your shoes. I do not envy your decision. I envy your freedom to choose."

They stood regarding each other until Miriam looked toward the house and broke the silence. "Do you think everybody has given up on dinner and gone home?"

"No, they are waiting to see if we enter the house arm in arm or nose to nose."

Miriam softened her expression. "Let's keep them guessing. You enter through the front, and I will come in the back door. That will give them something to talk about at the next quilting party."

"Jah, they always need something to talk about," Kate said as, with a heavy heart, she made her way to the front door and Miriam went through the back.

Chapter Twenty-Two

It was after sunset when Kate removed the last of the quart bottles from the pressure cooker and carefully placed them on the wooden table covered with old newspapers. Kate, along with Anna, Mary, and Mamma, had washed, sliced, and blanched tomatoes all morning and boiled, packed, and processed tomatoes all afternoon. Canning commenced at sunrise and ended when the last bottle was pulled from the hot water in the evening.

This morning, Dat had set up the three-burner propane stove in the backyard on the cement patio. Once the tomatoes were prepared in jars, Kate brought them outside and put them in the pressure cookers. When cookers were filled, Mamma, Mary, and Anna prepared more tomatoes while Kate heated the cookers to the precise temperature and tended them with a hot pad and a timer. Once the tomatoes were properly processed, Kate placed the bottles on the tables set up under the trees. Then Mamma would bring out new bottles to fill the empty cookers, and the process would start all over again.

Putting her hands on her hips, Kate looked at the two tables filled with bottles of beautiful red fruit. She heard an occasional *pop* when a bottle cooled and the jar sealed properly. A very satisfying sound.

The work had gone on all day, but the fruits of their labor proved bountiful. One hundred and forty-four quarts to divide among their three households for the winter—an amazing feat for any day of canning.

Mamma stuck her head around the back door. "Bring in the last cooker, leibe, and we will wash it. Is it cool enough?"

"Jah, I think so."

"I'll send the boys out to load some of the cooler bottles in Anna's buggy. She needs to get along home."

With both hands, Kate gripped the handle of the heavy pressure cooker and carried it to the edge of the grass, where she carefully poured the hot water onto the dirt. As she turned to take it back to the house, someone called her name. Through the semidarkness she saw Aaron coming towards her with long, purposeful strides.

"I need to talk to you now," he said.

"Very well," Kate said. "Let me take this pan into—"

"No, we must talk right now."

Aaron's abrupt tone did not inspire Kate to cheerfully cooperate, but he seemed determined. She placed the pressure cooker on the burner and folded her arms. Aaron grabbed her wrist and dragged her to the side of the house, the one with no windows.

"Stop this, Aaron. What are you doing?" Kate said.

"Since Dat won't do anything about you, I must. You are in need of sore repentance, Katie. Do you understand what you are doing to our family? Ada says you were rude to Nathaniel's mother."

"Rude?" Kate said, annoyed but not surprised at Ada's version of yesterday's events. "It was not like that."

"Ada says you yelled at Miriam outside for twenty minutes while ten women sat in her living room. What did you say to Nathaniel's mamm?"

Aaron didn't deserve an explanation. "You can believe what you want. I don't have to justify myself to you."

"You must justify yourself to God. But you don't care about that, do you?"

"What do you know of my desires?"

She flinched as he put his hand on her shoulder and backed her firmly against the side of the house. "I know that you are pulling down this whole family with your abominable pride."

"I am in my rumschpringe."

"People talk. People recognize when a girl is on a bad path. More than once the bishop has told me how alarmed he is by your actions. He asked me to do what I can to redeem you."

Kate tried to shrug his hand off her shoulder. "Do you really care about my redemption? Or are you more concerned with how all this looks to the people in this community? Be honest, Aaron. Your own vanity is wounded by my supposed bad behavior. You care too much how other people see you."

Aaron tightened his grip on her shoulder. "Of course I care how the good people of this community see me. Us."

"Because you want to be bishop someday."

"Do not accuse me of thoughts that are not mine. A man must not act proudly, or no one will believe he is truly humble. If a man's neighbors see him choosing worldly ways, they will judge him to be worldly. It matters very much what people think."

Kate couldn't disguise her disdain. "Then you should be satisfied with yourself. No one could think you anything but pious and upright. Your father-in-law is the bishop. You are related to the most important man in the district, and that relationship gives you some power, doesn't it? You train your keen eye on everyone and delight in calling transgressors to repentance."

Aaron scowled. "I never tire in the fight against wickedness. It is everyone's duty to keep the community pure."

"You often inform the bishop about the sins of the Weaver family. That probably keeps you busy enough for five such men."

She had never seen such rage in his eyes. Aaron grabbed Kate's chin in his large hand. "Dat puts up with your impudence. I will not."

Kate cried out involuntarily.

"I refuse to let you shame this family," he said.

"Let go of me," she said as pain shot through her jaw. Aaron had strong hands, farmer's hands.

Elmer came tearing around the corner of the house. "Get away from her," he said with such harshness that no one hearing would have guessed Aaron to be his elder brother.

To Kate's great relief, Aaron released his grip and stepped back. Elmer came close and put his arm around Kate. "Are you all right?"

She nodded and massaged her jaw while Elmer turned on Aaron.

"You've got no call to come over here and upset Kate. Go home, Aaron."

"No little brother tells me what to do. Kate has gone astray. This is for her own good."

"When you stop being embarrassed and start loving Kate as your sister, then I'll believe you."

Aaron looked thoughtful for a moment, as if he were struggling against the sense of Elmer's words. But whatever inner turmoil he experienced didn't last long. "It vexes me to see what she's doing to all of us."

"You don't care about Kate half as much as you care about being minister someday," Elmer said, folding his arms and looking as smug as if he'd just revealed the world's greatest secret. "Wouldn't you be pleased as punch if you could sermonize to your heart's content."

"Don't you dare accuse me of pride. You know nothing, Elmer, nothing. You're unbaptized and foolish."

"I know enough to warn you," Elmer said. "In this community, those who seek the ministry are usually the last to be chosen. If you really want the job, you shouldn't be so obvious about it."

Aaron had endured enough. He turned his back on both of them and stormed off to his house without another word.

Elmer watched him go and then pulled Kate into a bear hug. Her composure dissolved into tears and she wept onto Elmer's shoulder, whose shirt smelled of cheese. Aaron hadn't been particularly nice, but she had no excuse for responding so crossly. *"Blessed are the meek.*" She obviously needed more practice. But, ach, his words had stung.

"That brother of mine," Elmer said, "tempts me to be angry sometimes."

"Only sometimes?"

"Yes, the times I actually see him."

They both chuckled.

"Jah," Kate said. "Those are the times I am tempted too."

Elmer lifted her chin with his finger. "Ach, your face is as red as a tomato. He squeezed hard, I think." Elmer squared his shoulders and frowned in the direction of Aaron's house. "Nathaniel is going to hear about this."

"No," Kate said. "He doesn't need any more strife where I am concerned. Promise me you won't say anything."

Elmer scowled then let out an exasperated groan and softened his expression. "I will be silent," he said. He pinched his lips between two fingers and marched away. "Unless compelled to speak," he added hastily before disappearing around the corner.

Chapter Twenty-Three

Nathaniel sat in the Yoders' living room paying scant attention to the minister. He wiped the sweat from his brow and glanced over at the other side of the room, where several women fanned themselves with their hankies or scraps of paper. Yoders' was the smallest home they met in for gmay, so the worshippers felt nicely cramped and toasty warm by the time services ended.

He should have been paying heed to the sermon about nonresistance, his greatest shortcoming, but all his thoughts and desires focused on the beautiful girl sitting across the room. She gazed serenely at the minister as he preached on and embellished his remarks with quotes from the Sermon on the Mount. Would Nathaniel ever tire of studying her face? Not likely.

But today, he noticed something amiss with his Kate. *His* Kate. That was the only way he thought of her now, like a priceless treasure. Her jaw was noticeably swollen, with bruises discoloring her otherwise-perfect skin. She looked a little like James Zimmerman the day after he got his wisdom teeth out.

Once they started into hymn-singing, he reached over and tapped Elmer on the shoulder. "What happened to Kate?" he whispered, keeping his head and his voice as low as possible. Two men next to him frowned in annoyance.

Elmer's face clouded over, and he scowled outright. "After services," he said. Nathaniel could tell he got the curt response not because Elmer was irritated by the interruption, but because a few short sentences in the middle of singing-time were insufficient to relate the story.

Nathaniel's curiosity grew.

After services, Elmer motioned for Nathaniel to meet him outside. Nathaniel nodded. Kate, arm in arm with her mother, filed out ahead as Nathaniel pushed Dat's wheelchair to the door. Kate turned to glance in Nathaniel's direction, and he winked at her unashamedly. Her face lit up in a disarming smile.

Three men helped Nathaniel lift the wheelchair off the stairs and onto the flagstones. Two other men stood by to help Nathaniel put his dat in the buggy. Outside, the muggy air of late July still felt cooler than the stuffy rooms where they held gmay.

Scanning the group of people, Nathaniel caught sight of Elmer standing with Kate, separate from everyone else. "Mamm," he said. "Could you take Dat to the buggy? I will be right there."

Mamm pushed the wheelchair away, and Nathaniel hurried to Elmer and Kate. "Hello, Kate. You look very pretty this fine morning."

Kate blushed and put her hand to her swollen cheek.

Elmer pinned Kate with a meaningful gaze. "Nathaniel wants to know what happened to your face."

Kate glared back at Elmer. "Does he?"

Elmer and Kate glared at each other, communicating thoughts Nathaniel could not hope to understand.

Elmer massaged the back of his neck and squinted at Nathaniel. "Aaron—"

Kate turned her face from both of them. "Don't, Elmer."

"What about Aaron?"

Elmer kicked the grass. "Come on, Kate."

Nathaniel held out his hand to silence Elmer. "Nae, if this makes her uncomfortable, I will not pry further."

Kate glanced at Elmer. "It was nothing. No use crying about the milk after the cow overturns the bucket."

Nathaniel studied her bruised skin and swollen jawline. This was not "nothing." It took all the willpower he had not to reach out his hand and caress her face right here in public. Ach, he knew if he had his way, he would pull Kate into his arms and kiss her again and again in front of everyone. But he wasn't going to get his way today.

The men had Dat settled in the buggy, and Mamm waited patiently in the front seat. "I must go," Nathaniel said, with one serious look at Kate. "You will come to the gathering at Millers' this week?"

"Jah, I will be there," she said.

He smiled to reassure her. "I will see you then."

She smiled back and took Elmer's arm. "See you then."

Frustrated and confused, Nathaniel trudged to his buggy, trying to keep dark thoughts about Aaron from his mind.

* * * * *

Later the next day, Nathaniel slipped into Aaron's stable, hoping to find Kate's brother there alone. "Aaron," Nathaniel called when he didn't immediately see the man in the dimness.

"Here," Aaron said.

Nathaniel followed the voice to the compartment where Aaron pitched hay to his horses. When Aaron caught sight of Nathaniel, he smiled widely and leaned his pitchfork against the wall. "Nathaniel," he said, extending his hand.

Nathaniel hesitated then grasped Aaron's hand tightly. He had come to deliver a message, not make an enemy.

"If you are here to help with the buggy," Aaron said, "My dat and the deacon helped me fix it already. One wheel hub wobbled something ugly, but I think we got it worked out. Thank you for coming, though."

"I didn't know about your buggy."

"Then come in and have a piece of coconut crème pie that Sarah made. It'll put some fat around your middle."

"I didn't come to eat your food. I came because I have something to say to you."

Aaron's eyes narrowed, and he slowly reached back and laid hands on his pitchfork. "Then say it," he replied, pitching hay with renewed purpose. Did he know what was coming?

Nathaniel placed a firm hand on Aaron's shoulder, compelling him to stop what he was doing. Aaron froze then stood up straight and stabbed the pitchfork into the bale of hay at his feet. "What do you want?"

"As a fellow citizen in Christ, I bear you no ill will. I know how tempers can flare in a heated moment." Nathaniel trained his eyes on Aaron, daring him to look away. "But don't ever lay hands on my Kate again."

"What I do in my own family is my business."

"Kate is the girl I hope to marry someday, so your treatment of her becomes my business."

"I am trying to keep her from shaming herself and our family. If you ask me, you should be courting elsewhere."

The hint was not lost on Nathaniel. Sarah Schwartz was a lucky girl. She had so many people working to get her married off.

"Whom I choose to court is truly my business," Nathaniel said through gritted teeth. "But I will not stand by and let you bruise Kate's feelings." He moved close enough so Aaron could feel Nathaniel's breath on his face. "Keep your hands off her."

He backed away quickly, too angry to trust himself any longer. Nathaniel reached over and handed Aaron his pitchfork. "Enjoy that pie."

Not shying away from Aaron's glare, he put his hands in his pockets and strolled out of the stable.

Chapter Twenty-Four

The buggy rolled along the main road into Cashton with Elmer at the reins and Kate, Mary, and Mary's little ones riding along. Mary sat up front with Elmer, and Kate sat next to Sadie in the back. Holding baby Luke tightly in her arms, Kate fussed and fidgeted more than the baby did. She bounced him up and down and played games with first his toes and then Sadie's toes and sang silly little rhymes to both of them.

Mary turned to watch all the activity behind her. "You are really in a state, aren't you, Katie?"

"I cannot help it. He doesn't even know I'm coming."

"Why so ferhoodled? You see him two or three times a week already."

Kate's heart leapt like a ballerina. "I know, but that doesn't matter today. We are going to his house to see him and his mamm together." How would he respond under his mother's watchful eye?

The outing came about because Mary needed some gripe water from Miriam for the baby, who'd seemed a little colicky of late. After a visit to the Kings', they planned to stop at the park because Sadie loved the swings. Elmer, who never passed up a chance to drive the buggy, had agreed to take them, and Mary had invited Kate to come along for obvious reasons.

"You don't think Nathaniel's mamm will be pleased to see you?" Mary said.

Sighing in frustration, Kate leaned back and ran her fingers across the baby's soft head. The constant pressure to make the most important decision of her life grew unbearably heavy as the summer waned.

Nathaniel had fallen completely mute about the impending semester, but his eyes reflected a desperate urgency whenever they were together.

She'd prayed and prayed until her knees ached, and she felt certain the heavens were not taking any more requests. Her academy schedule had arrived this morning. Was that her answer or just another stumbling block to trip her up and muddy the already-murky choices? She needed to buy music, find a place to live, and contact the academy for another grant. Her to-do list made her head spin.

Two years ago she had been so sure of herself. But now? Was the uncertainty a sign for her to keep to the path or get off it? And if she was on the right path, how could she bear to leave Nathaniel?

Elmer stopped at a crossroads before the turn into Nathaniel's lane, and the buggy bounced lightly as he prodded the horse forward.

Then a squeal of brakes and a terrified scream rent the air, and they were jolted violently to the right. Kate instinctively clutched the baby to her chest as the buggy tumbled onto its side and sent the passengers rolling like pebbles in a river. Shattered glass cascaded over them like rain.

The buggy came to rest on its side, and Kate felt like a misused rag doll. Slowly, painfully, she sat up, clutching the baby firmly with one arm and pulling Sadie to her lap with the other. Blood dripped from the little girl's nose. Sadie started screaming.

"Hush, hush, now," Kate said, kissing Sadie's forehead and holding her close. With the edge of her apron, Kate did her best to wipe the blood from Sadie's face.

Over the din of both children crying, Kate became aware of the noisy confusion outside the buggy. The horse whinnied and moaned, making sounds Kate had never heard from an animal before. Voices came into her hearing—some barking orders, some crying.

"My babies! Get my babies!" Kate heard Mary scream. At least Mary sounded unhurt.

Nathaniel's voice boomed from several feet away. "I'll get them. Stay calm, Mary."

"Kate's in there too," Mary wailed.

"Kate!" She heard Nathaniel roar, closer now, alarm tearing from his throat.

He thrust his head into the opening of the buggy, his eyes wild with fear. "Kate, are you all right?" he said, panting with every word.

She nodded, too shaken to speak.

"Thank the Lord, praise the Lord," he said, exhaling what must have been every bit of air in his lungs.

He held out his arms. "Cum, Sadie, I've got you."

Sadie leaned forward, and he lifted her out of the buggy. He hugged her tightly, and she lay her head on his shoulder.

Nathaniel briefly disappeared from sight then reappeared with empty arms. He reached out to Kate, and she handed him the baby. Their eyes held, and she saw concern etched on every line of his face. A distant siren hummed like an approaching storm.

"I'm coming for you," he said before disappearing once again, this time with the baby in his grasp.

With all the racket, Kate didn't understand most of what she heard. Nathaniel barked a few orders Kate could not decipher, and then he crouched and stuck his head into the buggy once more. Taking Kate firmly by the arms, he pulled her up and out of the crippled buggy. She cried out in pain before finding her balance and standing. Without hesitation, Nathaniel wrapped his arms tightly around her and pulled her close. She in turn threw her arms around him and buried her face in his neck. She could feel him trembling as she tried to catch her breath. He held her as if he had not the slightest intention of ever letting go.

A police car with sirens blaring pulled up to the overturned buggy, and Nathaniel reluctantly released his grip. He nudged her away and studied her face. "Are you hurt?" he asked, his hands on her arms.

"Just shaken."

Kate surveyed the accident scene. A bulky car sat next to the crushed front wheel of the buggy, which was partially pinning Rollie's hind leg. Elmer cut the harness loose, and the injured horse flailed then managed to jump up and away from the wreckage. Kate looked at Rollie's leg. It was bleeding a bit, but he seemed capable of walking on it.

Nathaniel took Kate's hand and led her away from the buggy. Mary sat on the ground, grimacing in pain as she held her right arm in her left hand. Sadie stood beside her, still crying. "Onkel Elmer," she cried, pointing to Elmer, who had blood trickling down the side of his face. "Mamma, Elmer is hurt!"

"Hush, liebe. Elmer will be all right," Mary said.

Nathaniel's mamm stood a short way off, trying to calm baby Luke, while Elmer stayed beside the distressed horse, whispering words Kate could not hear.

Nathaniel squeezed Kate's hand and went to Elmer's side.

Sadie pulled on her mamm's dress. Kate knelt beside them as Mary held her arm and gasped in pain.

"It's broken...I know it's broken," Mary said. "How will I ever do the canning?"

With a determined look in her eye, Miriam handed the baby to Kate. "Go and sit under the tree where it's cool. I'll see to your sister."

Kate managed to get both little ones to the grass inside Nathaniel's gate. She eased Sadie to the ground and sat cross-legged, cradling the baby, before pulling Sadie onto her lap. Both children were still crying, too frightened and shaken up to calm down. Kate wanted to bawl right along with them.

She looked to the road. Nathaniel was in a discussion with one of the policemen. Miriam and a paramedic tended to Mary, while another paramedic knelt by the car and talked to an old man who sat in the driver's seat with the door open, his legs resting on the pavement.

"Shh, shh," Kate said over and over. "Everything will be all right." But with the deafening sirens, the glaring police lights, and the surrounding chaos, Kate found it impossible to console the children.

Music had always been her first and last refuge from a sometimes-insane world. So she did the only thing she could think of doing.

She started to sing.

"'Be still, my soul,'" she sang softly. An old German hymn, not one from the *Ausbund* but one Maria had sung to comfort her baby. "'Be still, my soul; the Lord is on thy side. Bear patiently thy cross of grief or pain.'"

To her amazement and relief, both children stopped crying almost instantly and looked at her with wide, curious eyes.

"'Leave to thy God to order and provide; in every change, He faithful will remain.'"

The noise around them grew distant as she persevered, her voice clear and strong enough to drown out the confusion.

"'Be still, my soul; thy best, thy heav'nly Friend, thru thorny ways leads to a joyful end.'"

The children stared at her in rapt attention as she began another verse. "'Be still, my soul; thy God doth undertake to guide the future as He has the past.'"

Then something caught her completely off guard.

With every breath she took, a radiating warmth flowed into her body until, by the time she finished the second verse, she was filled to overflowing with light. The powerful warmth surged through her arms and legs, infusing her with a strength she had never before experienced. Kate looked down at her hands to see if she was, in truth, glowing, so on fire did she feel. The sensation encompassed her entire being, and for the first time in her life, she could see clearly. The clouds parted from her mind. Her struggles, her life, her *self* all came into view with perfect clarity.

"Leave to thy God to order and provide."

"Kate, thou art careful and troubled about many things, but one thing is needful."

"Be still, and know that I am God."

The fabric of her life had stretched and frayed until she almost didn't recognize herself. But in this moment Kate knew what God wanted for her. She had been born to the simple and Plain life and could not twist tightly enough to fit into a world that wasn't hers. She had been hoping God would fit Himself somewhere into her plans, instead of letting Him mold her into His own treasure.

Kate closed her eyes and began to hum. In a rush of insight and emotion, she saw herself singing to a baby—her baby—songs that would tell the baby she loved him. She heard the melodies she would sing to mend a skinned knee or comfort a wounded heart. There were no concert halls with crystal chandeliers or velvet upholstery, only the priceless love of children and her husband and her love for God and His love for her. She would put her hand in God's and walk through the valley of the shadow of death to bring precious souls into this world. To be a mother— the highest, holiest, most sacred calling she could have or aspire to.

Here was her answer. Right here, here in this wonderful, compassionate, flawed, and struggling community was where she belonged, possessed of the love of a good man and ready to give her all to her future family.

Filled to the brim yet lighter than air, she wanted to shout in jubilation, to rush to Nathaniel and tell him what she had discovered. To share the gift she had been given.

He must have sensed her gaze, because he glanced up and his eyes locked on hers. Even amid the swirling confusion, he didn't look away. His frown disappeared, and he studied her in puzzlement.

Did she look different? She felt different, as if she had traveled a thousand miles and a hundred lifetimes in a few short minutes.

The world around them ceased to exist, and they stared at each other across the tumult, communicating thoughts that could not be put into words. His eyes never strayed from her face, as if he were trying to read every line to understand what he saw there. She held her breath, almost unable to bear the intense rush of ecstasy she felt when his eyes were upon her.

"I love you." Her lips formed the words she was too overjoyed to speak.

Nathaniel must have understood. In spite of the circumstances, he smiled at her with his whole face.

The moment evaporated as suddenly as it had come. A policeman tapped Nathaniel on the shoulder, and the connection broke.

"Elmer has blood," Sadie said, distressed to see her uncle in such a state. A single tear made a trail down her cheek.

"Do not fret, leibe. The doctor will take care of him."

Kate watched as Nathaniel tried to convince the unsteady Elmer to sit down. Elmer's eyes were glossy and stared absently, but Elmer would not budge. He persisted in whispering words of comfort to his frightened horse. Nathaniel motioned for a paramedic to look at Elmer's bleeding head. Kate couldn't see the wound under Elmer's hair, but judging from the blood on his shirt, he would need stitches.

Another paramedic came to Kate and the children sitting on the grass. After rifling through his bag, he put on some latex gloves and gently sponged the blood from Sadie's nose and face with a damp gauze pad. He examined her carefully and decided she wasn't seriously injured before stowing his supplies and walking away.

A police officer helped Mary stand and led her to a waiting ambulance.

"Kate, can you take care of the *kinner*?" Mary said.

Kate nudged Sadie off her lap and slowly stood with the baby tightly in her arms. Grabbing Sadie's hand, she made her way to the ambulance.

"I will take them home with me."

The splinted arm hung helplessly at Mary's side, but she caressed Sadie's cheek with her good hand. "Be good for Kate and Mammi. I will be home soon."

Nathaniel and another paramedic guided Elmer to the ambulance. With concern, Kate hugged Elmer and kissed him on the cheek before he sluggishly climbed inside and sat with his head in his hands.

"I will go with them to the hospital," Nathaniel said. "Elmer needs stitches, and they think he has a concussion."

"Oh, thank you," Kate said. "I will send Dat as soon as I get home."

"The police will right the buggy and pull it to my yard to fix later," Nathaniel said. "Mamm will take the horse to our barn until your dat can pick it up."

He saw that Mary and Elmer were both comfortably settled in the ambulance before he turned to Kate. "They will be all right, I promise."

Nodding, she slipped her hand into his and squeezed tightly. "I'm glad you are going with them." Then she added, "Tomorrow, after services, I must see you."

Anticipation flitted across his face before he climbed into the ambulance with Kate's two siblings. "The day is yours," he said. "All yours."

Chapter Twenty-Five

Even from her bedroom at the back of the house, Kate could hear the car slowly driving up the driveway. The gravel crackled noisily beneath the tires, heralding the arrival of an automobile rather than a buggy.

Sluggishly she rolled out of bed, her body throbbing with the fresh ache of the accident. Her family would not be back in time from the hospital to make it to gmay, and Kate had stayed home to rest, fearing that if she attended church, she would snooze through the entire service. She felt physically miserable.

But her heart soared in delirious happiness, and when she shared her good news with Nathaniel, his joy would double hers. She would not be able to keep herself from floating off the ground.

Early this morning, Mary had gone home with a glossy white cast up to her elbow. Moses fetched the children from Kate's house, and then a friend drove Mamma, Dat, and both younger brothers to the hospital to be with Elmer. They wouldn't even think of Kate accompanying them after her ordeal of the day before. She'd fallen asleep just before sunrise.

Elmer got seventeen stitches and an overnight stay in the hospital for observation. The doctor wanted to be cautious about the head injury, Moses had told them.

Kate sighed. The trip to the emergency room alone would keep the family awash in hospital bills for months. She feared they would have to rely on the church emergency fund for some of the cost. But at least Elmer and Mary were going to be fine.

Being careful of her sore shoulder, Kate slipped her emerald-green dress over her head and quickly smoothed her hair under her kapp. She didn't bother with shoes. Whoever her visitor, he would have to endure Kate with bare feet. She shuffled down the stairs and to the front door, aching from head to toe and fingertip to fingertip. Better take some Tylenol before going back to bed.

Kate opened the door wide enough to peek her head out. Buggies already rolled down the road on their way to *gmayna*. A familiar rusted red truck sat in front of her house, its driver leaning against the hood with his arms folded across his chest, just waiting for Kate to emerge from her house. He caught sight of her when the door creaked, and he flashed his dazzling white teeth in her direction.

"Carlos!" she squealed. Disregarding her achy body, Kate half tiptoed, half ran to Maria's brother, who opened his arms to receive her. She stopped short of touching him. Hugging an unmarried Englischer was decidedly improper for an Amish girl.

He threw his arms around her, lifted her off the ground, and twirled her in a circle. Laughing, he set her back on her feet, held her at arm's length, and studied her closely. "You didn't think I would let you off the hook for a hug just because you are dressed like that, did you?"

Kate rolled her eyes but let the joy at seeing him show on her face.

"You look like a pilgrim from my fifth-grade Thanksgiving pageant," he said.

"A pilgrim?"

"Just giving you a compliment. You look pretty no matter what you wear."

"Cum, cum to the house. I will make you some coffee."

"We don't have time." He wrapped his hand around her elbow as if to guide her somewhere. "I've come to take you to Milwaukee."

"Milwaukee? Carlos, I am not ready to go back." Kate shook her head and shrugged his hand from her elbow. "I am not planning on going back at all, truth be told."

Carlos didn't seem to hear her. "Jared's dead."

Kate held her breath and closed her eyes. In that moment, the avalanche of remorse almost buried her alive.

I killed Jared Adams. Oh, Nathaniel, I should have told you. What will you think of me now? Why has God done this?

Kate stared at Maria's brother until she composed herself enough to speak. "When?"

"Last week."

"How is Maria?"

Carlos took Kate's hand in both of his. He pressed the back of her hand with his thumb. "She needs you."

Kate swallowed hard.

As the Lord wills.

"*Be still, and know that I am God.*"

Be still.

Kate drew her breath in spasms, as if she had just finished sobbing for an hour. "Send Maria my love, but I cannot go with you."

"But you've got to."

"God wants us to live the lives He has granted us. I belong here. The people I love are here. The life I want to live is here."

"Jared's parents want Alex. Twice they've tried to take him from the day care—so far unsuccessfully, but if they find someone willing to hand him over, Maria may never get him back."

"How can they do that?"

"Maria is so nervous they're going to snatch Alex, she refuses to take him back to day care. Without day care, she can't work, and if she loses her job it will be harder to keep custody. Can't you come take care of Alex? For a few weeks until the custody hearing?"

"Hearing?"

"Jared's mother is fighting for custody of Alex. We need you to testify. Your testimony could save him."

Kate thought of Maria, struggling desperately, feeling alone and forsaken. How could Kate turn her back on a friend? "For just a few weeks?"

"The hearing is September first. Four weeks away."

Kate glanced up as the Yutzy family trudged down the road to church. Barbara Yutzy waved and stared at Kate and her visitor before fixing her eyes to the ground and quickening her pace. Several other families passed the house, some in buggies, others on foot.

Kate took a deep breath and made her decision. "I will come with you, Carlos."

Carlos smiled and gave Kate a cursory hug. "Good girl. Get packed. We need to leave in ten minutes."

"Ten minutes? Nae, my parents need to know where I am going. We cannot leave until they come home. And Elmer. I cannot leave without seeing Elmer."

Carlos glanced at his watch. "I can't spare the time. I have to be back to work at noon, and that barely gives us enough leeway as it is."

"Can you come back for me later in the week?"

"Don't you understand? Maria won't send Alex back to that day care, and we both have to work tomorrow morning. We need you now."

Kate groaned in frustration. "I cannot just leave."

"Write them a note."

Kate stood in her yard, feeling control slip from her grasp.

"Come on, Kate."

Surrendering to her circumstances, Kate ran to the house. The need was urgent. She would care for Alex until the hearing, and then her testimony could help Maria keep her baby.

Hurriedly, Kate packed her other dress and kapp into her small bag. She hesitated when she caught sight of the jeans and T-shirt at the bottom of her drawer. Should she take the Englisch clothes, just in case?

Shaking her head, she stuffed them into her bag. She could bequeath them to Maria on September first.

Sitting at the kitchen table, she wrote two letters—one to her parents and a longer one to Nathaniel.

"Nathaniel, I must go back to Milwaukee for a few weeks. Maria is fighting for her child, and I must help her. I want to tell you everything, all I have felt in the last twenty-four hours, all I feel in my heart for you. Please be patient. I promise to return. And I will return for good."

She had the courage to write her deepest assurances.

"I love you, Nathaniel. I love you forever."

She couldn't bring herself to tell him Jared was dead. That revelation required a face-to-face interview. She could only hope he would see it in his heart to forgive her and still want her for his wife. She buried such notions deep into her heart. How could she bear the thought of anything else?

Kate set her envelopes, along with Maria's address, carefully on the table in plain sight, so that Mamma would see them first thing when she walked through the door.

Carlos leaned against his truck as if he hadn't budged from the spot since his arrival. Kate handed him her bag, and he grinned. "You are the most low-maintenance girl I've ever met." He tossed the bag into the cab of his truck and then put his arm around her. "Did you pack anything in that bag?"

A movement to her right caught Kate's attention. Aaron stood with both hands on his porch railing, scrutinizing Kate and the dark stranger by her side.

"Aaron!" Kate leaped up his porch steps, more eager than she had ever been to talk to her brother. "You are not at church."

"Three boys are sick," he said, not taking his eyes from Carlos.

"Aaron, please listen. I must go back to Milwaukee."

"Who is that man? You should not be alone with him."

Kate turned her head to glance at Carlos. "He is Maria's brother. Aaron, look at me. Maria's boyfriend, Jared, is dead. Tell the family I am sorry to leave like this. Be sure to tell them I am sorry." Unbidden tears fell. "Tell Nathaniel I have made my choice. Aaron, are you listening? Tell him I have made my choice and will be back in four weeks." Her frustration rose as Aaron kept his attention riveted on Carlos. "I left two notes on the table. Please make sure Mamma and Nathaniel get them. I'll be back soon. Please see that they get the notes."

Aaron stroked his beard. "He was hugging you."

"He cannot help himself."

Aaron did not change his expression.

Kate sighed in exasperation. "Please make sure they see my letters."

He persisted in silence, and she slowly marched down the steps and got in the truck. She didn't need to depend on Aaron to deliver the notes. Mamma would see them without his interference.

She kept her eyes glued to her house as Carlos backed down the driveway. The three apple trees in the front yard were already laden with small green fruit. By the time they were ready to pick, she would be home. Home for harvest. A cold, unexpected chill trickled down her spine. Lord willing, home for good.

Chapter Twenty-Six

Nathaniel guided his buggy up Weavers' lane after gmay. Kate had not been in church today. He hadn't expected to see her. After her ordeal yesterday, she deserved to stay in bed for a full week.

He passed the birdhouse that stood securely on a post on the fence separating Weavers' yard from the lane. He couldn't help smiling. She had accepted his gift. Now he hoped she would accept his heart.

The horse slowed in the gravel. The pace sorely tested Nathaniel's patience. Service had lasted for an eternity, and he shouldn't have to wait one more minute to see her. Something had happened to Kate yesterday afternoon. Her shining countenance amid the commotion of the accident had etched itself in his memory. Whatever had taken place in those few minutes had transformed her.

"After services, I must see you." The light in her face told him it was good news. His heart pumped wildly, unable to restrain his galloping hope. He had driven Mamm and Dat home from church with indecent speed.

Moses had come to fetch Mary last night from the hospital, and Nathaniel had stayed with Elmer until the Weavers came for him early this morning. The taxi brought him home in time to get Dat up for gmay. Nathaniel felt the fatigue clear through to his bones, but mere exhaustion would not have kept him from seeing Kate today. What amount of needed sleep could compare to the elation he knew every time he laid eyes on her?

Finally reaching the end of the lane, he secured the reins and leaped from his seat. He strode purposefully across the yard, reaching the front door in record speed. Not caring who he awoke with his enthusiasm, he knocked loudly enough to rouse the entire household.

"Cum reu," he heard Aaron call.

Opening the door wide, he came face-to-face with Kate's parents and Aaron in the middle of the kitchen. His high spirits crashed to the floor. Tears streamed down Emma's face. Solomon, slumped over like an old man, had his arm around his wife, his mouth twisted into a wretched grimace.

Nathaniel caught his breath. "Is it Elmer?"

Solomon looked at Nathaniel as if seeing him for the first time. "Nae, Elmer is resting. We just brought him home. The doctor said he will be all right."

Kate's parents stared at Nathaniel, and deep sadness reflected in their eyes.

"Sit down, Nathaniel," Emma said, motioning to a chair at the table.

An emptiness rushed into his lungs, and Nathaniel felt as if he were going to be sick. "Has something happened to Kate?"

Emma and Solomon looked to Aaron, who pulled a chair from the table and sat. His parents followed suit.

"Sit, Nathaniel," said Emma. "You need to sit."

Nathaniel slowly pulled a chair from the table, never letting his eyes stray from Aaron's tortured face. Why had he ever believed that Aaron didn't care for his sister?

"A man came for her this morning," Aaron said.

"What man?" Nathaniel stared in confusion at Aaron. "Where did they go?"

"She put her travel bag in his truck, and they drove away."

Nathaniel's mouth went dry. "I don't understand. Who was this man?"

Aaron rested his elbows on the table and laced his fingers together. "I am sorry, Nathaniel. I called to her, chastised her for being alone with an Englischer. But you know how she is. Will she ever listen to my counsel?"

Nathaniel leaned forward. "What did she say?"

Emma sniffed and wiped her nose with her hanky. Solomon grasped her hand and held on like a lifeline.

"I think she did not expect anyone to see her make her escape," Aaron said. "She started to cry, saying 'I'm sorry. Tell everyone I'm sorry.' She kept saying that. She said, 'Tell Nathaniel I have made my choice, and I am going to Milwaukee.'"

Aching for a denial, Nathaniel stared at Aaron in disbelief. Every muscle in his body pulled so taut he thought he might snap. "But are you sure? Why didn't she tell me herself?"

Aaron leaned back and folded his arms. "I suppose she did not have the courage. Or maybe she thought it would be easier for you. That you would not want to shame yourself in front of her."

Nathaniel buried his face in his hands, and when he looked up, the faces around him were a blur of color and line. So, that was it? After all the months of waiting and dreaming, agonizing and hoping, she had left him? He was completely incapable of wrapping his mind around that horrible thought. The Weavers' kitchen tilted violently, and Nathaniel clutched the table for support.

Aaron reached over and patted his arm. "It is better this way. For all of us. Kate's worldly ways shamed our family. Who knows how many young people she influenced with her bad example? It is better she is away. It is better she stay away."

Nathaniel couldn't focus, not even to protest the injustice of Aaron's words. He couldn't form any rational thought but one.

Escape.

I've got to get away from this place.

Not knowing how he was able to stand, he walked to the front door and turned the handle. With pain saturating his very soul, he exploded out of the house, shoved himself into his buggy, and drove far away.

Chapter Twenty-Seven

"Maria, this fridge is an outrage," Kate said. "How do you survive on a half gallon of milk and a jar of pickles?"

"I've been spending a lot of time at Carlos's apartment. Jared's mother knows where I live. Carlos is a bachelor. We go out for fast food a lot."

Kate clicked her tongue in reprimand. "And what does the baby eat?"

Maria pointed to her chubby son, sitting in his high chair and eating Cheerios from the tray. "Does he look like he's malnourished?"

Grinning, Kate tousled Alex's hair. "He passes my inspection."

Maria spread her arms and squeezed Kate tight. "I'm so glad you're here. I was a nervous wreck without you. Jared's mother has gone to the day care twice to try to take Alex away." Her whole body trembled.

"What do you know about the hearing?" Kate said.

"My lawyer says no judge in the world is going to take a baby away from his mother unless the mother is unfit. That's why I need you to testify."

"Jah, of course."

Maria lifted Alex from his high chair, and she and Kate sat on the sofa in the small space next to the kitchen that passed for a living room.

"I'm frightened," she said, clutching Alex to her heart.

Kate placed a hand on Maria's arm. "Everything will turn out right, Lord willing."

"Be still, and know that I am God."

They sat in silence for a few minutes, Alex wriggling to be set down. Maria loosened her hold on him and let him play with her necklace instead.

"I missed you bad, Kate," she said.

"I missed you too." Kate reached out and stroked Alex's silky cheek. "I can only stay until the hearing is over. I hope you are not disappointed."

"Of course, I want you to stay. Carlos has a major crush on you. But it would be selfish of us to keep you away from where you truly want to be. Go back to Nathaniel and make a dozen babies and bake bread and sew quilts. You'll be in Amish heaven. Who am I to begrudge you your happiness?"

"Thank you," Kate said, her face relaxing into a smile. "I hoped you would understand."

Carlos burst through the front door and spread his arms wide. "Here I am, girls. Now the fun can begin."

"Don't you ever knock?" Maria said, rising and hugging her brother while Alex wriggled between them.

"Don't you ever lock your door?" He took the baby from Maria and tossed him into the air. Alex giggled with glee.

Maria snatched Alex away before Carlos could toss him again. "My son is not your ball."

"So," Carlos said, clapping his hands together and ignoring his sister, "I'm going to take both of you out to dinner."

"I can't afford it," Kate said.

"Me and Maria already discussed it," Carlos said. "You're babysitting for her, so we're supporting you—until you start school and custody is settled."

Maria cleared her throat and glanced at Kate. "Or until you go back to Apple Lake."

Carlos feigned astonishment. "Go back to Apple Lake? Why would you ever want to do that?"

Maria turned her back on her brother and rolled her eyes at Kate. "Don't listen to him," she whispered.

Kate stood and headed for her temporary bedroom. "Before we go, can I use your cell phone to call Nathaniel? I left so suddenly today, and I want to make sure he got my message."

Carlos pulled an imaginary dagger from his belt and stabbed himself in the heart. "Who can think of Nathaniel when Carlos is before you?"

Rolling her eyes again, Maria pointed to her phone sitting on the counter. Kate smiled indulgently at Carlos, took the phone into the bedroom, and closed the door.

Sitting on the bed, she dialed the number to Nathaniel's workshop. The phone rang and rang. Kate swallowed her disappointment. It was Sunday. How could she expect him to be in his shop on Sunday?

"This is King's Cabinetry. Please leave a message."

Kate's heart skipped a beat. Just hearing his voice was a thrill.

"Nathaniel, I am sorry I left so suddenly today. Please call me when you get a chance. I am staying with my friend, Maria. Her number is 555-432-8492."

She wouldn't give away her good news over the phone. She wanted to see the look in his eyes when she told him. She wanted him to see the look in hers.

* * * * *

Nathaniel's movements echoed against the walls of his dark workshop. Not even a hint of moonlight illuminated his surroundings as he felt for the matches in the table drawer. Although blind in the darkness, he knew exactly where the propane lamp stood steadfastly in the corner of his shop. He made his way to it and struck the match. Light hissed out of the blackness, bathing his workshop in line and murky shadow.

He had driven his buggy barely three miles out of Apple Lake before pulling it off to the side of the road and heading nowhere in particular on foot. He had walked all day, trudging through muddy pastures and thick stands of trees, exerting his body to keep his mind empty.

Long after dark, he finally surrendered to the welcome fatigue and drove slowly home. But he would not get any sleep tonight. His very skin seemed worn raw with painful emotion.

A single red dot blinked on and off on the far wall like a lone stoplight on a deserted highway. He stumbled to his answering machine, dazed and exhausted, and pushed the button.

Dizziness almost overcame him when he heard her voice.

"Nathaniel, I am sorry I left so suddenly today. Please call me when you get a chance. I am staying with my friend, Maria. Her number is 555-432-8492."

He staggered to a chair and stared numbly at the machine as the nice woman inside the box droned on and on. "To erase this message, press seven. To save it, press nine." Nathaniel didn't have the will to stand. After several lonely beeps, the machine gave up trying to get a response and fell silent.

The quiet had always been Nathaniel's friend, enveloping him in a warm blanket of his own thoughts. But now it seemed to press in on him like an invisible shroud, stealing the very air around him.

His moan cut the silence like a wounded beast throwing its anguish to the sky. "Oh, Nightingale," he cried, "don't call me. Don't call me." The fragile dam holding the flood at bay snapped and released the torrent. Burying his face in his hands, he sobbed until every last ounce of his strength was spent.

Chapter Twenty-Eight

The diminutive clerk slowly counted out Nathaniel's change. "Take this receipt to the back, Nathaniel, and the boys will load the bags in your wagon."

"Denki," Nathaniel said, unable to remember the man's name. He didn't really even want to try. What did it matter?

The clerk managed a wan smile. Without meeting Nathaniel's eyes, he said, "Have a gute day yet." Was it his imagination, or did everyone Nathaniel encountered give him that same pathetic smile? Was no one brave enough to look him in the eyes? Did they all have to conceal their pity with fake cheerfulness and forced conversations?

Nathaniel clomped his boots heavily on the store's cement floor as he walked to the door. Every step, every movement of his body took so much effort. His foot clanked against a bucket of birdseed, and two men at the counter glanced in his direction and then put their heads together and exchanged hushed words. Nathaniel pretended not to notice.

The bell tinkled weakly as he stepped out into the sunlight. He squinted, letting his eyes adjust to the glaring brightness of noon. Why did the days have to be so sunny? He just wanted to bury himself in a shadowy corner of his workshop and absorb the darkness.

Nathaniel walked around to the back of Troyer's Feed and Supply, where his wagon and team stood ready. The Troyer brothers, neither a day over fourteen years old, met him at the back and loaded his bags of feed into the wagon.

"When do you have to go back to school?" Nathaniel asked, giving them a hand. If he wanted to ever feel cheerful again, he had to start acting cheerful.

Adam smiled at him tentatively. "Two weeks. This is my last year. Abraham has to go two more years yet."

"Almost done, then."

"Jah, and after that, I work for my dat full-time."

They loaded the last of the bags and shook hands. "Denki," Nathaniel said. "I will see you next time."

Nathaniel stood and watched the boys saunter back to the warehouse. He wished he could go back to the days when he had no other care in the world besides how quickly he finished his chores. He furrowed his brow. That kind of happiness seemed impossibly long ago.

Before Nathaniel climbed up to the seat of his wagon, he felt a tap on his shoulder. He turned and immediately felt a mixture of elation and gloom.

"Elmer," he said, forcing the name out of his throat before it choked him.

Elmer, with his head still in a protective bandage, gave him a defeated look, threw his arms around Nathaniel's neck, and sobbed uncontrollably. Nathaniel folded his arms around Kate's brother and held on with a vice grip.

They stood like that until Elmer found his voice. "I don't understand, Nathaniel. I don't understand why she would leave like that without even saying good-bye. I was in the hospital. She didn't even wait to see me out of the hospital."

Nathaniel wanted to say something, but he had no words of comfort to give.

Elmer pulled away and wiped his eyes. "Have you heard anything from her? It's been a week. We expected at least a letter by now."

Nathaniel was silent as he thought of the three messages sitting on his answering machine. More than once he had come dangerously close to picking up the phone and calling Kate, but he resisted because he knew exactly what she wanted. She wanted to apologize, to relieve her mind and burden his with an explanation. But he refused to talk to her until he felt he could reasonably converse without bawling like a baby or begging her to come home. For her sake as well as his, he would not let her see the devastation she left behind. He wanted to be able, with composure, to tell her that her family would be okay, that he would be okay—to hide how badly she had hurt him and avoid making her feel worse than she already felt. He knew how agonizing the decision had been for her.

"I haven't had a letter," Nathaniel said.

"Aaron practically camps by the mailbox every day waiting for the mailman, but we haven't heard anything. I just don't understand."

Nathaniel took off his hat and ran his fingers through his hair. He had given up trying to understand. "She decided to go back to school, and she couldn't face telling us. So she left."

"The Kate I know would have courage enough to explain." Elmer wiped his eyes again. "I don't understand."

Nathaniel had nothing to give Elmer. He couldn't reach inside for assurances that weren't there. They stood staring at each other. "Got to get back to the shop," he finally said, taking a step closer to the wagon. "Tell your parents hello."

Elmer furrowed his brow. "Why don't you go get her?"

Groaning, Nathaniel massaged the back of his neck. "Ach, no, Elmer."

Elmer jumped in front of him before he could climb into his wagon. "Go find her. Talk her into coming back." Nathaniel shook his head vigorously while Elmer persisted. "If anyone could convince her, you could. I know she would listen to you."

Nathaniel folded his arms across his chest and gave Elmer a stern look. "She spent the better part of two years making this decision. It was, and will ever be, the hardest decision of her life. I want her to be happy. How happy would I make her if she knew how miserable her decision has made me?" That grief kept him pacing his room at night, made him unable to eat or work or...pray. "She left without talking to us in person because she did not want to see that pain."

Elmer, breathing heavily, leaned against the wagon for support. "You are trying to be noble," he said quietly.

Nathaniel shook his head. "I am trying to survive."

"Today I wish you were not such a good man."

They stood for a long time, staring up at the shade trees that towered over Troyer's property. A light breeze shuffled through the leaves.

An approaching team and wagon jolted Elmer from his thoughts. He rubbed his eyes and glanced toward the street. "I'm going," he said, "before anyone sees me like this." He bolted for the cover of the trees behind the warehouse.

A buckboard pulled up to the warehouse and creaked to a halt. "Hullo there, Nathaniel."

Junior Yutzy and Emmanuel Schwartz jumped from the high seat.

"Antique, isn't it?" Junior said, smiling and motioning to his wagon. "This thing is so old, my *dawdi*'s dawdi used it back in the day. Every time it breaks down, we patch it up and put it back on the road. If I took a match to it tonight, no one would be the sorrier."

"Jah, very old," Nathaniel said. "I can hear it complain from a mile down the road."

Emmanuel Schwartz came around the other side and took off his work gloves. "Hello, Nathaniel."

They shook hands. Emmanuel Schwartz, Sarah and Ada's brother, had grown so tall that he could see eye to eye with Nathaniel.

Of a solemn disposition like his dat the bishop, Emmanuel examined Nathaniel's face as if he were trying to look into Nathaniel's soul. His frown made him look much older than his seventeen years. At least he wasn't afraid to meet Nathaniel's gaze—or to tackle a topic straight on. "I am very sorry about what happened with Kate," he said.

The sincerity in his tone caught Nathaniel off guard. He couldn't brush off such heartfelt sympathy. "Denki," he said, meeting Emmanuel's eye. "I—I was very sad, but, Lord willing, the pain will go away in time. I hope she will be happy now."

"You are a gute man, Nathaniel," Junior said, glancing at Emmanuel. "If it were me, I do not know if I would be able to forgive her."

"There is nothing to forgive," Nathaniel said. "She chose the path she thought God wanted her to choose."

"Nae," Junior said. "I'm referring to the boyfriend. The man who came to get her."

Nathaniel stared at Junior in confusion. "He wasn't her boyfriend."

Junior's eyes darted from Nathaniel to Emmanuel. "We passed by the Weavers' house on the way to gmay last week. Kate and the man were standing by his truck, hugging."

Nathaniel rubbed his forehead. "Who was he? Did you see his face?"

"Dark skin. Young like Kate. I don't know. Their touching, it seemed improper."

Nathaniel felt the tension pull at his shoulders. "You think it was her boyfriend?"

Junior looked at Nathaniel's face and suddenly didn't seem so eager to share what he knew. "We were passing by. I didn't get a good look. We were just passing. The Herschbergers saw them. Ask Marvin."

Emmanuel held his hand up to hush Junior.

Nathaniel tried a reassuring look. "Thank you for being concerned." He climbed into the seat of his wagon. "Everything will be all right. Everything will be all right, Junior. Good luck with your wagon. May it give your family a hundred more years of service, Lord willing."

Junior cracked a smile. "Denki, Nathaniel. But I hope not. Perhaps today I will drive it into the lake."

* * * * *

Nathaniel was waiting in the barn when Aaron came to fetch the Weavers' horse and buggy. In spite of the paralyzing emotions swirling in his head, Nathaniel had repaired the shattered wheel, replaced the broken glass, and framed a new storm front. It was as good as new. Better than new, even, or Nathaniel wasn't worth his salt as a carpenter. Aaron had promised to stop by Nathaniel's later today and drive the buggy home.

A thin streak of afternoon sun materialized across the floor as Aaron stuck his head around the barn door. "Nathaniel, how are you? I've come for dat's buggy."

Nathaniel's frustration grew with Aaron's blatant cheerfulness, and he decided not to beat around the bush. "Why didn't you tell me about Kate and the man?"

The question seemed to throw Aaron off guard, and he sauntered farther into the barn. "What exactly didn't I tell you?"

"Did they hug?"

Aaron seemed thoughtful. "They were very happy to see each other," he offered, studying Nathaniel's face.

Nathaniel let out a heavy breath. Could anything in his life get worse? "Why didn't you tell me?"

He could see Aaron weighing his words carefully, debating what he should say and what he should not. "I did not want Kate to be hurt by such talk."

Nathaniel folded his arms and eyed Aaron skeptically. "You are not telling me the truth."

"You accuse me of bearing false witness?"

"Kate's reputation has never been your concern."

Aaron scowled and took a few steps away from Nathaniel. "Hiding the truth can sometimes be the best thing," he said, measuring each word before it came out of his mouth. "The harlot Rahab hid the spies of Joshua and lied to the king to save their lives. She and her entire family were spared because of her deceit."

"So you are protecting your family?"

Aaron sat on the workbench, rested his elbows on his knees, and stared at the ground. "I did not think you would believe my story of the excitement I saw in her face when that man touched her. It would paint a very unflattering picture of Kate."

Defeated and tired and growing more despondent by the hour, Nathaniel sank next to Aaron on the bench. It took Nathaniel every ounce of humility he had to look Aaron in the eye. "Why wouldn't she tell me?"

"Who can say?"

"Is she someone I only thought I knew?" Nathaniel whispered, more to himself than Aaron.

"I know she got many letters from Milwaukee."

Nathaniel buried his face in his hands. "Why did she even come back? Why, if she had a boyfriend and a better life in Milwaukee, would she come back to torment us?"

"You saw her injuries. She came back to get away from trouble."

A sick, nauseated feeling washed over Nathaniel. "Do you think that man, that boyfriend...?" He could hardly shape the word in his mouth. "…that boyfriend hurt her? That she left him in Milwaukee and later decided to go back to him?"

Aaron threw up his hands. "I do not know. How can I guess of the wickedness in her heart?"

The wickedness in her heart. If Aaron had said those words a week ago, Nathaniel would have responded with outrage. But now he did not know what to think, did not know how to defend Kate. Confusion, disgust, grief, all clouded his judgment. How could he ever get to the heart of the truth?

He didn't want to talk anymore. Without a word, he stood and led the Weavers' horse from his stall. Rollie had healed nicely, with no outward sign of any damage to the leg but a small scar where the hair would not grow back.

Aaron came up behind him. "I am indeed sorry to burden you with this," he said. "Kate's presence here did no one any good. Your mamm was against it. My parents felt the shame of her choices. Elmer and I disagreed over how to deal with her. She is too much in love with the world. You see that now. Perhaps knowing what she really is will make it easier for you to move on. To forget."

Nathaniel obstinately held his tongue and led the horse to the buggy. Aaron hesitated and then swallowed whatever he was going to say next. After they hitched up the horse, Nathaniel opened the wide doors and Aaron drove out of the barn and down the lane.

Why, even now, did Aaron's words anger him? Why was it so hard to hear the truth about Kate? Nathaniel closed his eyes as more questions than answers filled his mind.

He closed the barn door and took the long way back to the house. As he walked, it was Elmer's voice, not Aaron's, that echoed in his head.

"Why don't you go get her?"

Nathaniel pictured Kate's face, beautiful and serene. Would seeing her again bring him comfort or only compound his torment? Perhaps sharing what was in his heart and letting her do the same would bring him some measure of peace. And if Nathaniel desperately needed anything, it was peace.

He should talk to her—not on the phone where so much could be hidden, but face-to-face. He wanted to see her. Look into her eyes, no matter how painful, and find the truth.

Lord willing, the truth would set him free.

Chapter Twenty-Nine

Kate wiped the gooey green paste from her apron and then swiped the rag across Alex's face. "Okay," she said, "I swear I will never feed you green beans again. And I will wear a rain poncho when we try the squash tomorrow."

Dodging his busy hands, she carried Alex to the sink and ran his fingers under the water. Some messes were too tricky for a dishrag. Once Alex was sufficiently clean, she let him down and he crawled around the kitchen opening cupboards and emptying them of their contents. Kate smiled to herself. The only babies cuter than Alex would be her own—and Nathaniel's, Lord willing.

She heard a key at the door. Maria blew in, dressed in her waitress outfit and carrying the day's mail. "How did Alex do today?" she said.

"Gute. He would not eat his beans, but he took a two-hour nap."

"The apartment looks so clean," Maria said. "Are you sure you don't want to stay for another year or two?"

Kate spread herself on the sofa. "I just tidied up a bit. How was your day?"

Maria shuffled through the mail. "Best day ever. I didn't hear from Jared's mother once, and a very nice old man left me a twenty-dollar tip. Hey, look…a long-lost letter from Apple Lake."

Kate took in a sharp breath and practically leaped off the sofa. "Finally," she said, grabbing the envelope from Maria. "It's been two weeks, and I've sent four letters."

Her mood deflated slightly when she saw the return address. "Aaron?

What does Aaron want? He never wrote to me when I was at school."
Even knowing whom it was from, she ran into her bedroom and eagerly
opened the letter. "Why hasn't Mamm written?" she murmured.

> *Kate,*
>
> *Mamm and Dat were not happy that you left so suddenly,*
> *especially with Elmer still in the hospital. Elmer feels better. I*
> *must tell you how much happier Dat and Mamm are without*
> *you in Apple Lake. You know how the gossip upset Dat. Our*
> *parents seem at peace without having to answer for your*
> *transgressions.*
>
> *Nathaniel was sad when you left, but he, too, is coming*
> *to see you in a different light—the improper touching you did*
> *with the man who drove you to Milwaukee is no secret. Your*
> *worldliness is a stumbling block for him. How can he be a good*
> *church man with a wife he must always be reining in? Better*
> *for you to let him give his love to someone more suitable.*
>
> *Elmer says they want you to be the main part in the opera*
> *at the academy. You have a great career ahead of you. You*
> *were meant for greater things than our way of life. We will*
> *miss you, but everyone will be happier this way.*
>
> *Aaron*

Shaking violently, Kate paced around the room. Nathaniel had
heard about Carlos's behavior when he came to pick her up. Had he
jumped to conclusions? Her parents were happier without her there?
Everyone thought she was wicked?

Her world bounced and turned over and over like a rubber ball
rolling down a bumpy hill, leaving her confused and bewildered. She
fell across her bed and wept quietly. How had everything gone so horribly wrong?

Chapter Thirty

Nathaniel walked through the large wooden doors of the Milwaukee Music Academy. The lobby smelled of soap and furniture polish. He followed the signs to the main office and tentatively stuck his head through the doorway. A line of about a dozen students snaked in front of a large desk, where a young man with thick glasses and freckles sat typing furiously on his computer. Not knowing what else to do, Nathaniel took his place at the back of the line.

Many eyes turned curiously to gawk at him. He didn't mind. The Amish were used to Englischers staring at them wherever they went.

The boy at the front of the line argued with the one sitting at the desk. "I did not sign up for Music Theory, Part Two," he said.

"Fill out this form and pay the ten-dollar fee, and you will get the class change by e-mail tomorrow," said the freckled young man.

"I shouldn't have to pay ten dollars. It was your mistake, not mine."

Nathaniel's heart sank lower the longer he stood there. At this pace he would be waiting in line for two or three hours, and he was desperate to find Kate before the last bus left for Apple Lake tonight at seven.

Kate's mamm had gotten teary when Nathaniel told her where he was going, and she begged him to take Kate a letter and her mother's love. Emma gave him Kate's last-known address. "But she does not live there anymore," she said. "We had three letters returned. We do not know how to contact her."

A tall redhead filed in line behind him without even looking up from the phone in her hand. She punched the screen with such dexterity that Nathaniel couldn't help but be impressed. *This is the world Kate knows,* he thought with regret. *I do not belong here.*

The boy at the desk raised his voice in protest of another fee he shouldn't have to pay, and the redhead looked up from her phone. She glanced at Nathaniel and did a double take.

"Are you going to school here? If you are, you've seriously got to get some new clothes. Suspenders are not in."

Nathaniel shook his head. "I am Amish. I am looking for—"

"Amish! I know one other Amish person in the whole world. Her name is Kate. Are you related?"

Nathaniel didn't mean to raise his voice. "Kate Weaver?"

"Don't look so worried. I saw her yesterday." The girl gazed at him narrowly. "You're not Nathaniel, are you?"

"Jah. How did you know?"

"I should have guessed. Kate talks about you all the time. Tall, handsome, very nice eyes, dresses like a pioneer..."

"Do you know where she is?"

The girl smoothed a lock of hair behind her ear. "It's about time you showed up. She's been trying to call you for three weeks. Don't you ever check your messages? She's been pretty down about not hearing from you."

Nathaniel looked away. *Kate has been depressed? She should try walking in his shoes.*

"Can you tell me where to find her?"

The girl looked at her phone. "It's almost noon. Maria is at work, so Kate will be with Carlos and her baby."

Carlos and her baby?

The girl punched her phone screen then pulled out a pen and paper from her purse. "Here is the address," she said. "It's close enough to walk. I'd take you there myself, but I've got to get my schedule figured out."

Nathaniel nodded and walked quickly out the door. With his long strides, he soon covered the distance to the building where the girl said Kate lived. Standing across the street, he looked at the scrap of paper in his hand. He watched a car pull up to the front of the building, pick up a passenger, and drive away. He studied the mature trees in front. Three maples and an oak. Good furniture wood.

This was the strangest feeling of all. The fear wrapped itself around his throat and left him paralyzed, unable to take one step forward to his goal.

He could hear his heart beating thunderously through his chest. Instead of crossing the street, he sat on a bus-stop bench and stared at the apartment building.

He held his head in his hands. His courage had never failed him before. The apostle Peter had walked on water; Paul appeared before King Agrippa; Stephen testified to an angry mob bent on taking his life. How could Nathaniel give in to fear?

The answer came easily. He feared what he would find—that the Kate he knew would cease to exist and leave in her place only shattered dreams and unfulfilled hopes. If Kate fell, Nathaniel would cease to believe that there was any beauty left in the world. That thought kept him from crossing the street and knocking on her door. He wanted to hold tightly to his illusions, if only for a little longer.

He didn't know how long he sat there, but he could not move. Buses came and went while he waved them on.

He held his breath when he saw her. She was too far away, but in his mind's eye he imagined her brilliant green eyes and creamy skin. He had memorized every line, every curve of her face, until he could see her without opening his eyes. He was puzzled to see her in her kapp and Plain dress. Why did she still wear that?

She stood in the archway connecting two buildings and motioned for someone to follow her. A man with coffee-colored skin appeared, holding a chubby baby in one arm while pushing an empty stroller.

Nathaniel's blood heated up. Was this the man who had hit Kate and left her with bruises all over her face? If so, she did not act frightened or threatened now. She looked all too happy in his company.

Nathaniel almost crossed the street right then to warn the man not to hurt Kate again. But he reconsidered. The last time he'd protected Kate, he'd ended up doing violence. He would not let himself be tempted again. If Kate wanted protection, she should not have gone back to that man.

The man said something to Kate and her laugh carried all the way across the street, torturing Nathaniel with its deceptive sweetness. Still, he could not pry his eyes from the scene.

Kate took the baby out of the man's arms, hugged it tightly, and kissed it lovingly on the top of the head. After buckling the baby in the stroller, she started pushing it up the street.

The man put his arm around Kate as they walked. "Stop it," Nathaniel heard her squeak. She shrugged the man's arm off her shoulders and giggled. Smiling, he tried again, and she quickened her pace to avoid his teasing.

Nathaniel's mouth went dry, and he found it impossible to swallow. He watched Kate and her boyfriend with her baby walk up the street and out of sight. A bus pulled up to the curb, and Nathaniel leaped from the bench and climbed in. He didn't care where it was going.

* * * * *

It was a few minutes before midnight when Nathaniel stepped off the bus in Apple Lake. He breathed in the tepid air and let the wind pound against his face. He had no recollection of the journey home.

Chapter Thirty-One

The phone rang twelve times before the machine picked it up. These days, Nathaniel didn't ever answer his phone. "This is King's Cabinetry. Please leave a message."

"Nathaniel, this is Kate. I'm not sure you got my other messages. Please call me no matter if it is early or late. The number is 555-432-8492. I will be awake. Please call me."

The seventh message from her in three weeks. He marched to the answering machine hung on the wall next to the phone and firmly pressed the ERASE button. He wished it were as easy to erase her from his thoughts.

"Nathaniel King, must you work so hard that you don't even have time to eat?"

Nathaniel glanced up to see Sarah Schwartz standing in the doorway with a plate of food.

"Tell Mamm I will eat something later," he said, not bothering to meet Sarah's smiling eyes.

"Your mamm insists you are lying when you say that and made me promise to watch you clean this plate before I go back into the house."

She came closer and held the plate of steaming potatoes and corn out to him. He ignored her and ran his hand along the smooth edge of the tabletop he had been sanding.

"I made an oath, Nathaniel, and I won't break my word, even if I have to stay here all night and force-feed a stubborn man."

Nathaniel hesitated then turned and wiped his hands on an

available rag. Sarah handed him the plate, and he reluctantly sat at his desk to shovel in what he could. The corn was so buttery, it practically glided down his throat. Leave it to Mamm to try to fatten him up.

He hid his irritation as Sarah sat on the edge of his desk and watched him eat.

"I've heard you're keeping the cabinetmakers mighty busy these days. Miriam says you don't even hardly sleep."

Nathaniel didn't slow his eating, even to talk. "Lots of orders to keep up with."

"You keep this room very clean. That must be almost impossible, with dust flying everywhere."

Nathaniel didn't respond.

Sarah studied him for several more seconds before she got up and strolled around the workshop. "I love to see the things you can make from a plain block of wood. And the smell is wonderful-gute. Dat took me to a cedar factory once. I thought I was in heaven."

Chewing faster, Nathaniel tried to shorten the time of Sarah's visit. She showed up at the house almost daily now, so willing to help Mamm in any way she could. But Sarah could not help Nathaniel. He was past all rescue.

"Oh! Look at this beautiful rocker."

Nathaniel's gaze flew to the corner of the room.

"Is this for the auction? It looks like you are almost finished with it."

Nathaniel froze in place. "That one is not for sale."

Sarah ran her hand along the armrests and nudged the chair back and forth with her finger. "Can I sit?" she asked.

He nodded curtly.

"It's so smooth, like silk." She rocked back and forth and leaned against the slats, where she would find perfect comfort for her back and shoulders. "I love this, Nathaniel. It would be wonderful to rock a baby. I could sit for hours and never get sore." Closing her eyes, she rested her head against the back of the chair and continued to rock, humming an unrecognizable tune.

Why did something always have to remind him? Couldn't his memories leave him be? He never wanted to hear so much as a lullaby ever again.

Nathaniel jumped from his chair and strode to the door of his workshop, expecting Sarah to follow. Turning to find her close behind, he presented her with the empty plate. "This should satisfy Mamm."

Sarah took the plate. "Jah, she will be pleased."

He rested his fist on the doorframe. "But next time, don't ask me to make good on your promises."

Sarah couldn't quite hide her confusion under her smile as she stepped back and slipped into the house.

Nathaniel shut the door and wandered to the corner of the room, not taking his eyes off the unfinished rocker. All it lacked was a rich, dark stain and a coat of varnish. He nudged it lightly, and it glided back and forth smoothly, the fluid movement a testament to the care he took in crafting it. His finest work, forever unfinished. Forever tainted.

Clutching the back of the rocking chair, he lifted the heavy piece over his head and smashed it into the cement floor. With an earsplitting *boom*, the joints cracked and groaned but did not break. Again and again he beat the chair into the floor until it finally surrendered to the abuse and exploded into a jumble of slats and splinters.

Purposefully, he gathered up the bigger scraps that refused to be defeated, took them outside, and hurled them haphazardly in the direction of the woodpile. They clattered and banged as they hit the barn, the fence, and the compost bin—everything but the woodpile. The seat, which he couldn't break even with every ounce of his pent-up emotion, he took to the chopping block and reduced to kindling with eight swings of his ax.

Panting heavily, Nathaniel tromped back into his workshop,

stormed across the room, and ripped the answering machine from the wall. He refused to listen to one more message from that golden-throated deceiver. She wanted to relieve her guilty conscience, but he wouldn't be enticed again. Staggering at the thought of how utterly blind he had been, he pounded the thing against his desk until it disintegrated into a mesh of wires and plastic. He scooped up the pieces and tossed them into the garbage.

How had he not even felt an inkling of who Kate really was?

Because he had let her play him for the fool he was.

Mamm and Aaron had tried to warn him, but he had been beguiled by the dream of something that didn't really exist. He remembered telling his mamm that he shouldn't give up chasing his dream because of the pain down the road. How wrong he had been. His life would have been infinitely better had he never known Kate Weaver. The pain of losing her flowed through every blood vessel in his body, throbbed with every beat of his miserable heart. Would the weight of her betrayal crush him in the end?

Too late, he had learned the brutal truth. Kate had been away for two years. It would have been easy for her to fall into the ways of the world. A young, inexperienced girl with hardly any money and no friends would have found safety with a boyfriend. How long would it have taken her to justify sleeping with him to keep him happy? Nathaniel staggered. The thought of Kate cheapening herself sent him reeling.

Nathaniel even felt a little sorry for her. She probably couldn't fathom what she had gotten herself into. He might have been able to find it in his heart to forgive her if the deception hadn't wounded him so deeply.

As distressing as it was that she would become pregnant, it was even more reprehensible to Nathaniel that Kate would be willing to abandon her child to flee to the safety of the Plain community. All those letters she received, the worry in her eyes, were for her child left in who-knows-what kind of care. Kate had not been brave enough to bring the baby home with her and face the consequences of her mistakes. And he had been all too willing to believe her to be sincere and innocent.

Her behavior this summer had a logical explanation. The fresh bruises weren't from fighting off some boy she barely knew, but from an argument with her own abusive boyfriend. She needed a place to escape while things cooled off with the boyfriend. Apple Lake was the perfect solution. Nathaniel, the perfect dupe.

With his strength briefly spent, he sank to the chair at his desk and allowed his breathing to return to normal. A moist, warm sensation propelled Nathaniel's fingers to his forehead. He pulled back his hand, dripping with blood. An errant splinter of sharp wood must have struck him as he destroyed the rocking chair. With his fingers, he explored the wound—a two-inch gash across the edge of his forehead up past his hairline. It would sting for a while.

Good. It felt deeply satisfying to bleed Kate out of his system. Even if he bled himself dry.

Chapter Thirty-Two

Kate came in from a visit to the mailbox and plopped herself onto the sofa. She sat with her arms folded, staring at the wall. In spite of Maria and Carlos and the baby, she felt so isolated she thought she might scream. Were her parents that busy, that happy to have her away? Why didn't they write one word of encouragement or love? Their silence spoke louder than any scolding ever could.

And was Nathaniel truly having second thoughts, as Aaron had said? Had he learned the truth about Jared and been unable to forgive her? Kate pinched herself to hold back the tears. Maria would worry if she saw Kate crying, especially two days before the custody hearing.

Someone knocked softly. "Kate, it's Shannon," she heard a muffled voice say.

Kate unlocked the dead bolt and opened the door. Shannon stood in the doorway, her pointy-toed boots making her feet appear about three inches longer than they truly were. Kate noticed how Shannon's hair seemed to blow whimsically around her face whether there was a breeze or not, and when she stepped over the threshold in her sky-blue leather jacket, the room brightened considerably.

Inviting herself to sit, Shannon stuffed her phone into her purse and grabbed Kate's wrist. "Well, what did he say?"

"Who?"

"Nathaniel. What did he say?"

Kate sank next to Shannon on the sofa. "I still haven't been able to reach him."

Shannon squinted and frowned in confusion. "No, I saw him on Wednesday. I told him it was about time we heard from him."

"He was here? In Milwaukee?" Kate said.

"He came to the academy looking for you. I sent him to Carlos's place because that's where you usually are on Wednesdays."

Kate's heart hummed in anticipation. "I didn't see him…but I was there." She paused and put her hand over her mouth in dismay. "We went for a walk with Alex. Do you think he came while we were gone?" Kate burst into tears.

Shannon reached into her purse and pulled out a lemon drop for Kate. "Look, you need to call him again. If he won't answer the phone, leave him a very long message. And then, if he's not on the first buggy out here, believe me, you're better off without him."

"I can't do that," Kate said. "His phone has been disconnected."

Shannon gave Kate a quick hug then took out her phone and punched the screen furiously. "What's the name of his business?"

"King's Cabinetry."

Shannon stared at her screen and then her thumbs went wild. "Aha. Here it is. I'm amazing, really." She pulled a sparkly pen out of her purse and wrote a phone number on the back of an old receipt. "Try this one."

Kate sprinted into her bedroom with the phone number firmly in her fist. Then she sprinted back out.

"Here," Shannon said, waving her phone in the air, "use mine."

Back in her room, Kate's hands shook as the phone rang twice.

"Hello? King's Cabinetry."

Her heart leaped to her throat when she heard that deep voice. Oh, how she wanted to return to the safety of his arms!

"Nathaniel," she stuttered.

A long pause on the other end.

"Nathaniel?"

"How did you get this number?"

A sense of urgency drove her forward. "I want you to hear the whole story about Jared."

Another formidable silence.

"I know about what happened with the boyfriend."

Kate's heart raced. "Did Aaron tell you?"

"I forgive you."

Kate had never heard less forgiveness in her entire life. "I want you to hear it from me. I want you to understand."

"It doesn't matter. I forgive you. Do not call me again. I won't answer."

The *click* on his end of the line was deafening.

Chapter Thirty-Three

Kate looked in the mirror. Repeated splashing of her face with cold water had no effect on her puffy, bloodshot eyes or her sallow complexion. She buried her face into the soft towel and breathed in the scent of spring-fresh laundry detergent. Ach, if everything in life could be as utterly lovely as newly washed hand towels and daintily perfumed soaps.

She pressed the towel to her eyes as another wave of despair washed over her. *To despair is to turn your back on God, Mamma would say.*

No, true despair was when God turned His back on you. And God had truly abandoned her. She clung to the edge of a cliff with her frail faith, the whipping wind on the verge of blowing her into a black abyss.

Her breath came in stutters and spasms, the effects of crying still hanging over her. After the devastating phone call, Shannon and then Maria had slipped into Kate's room to give her comfort, but she had sent them away. It was impossible to share her pain with anyone, and Maria's sympathetic reassurances only made things worse.

Nathaniel. Everything inside her cried out for him.

Despite what he had told her, she knew his unblemished soul must abhor the thought of her taking a life. He could not bear such knowledge, and so he had to cut Kate out of his heart like a cancer.

Would she ever remember what it felt like to be happy?

No longer able to avoid her friends, Kate refastened the pins in her kapp and wandered into the living room, where Maria carried on a hushed conversation with Shannon. Alex sat on Maria's lap, sucking his finger. Both friends looked up expectantly when she entered the room.

Kate folded her arms. "He said he forgives me." With supreme effort, she kept her composure. "And to never call him again."

The ticking of the clock on the wall grew exceptionally loud.

"That jerk," Shannon muttered. Then louder, "That utter and complete jerk. And to think I was nice to him." She slammed her iPhone on the end table with such force that Kate fully expected it to break into a thousand pieces. "I really hoped he would be different."

"He is different. I'm the one who doesn't deserve him."

"Don't you dare blame yourself for this," Shannon scolded. "You deserve much, much better. I'm bringing over a pint of Ben and Jerry's. Chunky Monkey. Eat the whole thing by yourself. That's the only way I know to begin the cleansing process."

"I don't want to cleanse. I want Nathaniel."

Shannon handed her another lemon drop from her purse. "I'm sorry, Kate."

"Just when I thought God had given me an answer, that I knew where I was supposed to be, everything fell apart."

Maria moved to sit next to Kate. "As soon as the hearing is over, we'll get you home and you can sort everything out."

Kate turned her face away and wiped her eyes. Maria didn't understand. There was no home to return to.

Shannon glanced at her phone. "Oh, Kate, I'm sorry. I have to go. I'll bring that ice cream over," she said, before giving Kate a sisterly hug and walking out the door.

"This is all my fault." Maria cradled Alex in her arms and rocked him back and forth. "Right after the hearing is over, I'm coming with you to Apple Lake and explaining things to Nathaniel."

Kate clutched her chest, as if trying to scoop up the pieces of her shattered heart. No use in trying to repair it. She wasn't even the same person anymore. "I must accept what is," she said quietly.

Alarm flickered across Maria's face. "What do you mean?"

"I am the one who must control my life. Not Nathaniel, not the Church, not God."

"We must all surrender to God," Maria said.

"I do not need God interfering in my life. Hasn't He done enough?"

"You expect Him to make things easy for you?" Maria said, with uncharacteristic boldness.

"I don't expect anything from God anymore."

Maria reached out and caught Kate's wrist. "You're confused and upset about Nathaniel, but I believe you will come to see God's loving hand in all of this."

"I'm not going back," she said. "God has made himself perfectly clear. I have a choice, and I choose not to be baptized."

Maria stared at her in dismay.

Kate picked Maria's phone off the table. While she pressed buttons, she slid the pins out of her hair and pulled the kapp off her head. "Hello, Dr. Sumsion? This is Kate. I've changed my mind about the academy. Is the part of Juliette still mine?"

Chapter Thirty-Four

"Did you ever see Jared Adams hit Miss Trujillo?" asked the judge.

"Twice," Kate said.

The small room was so still, Kate could hear the judge breathing softly as he looked over the documents in his hand. Jared's mother sat with her meticulously manicured hands intertwined in her lap, never taking her eyes from the judge. Her platinum-blond hair seemed out of place, highlighting her aging face. Jared's father, tall and thin, looked as if he would rather be anywhere else in the world. Two attorneys in suits and ties flanked Jared's parents, while Maria's lawyer sat between Maria and Carlos and stared at the papers in the judge's hand.

The judge sat at a conference table face-to-face with Kate. "Did you ever see Miss Trujillo strike Mr. Adams?"

"Yes," Kate said. She sensed, rather than heard, Jared's mother hold her breath. "On April tenth. I was at the apartment. He had called her earlier in the day, wanting to see her, and she told him if he bothered her again she would call the police."

"Did she lure him to the apartment as his family asserts?"

"No, we wanted him to leave her alone. When he came over, we both fought him off. I pushed him into the counter and knocked him out," Kate said, her heartbeat pounding in her ears. She wadded the bottom of her skirt in her fist.

And for that, I lost everything.

"He later died of these injuries," said the judge.

"Yes."

"What is your opinion of Miss Trujillo's character?"

Kate glanced at Maria, who smiled reassuringly back at her. *"Don't sugarcoat the truth,"* Maria's lawyer had told her.

"I could not approve of her relationship with Jared. A woman should marry before…having relations with a man."

"I understand," said the judge. "But the Adamses want me to rule that she is an unfit mother. We have heard their opinion. I want to know yours."

"There is no mother as devoted to her child as Maria is to Alex. I have never heard a cross word from her. She is kind and loving and very careful for his health."

The judge laid his substantial stack of papers on the table. "Miss Weaver, let me hear something that hasn't been rehearsed a dozen times with Miss Trujillo's attorney."

"Every word is true."

The judge pinned her with a stern eye. "Have you got anything else?"

Kate hated the memories. "Three weeks after Alex was born, he got colic and cried for hours at a time. Jared lost patience and went to grab Alex from the crib. Maria stood in his way and wouldn't let him touch the baby. Jared cracked two of her ribs."

Jared's father hunched over and cradled his head in his hands.

"She would die to protect Alex," Kate said. "So she moved out. Alex is her life. It would destroy her if you took him away."

The judge looked at Maria, then at Jared's mother. "My job is to determine what is in the best interest of the child. No one else."

"I do not understand why they want to take Alex away from his mother," Kate said.

"She killed my son," said Jared's mother, unable to contain herself.

The judge looked over his glasses. "It is not your place to speak, Mrs. Adams. The police determined the incident self-defense, and I have no compelling evidence to suggest otherwise." He held up his hand. "And I'm not interested in hearing any more character witnesses for your son." Removing his glasses, the judge took a deep breath and gazed at Jared's mother, his eyes reflecting surprising compassion. "I am sorry for the loss of your son. To lose a child is unbearable. Can you see how taking Miss Trujillo's son would be just as unbearable for her?"

Maria, stoic up to this point, let a tear slip down her cheek. Kate blinked rapidly.

The judge tapped his pile of papers on the table and looked at the Adamses' lawyers. "You've paraded friends and family of the Adamses in here, listing all the advantages they can offer their grandson. But you left out the most important thing. They can never give him a mother. In cases such as these, as you well know, the burden of proof rests on those who would take the child from his mother, especially where no father is present. Granted, I have indulged you in this because of the Adamses' standing in the community, but I think enough is enough. Seeing no evidence to the contrary, I am granting Miss Trujillo full custody."

Both Maria and Jared's mother burst into tears while the judge made a hasty exit.

Kate ran around the table and threw her arms around Carlos and Maria at the same time. They laughed and cried and tried to ignore the sobs coming from the other side of the room.

"Thank you," Maria said, holding tight to both her brother and Kate. "I am so relieved, I think I might throw up." The emotion that Maria had bottled up for weeks overflowed, and she couldn't stop the tears. Half a box of tissues was not enough to contain her joy.

Kate suddenly felt her legs go weak. Alex and Maria were her only family now. The breathless thought of what might have happened almost overcame her.

Jared's father, with his arm wrapped around his wife, left the room, with their attorneys following close behind.

"He kept asking you questions," Carlos said, taking Kate's arm and nudging her into a chair. "You looked as white as a sheet. I thought you were going to pass out." Carlos laughed in relief. "He believed everything you said, though. You have that look of pure goodness about you."

"What if he hadn't?" Kate said.

"Don't think about that."

Maria's attorney left to finalize the paperwork, and Carlos and Maria sank into chairs next to Kate.

"What should we do to celebrate?" Carlos said.

"I'm going to go home and eat cheesecake until it comes out my ears," Maria said.

"I'm going to memorize music for my first *Romeo et Juliette* rehearsal next week."

Carlos waved his hand dismissively. "Boring."

The door opened behind them, and they turned to see Jared's father standing in the doorway. The anguish on his face was easy to recognize.

They stared at each other in uncomfortable silence.

"She felt so helpless," he finally said. "She didn't know what else to do with all that grief."

He strode slowly to Maria and placed a piece of lined paper and two one-hundred-dollar bills into her hand. "For the baby," he said. "And my phone number. If you ever need anything—anything at all—please call."

He seemed to want to say more but instead nodded to Maria and was gone. Maria disintegrated into a fresh bout of tears. Kate and Carlos held her hands and let her weep.

Chapter Thirty-Five

First day of rehearsal. First day of school. *Should be fun,* thought Kate. *Should* be fun.

"Measurements for costumes will be taken on Monday," Mrs. Malkin said. "Specific times are on the handout."

Dr. Dibble stood front and center. "Music must be memorized in three weeks. That is the end of September. No exceptions. You can all be replaced if need be." He pointed to Kate. "Glad to see you have decided to join us and cut other distractions out of your life, Miss Weaver." He waved his baton at the attentive cast. "If any of you are serious about your careers, this is where it starts. I expect you to work harder than you've ever worked, but if you prove yourselves here, fame awaits." He adjusted his glasses and pointed to the accompanist. "You all have your music. I would like to start with the 'Prologue' and then skip all the way to 'Frappez l'Air.'"

* * * * *

Kate propped her elbow on the table in the cafeteria and leaned her head on her hand. Even she, with her simple upbringing, knew this constituted bad manners, but she didn't rouse herself enough to care. She was a week into school and already looked forward to semester break. Rehearsals for *Romeo et Juliette* were as Dr. Dibble promised— grueling—and her class load left her almost dizzy, but she refused to muster any emotion at all. When she allowed herself to feel anything, the pain of losing Nathaniel overwhelmed her. A single-minded numbness was her only refuge from the grief.

Chelsea and Shannon chatted away about *Romeo et Juliette*, Shannon with a sandwich in one hand and her phone glued to the other. How she managed to eat and surf the Web at the same time was a seven-day wonder.

Kate only barely paid attention to their conversation.

Chelsea tilted her head to look into Kate's face. "Kate, are you okay?"

"I guess the Ben and Jerry's didn't help," Shannon said.

"Carlos ate most of it."

"As far as I'm concerned, every guy in the world can go jump in Lake Michigan," Shannon said. "I'm sick of all of them." Then, suddenly brightening, she said, "Look, there's Carlos." She bobbled one of her curls and hastily put her purse on the floor. "For a guy that good-looking, you'd think he'd find a nicer-fitting pair of jeans."

Glancing behind her, Kate saw Carlos coming toward their table. He wore the same pair of baggy pants he wore almost every day, and they looked as if they hadn't been washed in weeks. Carlos liked the "scruffy look," with his face whiskery but not grown to a full beard. His ruffled hair completed the picture of a man who couldn't care less about his appearance but somehow managed to look attractive anyway.

As soon as he caught sight of Kate, he practically sprinted to the table and slipped into the chair next to her. "How are my favorite girls in the world?" he said.

"We're okay," Shannon said.

"Not you, Shannon," Carlos said. "I was talking about Kate and Chelsea here."

Shannon cuffed Carlos on the arm.

"Hey, you're definitely in my top one hundred," Carlos said. He tried to dodge another blow.

Carlos and Shannon considered each other for a moment before

Carlos cleared his throat and stuck his hand into his pocket. "A letter came for you today to my apartment."

"Me?" Kate said.

He handed her a crinkled envelope that had her mother's handwriting across the top. Kate laid it on the table and smoothed it carefully with her hands. "It's from Mamma," she whispered.

"Good," said Carlos. "I was beginning to think you didn't actually have a family."

Chelsea stood up. "Walk me to the rehearsal hall, Carlos. It's on your way."

Carlos and Chelsea walked away and still Kate smoothed the wrinkled letter over and over with her hand.

Shannon watched Kate expectantly. "Are you going to open it?"

"I'm afraid of what it will say."

"Do you want me to have a look at it first?"

Her fear seemed irrational, even to herself. "Will you read it to me?"

"Okay," Shannon said. She took a miniscule pink fingernail file from her purse and slit the envelope. Unfolding the single sheet of paper, she looked at Kate doubtfully. "Are you sure?"

Kate nodded.

Shannon glanced around her and swallowed hard.

"*Dear Kate, Nathaniel gave me this address and said this is where you are staying. I hope you are not angry at me for writing. We have tried to respect your wishes and leave you alone. I understand that you have made the choice not to join the Church and to stay at the academy. Your dat and I love you. If this is what truly brings you happiness, then we are happy. We will miss you terribly, but do not worry, we can manage without you. The grands are getting old enough to be a big help at harvesttime. Do not worry. We will be good.*

"*We long for you to visit us. You do not need to stay very long. I will not ask you to see anyone you do not wish to see. It is true, Nathaniel was* very unhappy when you left, but please do not worry about him. He will heal in time, Lord willing. He is already seeing Sarah Schwartz several times a week, and Aaron tells us that they like each other very much. He deserves much happiness. Hopefully he can find it with Sarah.

"The harvest will be shortly upon us. Elmer is not looking forward to the cider pressing, but Dat told him it builds muscles. If he wants to impress the girls, he will do the pressing.

"We love you and miss you. Please, write to us so we know you are safe and happy. We will look every day for your letter. Love, Mamma."

An ache of loneliness pulled at Kate from far away. "Nathaniel," she whispered.

Shannon folded the letter and placed it on the table. "So, that's it."

"When did I ever tell them I wished to be left alone?" Kate propped her elbow on the table and rested her forehead in her hand. "God is punishing me. And I cannot bear the chastisement."

"No, no. Don't ever believe that," Shannon said. "Not every bad thing that happens to you is because some celestial being is angry. I think it would be much more like God to be merciful than vengeful, don't you?"

Kate straightened and looked at Shannon in wonder. She seemed to recall having this very conversation with Nathaniel's mother. Except at that time, she was attempting to convince Miriam of God's mercy. And here was Shannon, trying to convince her.

But she didn't believe it anymore. After all she'd been through, she'd be naive to let God run her life. She'd seen where that had taken her.

Chapter Thirty-Six

Nathaniel sat in silence, eating his obligatory helping of potatoes and corn, when he heard a soft knock at the back door.

"I'll get it," Mamm said, hurrying into the room, as if she constantly stood at her post just inches outside the kitchen doorway.

Two little boys, no more than six years old, stood on the back porch and looked longingly into the house. "Can Nathaniel play?"

"Nathaniel, you have some visitors." Mamm opened the door wide and glanced at Nathaniel expectantly.

He rose slowly and dropped his napkin on the table. "Hello, Toby. Who is your friend?"

"My cousin Yost," said the first little boy. "He wants to play baseball."

Nathaniel went to the door and his mamm backed away. "I'm sorry, Toby. I can't play tonight."

Toby stared at Nathaniel with wide, puppy-dog eyes. "My dat bought a new bat."

"Tonight's not a good night," Nathaniel said.

"Yost ain't gonna be here long," Toby said, "and he wants to see you hit."

Yost grinned, revealing a sparse collection of teeth, and he nodded enthusiastically.

"Sorry, boys. Maybe some other time."

Yost turned and clomped down the porch steps, but Toby held

his ground. "You never play anymore," he said putting his hands into his pockets and planting his feet. "Just for a few minutes?" Toby said, pitching his voice a little higher for dramatic effect.

Nathaniel studied Toby's face. He frowned and tapped the boy's hat brim up a few inches. "It's like this, Toby. I've got to start acting like a grown-up now, and that means I'm not going to play ball with you anymore."

Toby hung his head as if he'd found out he had to go to school for the rest of his life. "But you are the best player."

"You'll have to find another best player."

Toby shuffled his feet, gave Nathaniel one last disappointed look, then turned and trudged down the steps.

Nathaniel closed the door and turned to see his mamm watching him in concern. "You love baseball."

Nathaniel rubbed the back of his neck. "What do you want me to do, Mamm? Do you want me to go out there and play with them?"

"If you want to play, go play."

"Will that make you happy?" Nathaniel said. "I'll do whatever you want me to."

"I want you to do what *you* want. When I see you so miserable, I know that the only thing I want in life is to see my son happy again."

"Do you really believe that? Because three months ago I was deliriously happy. And that wasn't good enough for you. She wasn't the girl you wanted, so you resisted. You tried to separate us, without regard to my happiness."

"I was right, wasn't I?"

Nathaniel threw up his arms. "Yes. You were right. And aren't you delighted about it?"

"I am glad she isn't here to break your heart."

"Too late."

Mamm took Nathaniel's face in her hands. "I want you to heal.

I long to see that smile that was always there, which I haven't seen since she left. I want your life to work out well, Lord willing."

He turned away from her. "Then you should be quite pleased with yourself. Everything you've schemed and planned for all these years is coming to fruition. By this time next year, I'll be published with the bishop's daughter—the girl of your dreams."

"She is worthy of your affection. Kate was not."

"How satisfying it must be for you to say 'I told you so'—the phrase every mother would love to be able to say to her son."

"Nae, I never wanted things to turn out like this." Mamm reached her hand out to him. He backed away. "I don't mean to make light of what you are going through, but when that feeling subsides—and it will—you will be able to judge what you really want, what will truly make you happy."

Nathaniel staggered and leaned against the kitchen counter for support. "I don't live for my own happiness. There is no such thing anymore."

"In time, you will be glad things worked out as they did. You will realize you didn't really love her."

Nathaniel stared at his mother in disbelief before his incredulity melted into resignation. If it made Mamm happy to believe that he had never been in love in the first place, let her believe it. In a few weeks she would start calling the whole relationship an infatuation, and in a matter of months, she would cease to think of it as more than a passing acquaintance.

His relationship this summer had been an uphill battle against Mamm and the Amish community and, it seemed, the world at large. But it pained him that his own mamm could discount his feelings simply because she wished to.

However, his disappointment in Mamm paled in comparison to the powerful anguish swirling like a tornado inside his head. In moments of weakness—which came every minute of every day—the wounded man deep inside him cried out for *her*. Nothing could subdue the need.

He took a deep breath to clear his head. He was late for his Scrabble date with Aaron, Ada, and Sarah. As penance for his tardiness, he'd give Sarah a big kiss.

Anything to make Mamm happy.

Nathaniel ran his fingers through his hair then bolted for the door. He had to get out.

Chapter Thirty-Seven

"Kate, those runs are atrocious."

Kate massaged the back of her neck. "I'm sorry, Dr. Dibble. I didn't sleep well last night."

"Come down here." Dr. Dibble was a small man, short and thin, and had been teaching at the academy for what Dr. Sumsion swore was over a century. He sat in the darkened auditorium in the exact middle seat, shouting instructions to his singers like a disembodied spirit.

Kate shuffled off the stage and down the steps to the seat next to Dr. Dibble. He tapped his pen on the score in his lap and peered at Kate over the top of his glasses. "Four weeks of rehearsals and you haven't sung these passages correctly yet." He pointed at the measures in question. "This entire show falls on Juliette's shoulders. If you can't work out this mental block with 'Je Veux Vivre,' I've got three girls standing in the wings to take your place."

"Jah…Yes, I'll do better."

"Good. Now go do it again. Rosemary, take it from the top."

Kate sighed and plodded back up to the stage. If she didn't feel so drained and depressed all the time, she'd be able to muster some sort of joyful emotion for "Je Veux Vivre" or, as she reminded herself of the English translation, "I Want to Live." Dr. Dibble seldom complained about Kate's death scene. Her performance, he told her, was right on the money.

The piano plinked along merrily while Kate concentrated on her breathing technique for the first run. Out of the corner of her eye, a figure entered the side door of the auditorium and sat in the front row on the end seat. She chanced a look in that direction. *Elmer!* In full Amish garb, sitting comfortably in his chair, smiling at his own cleverness.

Kate nearly called for a halt to the music. She ached for just one hug from her brother. Instead, she let the thrill of seeing Elmer soar from her mouth to the back of the auditorium. The top notes spun from her head, and the trills escaped freely and effortlessly from her lips. "Je Veux Vivre." *I want to live. Take that, Dr. Dibble.*

The piano sounded the last decisive chord, and Kate actually heard the frail Dr. Dibble clap three times. His voice echoed through the darkness. "Much better. Take five minutes and we'll run through 'Ange Adorable.'"

Kate bolted down the steps and breathlessly flew into Elmer's arms. "This is the best thing that's happened to me in weeks," she said, laughing.

"That was a wonderful-gute song. I want to hear it again."

"What are you doing here?"

"I told Mamma that if I looked at one more apple, I'd be laid down till Christmas. She gave me leave to come see you. I paid for the bus, but I have to get back on it at seven o'clock."

"Ach. I've got rehearsal for another hour at least."

"Kate, is this him?" Chelsea stood on the stage, curiously studying the siblings.

Kate latched onto Elmer's arm. "This is my brother, Elmer."

Chelsea continued across the stage. "He's pretty cute for an Amish guy."

She disappeared behind the curtain as Elmer puffed out his chest. "See? Even the Englisch girls think I'm gute-looking."

"And you carry the sweet aroma of apples wherever you go. That must attract a lot of girls. Or bees."

Elmer tugged on Kate's ponytail. "You try swimming elbow-deep in cider for two weeks. My fingernails are permanently stained, I think." He held out his hands, palms down, for Kate to examine.

"Where did the bus drop you off?"

"At the north station. Then I took a city bus to the address Mamma gave me, and the man directed me here." Elmer looked at Kate anxiously. "Is that where you are living?"

"What address did Mamma give you?"

Elmer pulled a piece of paper out of his pocket. "This one."

Kate looked at the address. "Nae, this is Carlos's apartment. That is where Mamma sent her letter."

The color moved up Elmer's neck to his face. "Who is Carlos? Is he… Do you have a relationship with him?"

Kate made a face. "Nae, of course not. He is a friend, part of Maria's family. He takes good care of her. Like you do with me." She poked him in the ribs.

Elmer still seemed unhappy. He looked down at his shoes. "Why do your letters go to his apartment?"

"I do not know," Kate said. "I don't know how Mamma could have gotten that address."

Her sincerity must have placated Elmer. "He is not your boyfriend?"

"Why would you think such a thing?"

They both immediately fell serious. Silence persisted between them until Elmer grabbed her hand and pulled her to sit. "Nathaniel is dating Sarah Schwartz. I guess you heard."

"Jah."

"He didn't even try to win you back."

Kate cleared her throat. "Let us not mention such things." She ran her fingers through Elmer's tawny hair as tears stung her eyes. "How's your cut?"

He tilted his head and probed his scalp with his fingers. "Seventeen stitches. My hair will never lay straight again."

The memory hijacked Kate's senses: the noise, the singing, the look of unfettered eagerness in Nathaniel's eyes, the flash of revelation she would never experience again.

Pay no heed. Let it pass.

She forced cheer into her voice. "It seems like years instead of weeks since I last saw you."

"Not since the accident," Elmer said. He focused his attention on the empty stage. "Why did you leave without saying good-bye?"

A dark cloud settled over Kate. "I will regret that forever. I should not have been in such a hurry." She sniffed. "But it is better this way. Mamma and Dat are happier without me. I do not cause trouble for them. They no longer have to be ashamed of their worldly daughter."

Puzzlement and frustration etched lines onto Elmer's youthful face. "I do not understand you. You left Apple Lake because you thought it would make us happy?"

"That is why I stayed away. No one wants a proud, wicked daughter and sister."

Elmer growled. "Kate, that is Aaron talking. No one for a minute believes we are better off without you. No one." He averted his eyes and rubbed his chin. "Except for Aaron."

"Jah, he has told me many times." Kate thought of Aaron's letter. She knew what everyone truly thought. "I called Nathaniel on the phone. He made it clear he does not want me back either." Kate wiped the tears from her face. A man of peace did not want a wife who had caused the death of another human being.

Elmer laced his fingers with Kate's. "We avoid each other. He tried to help with the pressing once, but I made him feel unwelcome."

"How did you do that?"

"I told him he was unwelcome." A half smile flitted across Elmer's face.

"Don't treat him differently on my account," Kate said.

"Not after how he's treated my sister."

Kate found it impossible to speak.

"He's different, Kate. He and Aaron talk all the time about how a man must avoid the ways of the world. I begged him—'Call her up, go to Milwaukee and see her, do something besides pretend she doesn't exist.' He finally told me—'I loved your sister once, but she is not who she seems to be. It is better that she is gone.' I hate the sight of him." Elmer's irritation couldn't sit still. He jumped to his feet and paced in a small circle.

Kate rose and brushed an errant lock of hair from his eyes. Sighing, he put his arm around her shoulder. "It's good I'm not baptized," he said. "I am so weak yet."

Ryan ambled onto the stage. "Is Kate around?"

"Here," Kate said.

Elmer played with Kate's ponytail while studying her face. "So, is this what you have chosen?" he said, motioning toward the stage.

Kate lowered her eyes. "What else is left to me?"

"Your family. The Church. Your handsome younger brother."

"Singing is what I was born to do. I am very happy here."

Annoyance flashed in Elmer's eyes. "You think I can't see it? It is impossible to sit here for even five minutes and not see that you are swimming in sorrow. You're not happy here at all. Come home to us."

Kate turned her face from him. "I can't, Elmer."

"Your choice whether to be baptized cannot be made with regards to Nathaniel. It is between you and God."

"God has cut me off. I fend for myself."

"You talk like someone I don't know," Elmer said, picking up his hat.

"Meet the new me," Kate said. "Seizing the reins of my own life." She hesitated and then turned and marched up the stairs to the stage. "I couldn't be more pleased."

Elmer backed up the aisle, never taking his eyes from her until he donned his hat and disappeared out the clanking metal door.

Chapter Thirty-Eight

Elmer blew into Nathaniel's workshop like a hurricane. Nathaniel and Luke were boxing the last set of cabinets that would go out on the truck tomorrow.

Nathaniel caught sight of Elmer and groaned inwardly. He hadn't the restraint or strength to deal with Elmer's persistence today.

Elmer saw where Nathaniel stood and came straight to him. "Nathaniel, we must talk."

Taking a deep breath, Nathaniel glued on a patient expression. "Luke, can you finish up?"

Luke nodded without giving Elmer a second look.

Nathaniel led Elmer back the way he had come and out the door. The nippy air slapped at his face. They would have been more comfortable indoors, but Nathaniel wanted a short conversation and hoped the cold would encourage Elmer to be brief.

As soon as the door swung shut behind them, Elmer started talking excitedly. "I went to see Kate yesterday."

Nathaniel folded his arms to keep the ache from bursting out of his chest. "How is she?" he asked, pretending that he didn't really care.

"We misunderstood her. She thinks she is too much trouble. That is why she left the community. Don't you see? She didn't choose the world. She was being unselfish. For all of us." He waved his arms with great animation. "She thought you rejected her when you were really trying to be noble because you thought she made her choice."

"Things are complicated," Nathaniel said, with all the emotion of a man reading from the phone book.

"Don't you understand?" Elmer insisted. "She still loves you."

Nathaniel's heart almost failed him. If he believed that, if he believed she ever had loved him, he would crawl to Milwaukee on his hands and knees to fetch her back. If there were no boyfriend and no baby, nothing could keep him from her.

He passed his hand over his eyes. "I know what you want from me, Elmer, but I cannot give it. There are other circumstances that separate us."

Elmer glared at Nathaniel in astonishment. "Like what?"

For Elmer's own good, Nathaniel would not reveal the whole truth. Let Kate's brother believe what he wanted to believe. How could he tell Elmer of the forbidden relationship Kate had with a boy in Milwaukee? Of the baby that had come from that relationship? He would not be the one to destroy Elmer's opinion of his favorite sister. Kate would have to find the courage to tell him herself.

"Kate has made her choices." He cleared his throat and looked away. "She is worldly and vain and selfish. She is not the kind of woman I want for my wife. And I know she does not want me."

Elmer became more agitated with each word Nathaniel spoke. "Worldly? Vain? Kate is not these things." He paced back and forth then closed in on Nathaniel. "And you know it. Has Aaron poisoned you too? How can you spout such lies about my sister?"

"It does not make me happy to tell you this."

"It makes Aaron happy to hear you say it."

"I am sorry."

Elmer backed away. "Nae, you are not."

Nathaniel gave up. Nothing he said would make Elmer feel better. He shook his head in pity and opened the door to his shop. "I will not speak of this again." Elmer tried to say something, and Nathaniel held up his hand. "Never again, my friend."

The hurt in Elmer's eyes almost broke his heart. Better to escape before compassion betrayed him.

Nathaniel raised his hand to pat Elmer's shoulder but thought better of it and pulled away. "May you find peace."

He went inside and left Elmer standing there, staring at his own reflection in the glass door.

Chapter Thirty-Nine

Kate sat in Music Theory, barely able to stay awake, as the graduate assistant droned on and on about the rules of counterpoint and how Mozart broke them all the time. With her head propped in her hand, Kate gave in to the temptation to close her eyes for a minute. She deserved a little indulgence following her opening-night performance.

After two-and-a-half months of demanding rehearsals, *Romeo et Juliette* had opened to an enthusiastic audience. The crowd gave them a standing ovation after each act, and people practically leapt to their feet at the finale. She should have been floating ten feet in the air on adrenaline alone.

"Psst."

Kate opened her eyes and looked into the hallway, where the hissing had come from.

Shannon stood outside the open door, waving and pointing to a newspaper in her hand. She mouthed words Kate could not interpret. Kate shook her head and pointed to the clock on the wall above the teacher's head. Holding up three fingers, she formed the words, "Three more minutes. Hold on."

Shannon fidgeted and paced until the instructor dismissed the class.

Three of Ryan's friends lingered around Kate while she halfheartedly gathered up her notebook and pens.

"You were amazing last night," Brandon said. "You totally stole the show."

"Oh, thanks. And Ryan did great as Romeo," Kate said.

Blushing, Ryan's friend Keisha handed Kate two playbills. "Don't think this is dumb, but can I have your autograph? My mom asked me to get one for her too, because you're going to be famous someday."

"Sure." Kate signed her name on both playbills.

Brandon grinned sheepishly and produced the program from his pocket. "Me too?"

"After last night, you must be on cloud nine," Keisha said.

Kate forced the same smile she bestowed on everyone and gave the answer she knew was expected. "I am honored to play Juliette. It's the chance of a lifetime."

Shannon grew impatient waiting for Kate. She marched into the classroom, grabbed Kate by the wrist, and shoved the newspaper in her face. "Read this."

"Read what?"

"Right here, on page one."

"Which part?"

Impatient at Kate's apparent lack of interest, Shannon snatched back her paper and began to read. "'The Milwaukee Music Academy's production of *Romeo et Juliette*'...yadda, yadda, yadda...here it is. 'Kate Weaver's performance as the young girl is both heartbreaking and powerful. Her stunning vocals along with the wide-eyed innocence she brings to the role are the perfect combination for Juliette. This critic has never seen her equal. The performance was an unmitigated triumph.'" Shannon clutched Kate's arm and beamed. "I don't know what *unmitigated* means, but it must be really good. Oh, Kate, isn't this amazing?"

Was this what *amazing* felt like? Because all Kate felt was empty, like a deserted road in Apple Lake after midnight. Had she experienced anything amazing before Nathaniel came into her life? Was it so bad now because it was so good with him?

Keisha and a couple other students leaned in to read the review.

"One of the women on the board said it was the best opera the academy has ever done," Keisha said. "I heard some of them talking after the performance."

Where was the rush of elation that should accompany such praise? Kate had everything she had every wanted, more success than most of the kids at this school could ever dream of, and she couldn't care less.

Maybe down the road she would find what she truly searched for.

But she didn't have to waste her time looking. What, or rather *whom*, she wanted was sitting in a little workshop in the heart of Apple Lake, shaping blocks of wood with strong, gentle hands.

* * * * *

Kate sat in the empty dressing room in front of the full-length mirror. With her eyes closed, she listened to the muted sounds of the empty space: the vending machine down the hall that hummed and sputtered to silence in turns, the buzzing fluorescent light over her head, the subtle groans and creaks of the stage above as the crew arrived to set the show. Taking a deep breath, she wrapped her arms around herself.

November fifteenth.

Closing night.

Her soul felt as empty as the spacious dressing room.

Every night the audience stood in resounding ovation and threw her roses and teddy bears at curtain call.

"A masterpiece. Brava. A tour de force. When will we see you at the Met? Have you thought of studying in Europe?"

"You'd make a stunning Mimi."

"Your mother must be very proud."

"Yes, yes, your mother must be very proud."

Kate inhaled deeply, as if she had been holding her breath for a long time. She fluttered her eyelids to keep any mutinous tears from escaping. Dr. Dibble would not approve of self-pity.

She picked up a brush and ran it through her cascading tresses. No wig needed for the performance. Every night, Shannon came to the theater almost two hours early to curl Kate's hair and sweep it onto her head in perfect Juliette fashion. *Better get into a robe. Shannon will be here any minute.*

Kate heard the door open slowly. It stood on the other side of a dividing wall so curious eyes wouldn't be able to observe costume changes. "Shannon?"

"Leibe?"

Kate watched the reflection in the mirror as her parents inched tentatively around the dividing wall and into the room.

"Mamma! Oh, Mamma!"

She melted into her mamm's arms, sobbing and laughing at the same time like a child reunited with her mother after being lost in a crowd of strangers.

They stood like that until Mamma took Kate by the shoulders and held her at arm's length. "Let me take a look at you. It was the same last spring," she said with an affectionate scold in her tone. "You are too din. Don't they have a kitchen at this school where you can put some meat on your bones?"

Laughing in the delight of a hundred memories, Kate hugged her mamma again. Dat patted her on the shoulder, an unusual show of affection from him. "My Katie," he said. He stared at her as if she would disappear if he looked away.

"We hope you are not cross with us for coming," Mamma said.

"Cross? How could I be cross? I am so happy to see you, I think I will float onto the stage tonight. You got my letter?"

"Jah, leibe, thank you. We were so happy to finally hear from you," Mamma said.

"They told us at the ticket office that tonight is your last night," Dat said. "And that you are wonderful-gute." He turned to Mamma. "What is the word they used, *heartzly*?"

"Stunning," Mamma said.

"Jah. Stunning," Dad repeated.

Kate clutched both her parents' hands. "I have missed you so much. How is the family? How are all the brothers and sisters?"

Mamma nodded. "Joe and Ben have both grown three inches since the summer. Mary's arm is all better, and the children are gute. We pressed four hundred gallons of cider."

"Four hundred?"

"Jah, a very gute crop. Elmer did most of it, with the help of the twins."

"How is Elmer?" Kate said. "I am afraid he was angry with me when we parted."

Mamma and Dat looked at each other, and then Mamma looked down at the floor. "He had a hard time with your leaving. I worry for him."

"He loves Christmastime. At Christmastime I am sure we will see him happy again," Dat said. "Especially if you come for a visit."

Kate smiled wistfully. "I would like that very much."

"We miss you, Katie," Mamma said. "Can't you come home for good?"

Dat took Mamma's hand. "Now, hush, Emma. We will not trouble Kate with our selfish wishes."

"You want me to come home?"

Mamma dabbed moisture from her eyes. "What a question."

Shannon, holding her phone in one hand and a jar of applesauce in the other, appeared from behind the divider like a warm spring breeze. "Oh, hello," she said. "Are you Kate's parents?"

"Jah," Dat said. "Solomon and Emma Weaver."

"Nice to meet you." Shannon turned to Kate and gritted her teeth. "There's another one waiting for you down the hall. I'm afraid she's related." She held up the applesauce. "She gave me this. Made by real Amish people."

"Who is it?" Kate said.

Both Mamma and Dat shook their heads.

Shannon winced. "I don't know. But she's a talker. After two minutes I was looking for her OFF switch."

With a sense of foreboding, Kate led her parents out of the dressing room. A high-pitched screech echoed down the hall. Immediately they snapped their heads in the direction of the sound. There was no mistaking that voice.

Bewildered, Kate looked at her parents. "What is she doing here?"

Dat shook his head in disbelief.

They watched as Ada sashayed towards them with a wicker basket hanging over her arm. The spring in her step left no doubt that she was in very good spirits. Her eyes lit upon Dat and Mamma, and then her expression sparkled with recognition after examining Kate for a few seconds.

"Kate!" she squealed as she jogged forward to meet her wayward relative.

The occasion called for an embrace, so Kate reluctantly held out her arms to her sister-in-law.

"I am a lucky soul indeed to find you," Ada said. "This building has about a hundred hallways. I wasn't sure I was in the right place."

"What are you doing here?" Dat said.

"Last night I was halfway asleep when the idea came to me," Ada said, tripping over her words in an effort to get them all out at once. "Aaron was quite alarmed when he heard you were taking the bus to visit Kate today, and he asked me to follow you over and bring a little cheer. This morning I called Madeline Schwimmer from the phone at the grocery store, and she said she'd be delighted to drive me." Ada beamed with satisfaction.

Kate could only pretend to share her jubilation.

Ada's gaze traveled from Kate's bright yellow sundress to her rather frivolous orange heels, courtesy of Shannon's credit account at Nordstrom. "Look at you!" she gushed. "You're all made up and ready to take on the world." She leaned close to Kate and lowered her voice. "I think the fancy clothes suit you. Might as well be honest about who you are."

"You brought some of the applesauce," Mamma said.

Ada reached into her oversized basket and pulled out a jar. "Look what we did, Kate. Me, Anna, Mary, and Mamm Weaver. My sister Sarah came too. More than one hundred quarts in one day. I thought my feet were going to fall off, they hurt so bad."

Ada handed Kate the bottle. "From the MacIntosh apples?" Kate said.

"Jah," Mamma said.

Ada waved her hand in the air dismissively. "I don't know the kind. Mamm Weaver dumped the apples in the sink and told me to wash. Mary had to bring me a stool because I could barely stand on that hard kitchen floor of yours. Mamm saw how badly I suffered and told me to go put my feet up on the sofa. Ach, what a time we had!"

Out of the corner of her eye, Kate saw Dat flash a peculiar half smile.

"And look at this." Ada produced a small bottle of apple cider, a beautiful amber gold. "My boys were a big help to Elmer and the twins. And lots of neighbors dropped by, didn't they, Mamm Weaver? The Zooks, the Herschbergers...oh, too many to name. Nathaniel King lent a hand, but secretly I think he came over because Sarah was there."

Kate's stomach flipped at the sound of Nathaniel's name, but she did not betray any emotion to Ada. She refused to give Ada the satisfaction of knowing that the mere mention of Nathaniel King sent Kate reeling. Resolving to bury her curiosity so Ada wouldn't suspect, she nodded politely but didn't reply. As it turned out, her pretense didn't matter. Ada was eager to talk about Kate's one-time boyfriend.

"And, Kate," she said, patting Kate on the arm. "I don't want you to fret one bit about Nathaniel. He told Aaron that he has completely forgiven you and has not one iota of bad feeling left in his heart for you or the family."

Kate forced her throat open to speak. "That is very good of him."

"The whole community worried over him for weeks, but I'm convinced he has completely recovered. That boy won't slow down. He's joined two different youth groups, and he and Sarah go everywhere together."

Kate wanted to crawl into a hole. Did she look as distressed as she felt, even with a painful smile pasted on her face?

"Plus, Nathaniel loves Sarah's apple pies." Ada glance darted between Kate and Mamma, and she sighed in conspicuous contentment. "We'll have those two married off next year, Lord willing."

Mamma, who avoided confrontation at all costs, cast her eyes downward while Ada chattered away.

It was only with supreme effort that Kate kept her composure. A gaping hole in her chest quickly sucked every bit of light right out of her. Why was this news so devastating? She had already learned the brutal truth from Nathaniel's own mouth.

"Ada," Dat said, "Kate does not need to hear this. Leave well enough alone."

"I am just sharing the news. My boys adore Nathaniel. He plays Scrabble with us once a week and is already their favorite uncle," Ada said, prattling merrily.

Kate thought she might scream if she were forced to listen any longer.

"Nathaniel is a fine man," Ada said. "Don't you think so, Dat Weaver?"

Dat did not answer. He was studying Kate intently. What he saw in her face must have made him unhappy. His eyebrows loomed over his eyes like dark storm clouds.

He took Mamma's hand. "Ada, could you wait here while we find a vending machine for Kate? She needs something to eat before her final performance."

Ada pulled a bright green apple from the basket. "No need. I brought apples."

"She needs some sugar."

"I brought pie," Ada replied.

Still holding tight to Mamma, Dat grabbed Kate's hand and pulled them both away. "She wants something not in your basket."

Dragging Mamma and Kate with him, he plowed his way to the end of the hall, around a corner, then into the stairwell, where the metal door slammed behind them. The deafening *clang* echoed off the cement stairs.

Without saying a word, Dat pulled Kate to him and wrapped his thick arms around his daughter. Kate could not remember ever before receiving an embrace from her reserved father. Feeling as if she had run a marathon, she inhaled and exhaled with purposeful breaths until her heart slowed to normal and the vice squeezing her lungs relaxed.

"He hates Scrabble," she said.

Still holding tightly to his daughter, he said softly, "You still love him."

A pathetic sob escaped Kate's lips.

"Elmer said as much," Mamma whispered.

Dat stroked Kate's hair gently while Mamma came from behind and placed her hand on Kate's shoulder. "Then why did you leave us, liebe?" Dat's voice wavered. "Why?"

Kate tugged away from her dat's arms and wiped her eyes. "I tried to explain in the note. Maria needed me to testify for her son. Her brother drove me to Milwaukee. I told them I could only stay for a few weeks and then I was planning to return to Apple Lake."

Mamma and Dat looked at each other in confusion. "That is not what Aaron told us."

"Aaron?"

Without warning, Dat buried his face in his hands and moaned. "Aaron. My son. What has he done?" He sank to the steps and sat, face in hands, his stocky frame shaking with every drawn breath.

Care seemed to weigh Mamma down as she sat next to Dat and put her arm around him. "I am beginning to see."

"See what?"

Mamma motioned for Kate to sit next to her. She put her hand to Kate's cheek. "Tell us what happened, liebe. The day you left."

"Carlos came to get me. Maria needed me to care for her baby and then testify in a custody hearing. She might have lost her son if I had not helped."

Dat lifted his head.

Mamma nodded. "You saw Aaron?"

"Jah. I told him to tell you I would be back before harvest. And I wrote the notes for you and Nathaniel. I did not feel I could explain everything in my note."

"She wrote notes," Dat said.

Kate took Mamma's hand. "On the day of the buggy accident, I *knew.* I knew that the Lord wanted my future to be with our community, to be with my family and my faith and Nathaniel. I knew beyond a shadow of a doubt."

Mamma exhaled slowly. "Oh, my liebe, oh, my liebe."

"But then Aaron wrote and said you were happier without me, that my worldly ways were destroying our family. I doubted your love. I doubted my worthiness to live in the community."

Dat spoke in monotone syllables. "How many letters did you write us, Katie?"

"Five. But you never wrote back. What was I to believe?"

Pain filled their eyes as Mamma and Dat gazed at each other. "We sent you six letters, liebe," Mamma said. "All but one came back unopened. We never got any of yours or ever saw the note."

Kate grasped the import of what Mamma said. "You didn't?"

Mamma shook her head, tears rolling down her cheek. "Aaron brought in our mail every day for weeks. I thought he was being thoughtful."

"My son," Dat said, his hands clasped around his knees, his face a picture of agony.

Kate felt dizziness wash over her. She would not have imagined that Aaron, even with his rigid ideas, could do such a thing. "He sent me three letters. He told me the family was better off without me." Kate stared dumbfounded at the floor. "He must truly despise me to hurt me so. To hurt you so."

"He does not despise you as much as he loves himself," Dat said. "And desires to be bishop."

The three sat in silence, listening to the distant howl of the wind outside. A storm was blowing in.

"So this is why you decided to stay in Milwaukee? Because you thought we didn't want you?" Dat said.

"Jah."

To Kate's surprise, her mamm smiled. "Oh, liebe, now you can come home. Now you can come home. We will demand that Aaron confess his sin and explain to Nathaniel. You can come home!"

Kate slowly stood and leaned against the railing. "Nae, I cannot. I talked to Nathaniel on the phone. He knows that Maria's boyfriend is dead and that I caused his death. He forgave me but said he never wanted to talk to me again." Her voice cracked, and she walked around the small landing to regain her self-control. "He hasn't merely rejected me, Dat, he acts as if I meant nothing to him, ever. Am I of so little value?"

Dat pulled her to sit next to him again. "You are of infinite value."

"The Lord and Nathaniel have both abandoned me."

"How could our Lord and Savior abandon someone He bought with such a high price? Look at me, Kate." Dat reached out and held her face between his hands. "I am your father. I am an imperfect man with many faults, but I would never turn my back on you. You are more precious to me than all the treasures in the world. Now think of our perfect Father. It is not in His character or His nature to forsake one of His children. It is impossible. If you cannot see God that way, then you do not see the love a father has for his daughter. God's ways are not our ways. We cannot know why things happen. We can only trust that He knows all things. We must not trust in the arm of flesh, only God."

Kate stood up and turned her back on her parents. Slumping her shoulders, she lowered her voice to a near whisper. "Aaron has deceived us, Jared is dead, and I have lost Nathaniel. It does not seem like the doings of a being who loves me."

Mamma tried to grab her hand. She shrank from her mother's touch.

"Nothing is lost to the Lord," Mamma said.

"I am," Kate said. She looked into her mamma's eyes. "I will have a brilliant singing career. People from all over the world will know my name. I'll have everything I ever dreamed of." She depressed the latch on the stairwell door and slowly pushed it open. "Let God run other people's lives and leave me alone."

Chapter Forty

"There." Shannon stabbed one more bobby pin into Kate's hairdo. "I am amazing. We get started twenty minutes late and I still manage to make your hair look gorgeous with a half hour to spare."

Kate fingered a curl at the base of her neck. "Thanks, Shannon."

From behind, Shannon put her hands on Kate's shoulders and stared at her reflection in the mirror. "Now, if only we could fix that sadness as easily as I fixed your hair, that would be a real trick."

"I am fine," Kate said.

She stood and removed her first costume from the clothes hanger. Shannon, familiar with the routine, helped her ease it over her head and tightened the laces in the back. Kate raised her arms to make sure she had freedom of movement then dropped them to her sides and nodded at Shannon.

Shannon gave her a quick yet significant hug and turned to retrieve her own costume from the rack.

One of the girls from the ensemble stuck her head around the divider. "Kate, Dr. Sumsion's out here to see you."

Kate emerged from the dressing room and looked to her left. Mamma and Dat sat with Ada on a bench at the far end of the hall. They stared at her but were too far away to do anything but observe. She looked the other way and spied Maria and Carlos marching toward her, with Alex riding on Carlos's shoulders.

Kate knew she was glad to see them rather than feeling so. In her present state, she was incapable of mustering enthusiasm for anything.

She gave Maria a hasty hug. "Thanks for coming," she said.

"Hey, what about me?" said Carlos, spreading his arms for Kate.

"Sorry," Kate said. "You get a handshake."

Carlos glanced expectantly at the dressing room door. "I need a hug. Where's Shannon?"

Kate turned back to Maria. "Have you seen Dr. Sumsion? She was asking for me."

Someone grabbed Kate by the shoulder. Dr. Sumsion, wearing an elegant black formal, flashed her no-nonsense smile. "Kate, a woman from the Met is here to meet you before the performance. Come with me."

Kate followed Dr. Sumsion down the hall in the opposite direction of her parents. An elegant woman with snow-white hair, also in a black formal, stood waiting for them. "Kate, this is Mrs. Harriett LeFevre from New York."

Mrs. LeFevre held out a gloved hand. "Delighted to meet you, Kate. My assistant came to your performance on Monday and insisted that I fly out immediately and see it." Her earrings tinkled when she moved her head. "High praise, I assure you."

Kate tried to pay attention. Tried to be flattered by the compliment. The deference even Dr. Sumsion paid Mrs. LeFevre revealed how influential she must be. Kate made an effort to inject her expressions with more animation, more admiration than she felt. This woman could help her go places.

A tug on the back of her dress diverted Kate's attention. She turned to find a little girl no more than five looking up at her expectantly, holding a small notepad and a pen with a bright pink feather sticking out of the top. "Could I have your autograph?" she said timidly.

"Kate, we have things to discuss." Mrs. LeFevre's irritation at such a minor interference seemed excessive. "Perhaps we could find a private room, Dr. Sumsion?"

Kate took her lead from Mrs. LeFevre. Here was a woman she must impress. She looked down at the little girl. "Please, not now," she said curtly.

The little girl chewed on her index finger and looked at the ground. "But you are so pretty."

Kate glanced at an annoyed Mrs. LeFevre, and her own irritation grew. Couldn't the girl understand how vital this conversation was to Kate's future? "I'm right in the middle of something important. Go. Go find your mother."

The girl tried to hand her pen to Kate. She dropped it, and it made a small mark at the bottom of Kate's flowing costume. "I'm sorry," she said.

"Now look what you've done," Kate said, lifting the hem of her dress and examining the mark.

Distressed, the little girl turned and shuffled quickly down the hall to a woman standing at the other end, only a few feet from Kate's parents.

Mrs. LeFevre shook her head and went right on talking.

The little girl flew into her mother's arms. She talked to her mother with great energy, and the mother attended her with a look of calm concern. She produced a tissue from her purse and wiped the little girl's face.

While Mrs. LeFevre prattled on about what education Kate would need before going to Europe, Kate could see Ada and her parents attentively listening to the little girl. After the child finished her story, Ada knelt beside her and put an arm around her. Kate's sister-in-law reached into her basket, pulled out a shiny green apple, and handed it to the little girl. The girl smiled through her tears, took her mother's hand, and walked away, cradling the apple in her arm.

A small act of kindness from, in Kate's view, an unlikely source.

Why did Ada show kindness to a child and I did not?

I've got a few things on my mind at the moment. Like the fact that

I've lost my parents and my boyfriend. Like whether I am going to sing at the Met in five years.

But those thoughts could not hold her. What was wrong with her that she could not muster charity for anyone but herself?

Kate's surroundings blurred, Mrs. LeFevre's voice disappeared, and she heard her dear mamma's voice reciting Kate's favorite story. Not a typical bedtime tale, but one that Kate never tired of hearing.

"An old teacher spent months tutoring his pupils on the life of the Lord Jesus. When it came time for the final exam, the students arrived at the schoolhouse only to be told that the place for the exam had changed. Each rushed to the new location, worried that they would not have time to finish the test."

"Where are you thinking of completing your Masters?" Mrs. LeFevre was saying. "I have four recommendations, all excellent schools."

"Along the way, each student passed a crying child who had fallen off her bicycle, a farmer whose load of hay had toppled onto the road, and an old woman who mumbled to herself in confusion. But the students did not stop to help, the final grade their only concern."

Looking down the hall, Kate scanned the faces of those she loved: Mamma and Dat, Maria, Alex, Carlos, even Ada. But nothing erased the memory of the little girl pleading for a small bit of attention.

"When they reached the new location, the teacher greeted them in tears and informed them that they had all failed the class. Why? 'Because,' said the teacher, 'although you know many interesting facts about the Master, you do not know the Master until you live His teachings.'"

The force of the blow hit her like a ten-foot wall of water. From the outside looking in, it was a seemingly trivial interaction with a child she didn't know. But to Kate, it was a pivotal moment. How far she had fallen!

Not caring what Mrs. LeFevre thought, Kate took a few steps away from both ladies and stared in the direction the little girl had gone. She had sunk lower than she ever thought possible—not because of Jared's death, not because Nathaniel had cast her aside, but because she had hurt another human being. She had forgotten the Master.

The tears flowed. She covered her face in her hands, but even that wasn't enough to stifle the sobs that came from the deepest part of her being.

Mrs. LeFevre stopped droning and said something to Dr. Sumsion.

"Kate." Dr. Sumsion placed a firm hand on her back. "What's the matter with you?"

"Dr. Sumsion, I'm...sorry. I need...to...step out for a minute."

Kate did not wait to gain anyone's approval. She bolted for the nearest exit. The sobbing spasms refused to subside.

"But, Kate, curtain is in fifteen minutes."

Kate found the stairs and ran to the bottom floor into a deserted commons area and plopped herself on a sofa.

In the oppressive silence, self-condemnation piled upon her. How pitiful was her knowledge of the Savior. How feeble her faith. In her anguish, she had forgotten everything she had ever been taught, everything she'd ever believed. Her mind flew back to her first buggy ride with Nathaniel. Thinking of him made her catch her breath as she tried to remember what he had told her.

"Because God loves us more than we can possibly comprehend, He pushes and crushes us to stretch our faith beyond what we can see. If the way were easy, how could we grow into who He wants us to be? How could our faith become unshakable?"

When she closed her eyes, she could almost hear him speaking to her. *"Your heart is ready for God when you are in your darkest hour."*

What did she truly believe about following the Master? About giving her heart to the Lord?

The warmth of recollection spread through her as her mind flew to the day of the buggy accident. Her circumstances had taken a decided turn for the worse, but nothing could ever invalidate what she felt that day when everything became so clear to her.

Still the tears flowed. Bowing her head, she prayed with more fervor than she ever had before. "Dear Father, I am grateful for this dark hour, for now I am ready for Thee to change my heart."

"Did your grandma die?"

Kate blinked back her tears. The little girl, with apple still in hand, sat next to her, swinging her legs from side to side and looking with great concern at Kate's tearstained face. Kate looked around. The girl's mother stood in the doorway watching them, not inclined to interrupt.

"My grandma died, and Mommy cried and cried." The girl reached up and patted Kate on the cheek. "Did your grandma die too?"

Kate did her best to dry her eyes.

"Here," said the little girl, and she popped off the sofa and ran to the nearest tissue box. In a blur of blue ruffles, she returned with three tissues for Kate.

"Thank you," Kate said. She blew her nose and dabbed her eyes while the little girl sat patiently next to her.

"When Grandma died, we all sang a song. When I sang it, Mommy felt better. Do you want me to sing it to you?"

Kate nodded.

The precocious little girl slipped off the sofa and stood facing her audience of one. "'Be still, my soul; the Lord is on thy side.'" Her angelic voice rang through the empty commons area.

Kate felt her whole body go weak as the little girl sang several lines. Had she been standing, she would have crumpled to the ground.

"'Be still, my soul; thy God doth undertake to guide the future as He has the past. Thy hope, thy confidence, let nothing shake; all now mysterious shall be bright at last. Be still, my soul; the waves and winds still know His voice who ruled them while He dwelt below.'"

Disregarding the water gushing from her eyes, Kate tenderly took the girl by the hand. "Can I sing the next verse with you?"

The girl nodded.

In spite of her irregular breathing, Kate found her voice. "'Be still, my soul, though dearest friends depart, and all is darkened in the vale of tears; then shalt thou better know His love, His heart, who comes to soothe thy sorrows and thy fears. Be still, my soul; thy Jesus can repay from His own fullness all He takes away.'"

The little girl stopped singing altogether after the third stanza, her gaze frozen on Kate. "I saw you in the play last night," she said. "You are the best singer ever."

The girl's mother ventured near them. "I usually wouldn't bring a five-year-old to an opera," she said. "But my little sister is in the chorus and Haley begged me to come. I can't believe how still she sat through the entire performance." She walked over and patted Haley's head. "She was so sad when your character died. That's all she could talk about all day today. I brought her tonight so she would know you were really okay."

"Are you okay?" Haley asked.

"Yes," Kate said, with more conviction than she had felt in months. She squeezed Haley's hand. "I am okay."

Haley smiled.

"Thank you for your song," Kate said.

"You're welcome." Haley beamed. "I want to be a opera singer when I grow up."

Kate looked up at Haley's mother. "I am sorry about the autograph." She patted Haley's hand.

Haley ran her hand along the exquisite fabric of Kate's dress. "That's okay. Mommy said you were nervous for your show."

Kate held out her hand. "Can I give you that autograph now?"

Haley's mother pulled the notebook and pen from her purse and handed it to Haley who, in turn, placed it in Kate's lap.

Kate smiled and wrote a small portion of what was in her heart.

To Haley. Today you were an answer to my prayers. I think that makes you one of God's angels. You are a very special little girl. Love, Kate Weaver/Juliette

Kate handed Haley the pen and notebook.

"What do you say?" her mother prompted.

"Thank you," Haley said.

Haley's mother held out her hand to her daughter. "Come on, honey. We need to go find our seats. Good luck—I mean, break a leg tonight."

Haley took her mother's hand, looked at Kate, and held out the apple. "A lady gave this to me. You can have it."

Kate took the apple. How could she refuse a gift that had traveled such a long way?

Kate cradled the apple in her lap and played Haley's song in her head again. *What to do now?*

As she watched the young mother tenderly lead her daughter away, the answer came to her as gently as a wispy melody played on a flute.

"Choose that good part, which shall not be taken away from you."

"Be still, and know that I am God."

Chapter Forty-One

In spite of the fact that the opera started almost fifteen minutes late because the leading lady mysteriously disappeared mere minutes before curtain time, the final performance of Milwaukee Music Academy's *Romeo et Juliette* proved to be its finest. Kate played every scene with all the emotion of a farewell performance. Because it was.

She almost lost her composure during the death scene with Ryan, thinking of her affection for her friends at the academy, her love of opera, and what she was giving up with her heartrending choice. But her inner conflict lent that much more emotion to the scene, and she knew she would always remember it fondly as her finest performance.

When the final curtain fell, the applause was thunderous, deafening. Ryan threw his arms around her and kissed her jubilantly on the mouth. She hugged him back, and he helped her off her marble perch.

"Remember me when you're famous," he said.

The curtain went up, and she and Ryan swept hand in hand to the front of the stage for a bow. The applause never subsided as the ensemble and the other principles came onto the stage for curtain call. The curtain went down again and they stepped back, but the thrilled crowd kept clapping.

Kate and Ryan came out to the front again. Kate motioned to the usher at the front of the theater and, on cue, he lifted little Haley onto the stage. Haley walked politely and a little timidly to Kate. Kate turned Haley to face the audience, and Haley performed a perfect curtsy.

The audience laughed and clapped. Kate laughed with them. She scanned the faces of the crowd. Many of them were in tears but beaming at the same time.

She caught her breath. Her parents stood in the very last row of the theater, looking uncertain but smiling and clapping their hands as well. She couldn't believe it. Had Mamma and Dat seen the performance?

Kate couldn't help herself. She bolted down the steps and up the aisle to where her parents stood. They wrapped themselves around her and held on for dear life. The audience roared its approval.

Haley and Ryan stood alone. Ryan picked up a rose that had been thrown onstage and, with a show of supreme gallantry, presented it to Haley. Haley kissed Ryan on the cheek, and they walked off the stage holding hands.

* * * * *

With elbows linked and no intention of letting go, Kate stood close to her mother while a horde of admirers filed past.

"Splendid, absolutely splendid."

"We can't remember a better performance."

"How can you cry and sing at the same time? I couldn't hold back the tears."

"Wonderful, wonderful, and is this your mother? Are you Amish?"

Kate smiled with satisfaction and relief. "Yes, I am." At least she knew that much.

Her mother held on tighter.

The crowds thinned out, and Kate and her parents found themselves standing alone. "You got my message," Kate said.

Dat wiped some moisture from behind his glasses. "Jah. You want to be baptized."

"Jah," Kate said. "I want to be who God wants me to be."

"You were beautiful, Katie," Mamma said. "To think you can bring so much happiness to so many people. It makes my head spin. I finally understand why giving this up has been such a hard choice for you."

"But once it all became clear, it did not seem so hard." Kate and her parents gazed at each other, and Mamma squeezed her more tightly.

"Why did you come to my performance?" Kate said. "Does Ada know?"

Dat scratched his beard. "If we must sit in the front row of church for a few weeks, we must. I do not care what Ada knows."

"I felt so empty, watching you enter a place I could not go," Mamma said. "The bishop will do what he will do about it. I do not regret it for the world."

Kate spied Maria across the lobby. "Mamma, I must go explain to Maria. I will be back."

Dat sighed. "And I suppose we should find Ada. She did not come to the performance, but she stayed to see if we would have a wicked look to us after the opera. We will meet you back here in a few minutes."

Kate hadn't had a chance to change out of her costume yet, so she lifted her skirts and jogged to Maria's side before she could leave. "Where is Alex?"

"The babysitter took him home earlier," Maria said. "I wanted to bring him so we could get a picture before your last performance." She hugged Kate. "You sang so beautifully tonight. My voice is never going to be that good, but if you're my teacher, I'm sure I'll improve over time."

Kate didn't know any way to soften the truth. "I'm not coming back."

"You mean…to my apartment?"

"No, I am not coming back to the academy, Maria. I have made the decision to be baptized."

Maria clapped her hands in delight and then, as if thinking better of it, turned serious. "You know I'm going to miss you like my own soul, but I've sensed for a long time that the academy is not where your heart is." She draped her arm over Kate's shoulders. "I mean, you have this big curtain call with like a hundred bows and all you want to do is jump off the stage and hug your parents. It's obvious."

Kate smiled. "Give Alex a kiss for me every day."

"And you must write me at least once a week."

"I will, Lord willing," Kate said. Then she couldn't help herself. "Choose your friends wisely."

Maria didn't take offense. "Don't worry. I've learned my lesson. Alex is the only man in my life from now on. I promise. And Carlos. I guess Carlos counts for something."

Maria rifled through her purse and pulled out a small photo. She handed it to Kate—a smiling mother cuddling her chubby baby. "Are you allowed to have this? To remember me?"

Kate smiled at the memory of little Alex's cherubic face. "He is worth every bit of trouble, jah?"

"*Si*, the only good thing to come from me and Jared."

"Not the only thing." Kate pressed her hand to Maria's heart. "*This* came from our afflictions."

Maria closed her eyes and nodded. "I will never forget." She breathed a sigh and fished her keys out of her purse. "You will stay at my apartment tonight?"

"Jah, and then on to Ohio as soon as I can make arrangements."

"Ohio?"

"To my sister Hannah."

Maria glanced over Kate's shoulder and shook her head. "I don't know what that brother of mine thinks he's doing." She looped the purse over her shoulder. "Tell Carlos I'll talk to him in the morning." She squeezed Kate's hand and was gone.

Chelsea, Shannon, and Carlos charged Kate from behind. Carlos poked Shannon in the ribs, and Shannon giggled hysterically. "You were great tonight, Kate," she said between giggles. "I cried clear through the death scene from backstage."

Kate's parents, with Ada in tow, made it back to Kate's side. "That hard bench gave me a pain right here," Ada said, kneading her lower back. "I sat there for like as not three hours."

"Hey, Kate," Shannon said. "My parents are meeting me at Jean Chevalier's downtown for some dessert. Wanna come?"

"No, thank you," Kate said, putting her arm around her mother. "I have to get back to Maria's in good time tonight."

Shannon turned to Carlos. "How about you? Wanna come?"

Carlos, who had been smiling a few seconds earlier, glumly put his hands into his pockets. "I have to work early," he mumbled. "I'll see you later." He exited the building like a bull trying to escape the branding iron.

Shannon pounded her forehead with her palm. "Oh, Jean Chevalier's is the most expensive place in town. Why didn't I suggest the Dairy Queen? How stupid could I be?"

Kate watched Carlos through the glass doors as he trudged dejectedly down the steps. "He's *ferhext* for sure."

A faint smile emerged on Shannon's face. "Ferhext?"

"Smitten," Kate said.

Shannon sighed. "I wish. But he'd never actually ask me out."

"Why not?"

"He thinks he's from the wrong side of the tracks or something ridiculous like that."

Dr. Sumsion came bustling toward their little circle. "Chelsea, Shannon, good job tonight. Kate, Mrs. LeFevre says she'll call you next week. In spite of your little outburst beforehand, you exceeded expectations. Don't worry. You're not the first girl to let the pressure of a lead role get to her."

Kate tucked a lock of hair behind her ear and looked at the people surrounding her. *Might as well inform the whole world all at once.* "Dr. Sumsion, I know how much you have sacrificed so I could attend the academy. But the music in my heart sings a melody that I have ignored for too long. I ache for the place my heart and song have always been—among my own people. I'm sorry, but I won't be returning to the academy."

Out of the corner of her eye, Kate saw Shannon tilt her head to be sure she'd heard correctly. She smiled, produced her phone from her purse, and began frantically pressing the screen.

Dat took off his glasses and wiped his eyes.

Dr. Sumsion was silent for several seconds. "I can't pretend I'm not disappointed. You know I care for you, and I don't want you to wonder or regret what could have been."

Kate gazed steadily at Dr. Sumsion. "No amount of regret compares with knowing God's will and failing to do it. I am sure of what God wants me to do. Without a doubt, I have felt His guiding hand. Understanding what I give up and knowing that I choose freely makes my choice more precious to me."

Shannon looked up from her phone. "Now that she's going back, maybe she can win Nathaniel again. Although I wouldn't give Nathaniel King the time of day if I were Kate."

"Nathaniel King!" Ada said, delighted to share her good news. "He and my sister Sarah are practically engaged."

Shannon abruptly turned off her phone and stuffed it into her purse. "Nathaniel? Kate's Nathaniel?"

"I can't see as how you could call him 'Kate's Nathaniel' when he's been courting my sister for the last three months," Ada said, pursing her lips and blinking rapidly.

"He didn't take long moving on to greener pastures, did he?" Shannon said.

Ada lifted her chin. "It doesn't take a genius to see that Sarah is better suited to him. She is the bishop's daughter. Nathaniel is a person of importance in our community. I would not be surprised if he were bishop someday. But not if he married Kate—with her history of flitting about the world, performing in operas and such." Ada's gaze moved from one person to another. "Anyone with a lick of sense can see that."

No one spoke.

After a long pause, Shannon quit staring at Ada and rummaged through her purse. "You'll have to give him my congratulations for finding his perfect match." She pulled out a business card and wrote something on the back of it. "Give this to him for me."

Ada studied Shannon's handwritten message. "Proverbs 12:15. What's that?"

"A good-luck message."

"I'll see he gets it," Ada said, looking a bit confused.

"Now," Shannon said, "Kate and I are going to change clothes before the costume mistress comes for us with a shotgun."

Kate hugged Dr. Sumsion. Dr. Sumsion took a few seconds to hug her back. "I'm glad it's Friday," she said. "I need a good long weekend to work up the nerve to break the news to Dr. Dibble."

Shannon tugged Kate's sleeve, and Kate followed her down the hall.

"You have business cards?" Kate asked.

"Oh, I had some made up in case I wanted to give a guy my phone number."

"What did you write on the card you gave Ada?" Kate said.

"Proverbs 12:15. 'The way of a fool is right in his own eyes.'"

"I wish I could see Ada's face when she discovers what it says."

Chapter Forty-Two

After changing, Shannon and Kate rejoined Kate's parents and Ada in the lobby.

Shannon glanced at her phone and sighed. "I've gotta head out," she said. "I'll miss you like crazy, Kate. Plus, I'll need to find a new diction coach. If you ever need anything, call me." She paused. "Oh, I forgot. You can't call me. Send me a letter. Anytime."

"Shannon, I can call. There are phones where I live."

"Okay, then. Give me a ring." She held up her phone. "I always have it with me."

Kate laughed. "I can count on that."

Shannon gave Kate one last smile and then she was gone, blowing through the tall glass door like an Indian-summer breeze.

Choosing one path means rejecting another. Every choice involves regret and sacrifice and hope.

Kate went to her parents and touched Dat's elbow. "Ada, I need to talk to Dat and Mamma privately for a minute. You'll forgive me?"

"Take your time," Ada said, finding a digital clock above the box office window. "Madeline won't be here for another fifteen minutes."

Although a chilly November wind whipped the leaves around the academy building, Kate and her parents walked outside and found a place to sit on the steps.

Kate wrapped her arms around her legs and propped her chin on her knees. "What will you do about Aaron?" she said quietly.

Dat looked stricken at the mention of his eldest son. "I do not know yet. I will not speak to him until I am sure. The bishop might think a shunning necessary."

"The bishop? Aaron is married to his daughter."

Dat studied the cracks in the cement at his feet. "Bishop will do what is best for the community and the gmay. My challenge will be to forgive him."

Kate tried not to dwell on Aaron's sins. She had pressing concerns of her own. "Mamma and Dat, you know I love you," she said, shivering slightly in the cold.

"Jah. You know we love you," Mamma said.

"I want to see Elmer and Mary and the twins something terrible."

"Jah, no doubt," Dat said.

"But I'm not coming back to Apple Lake," Kate said.

The distressed look returned to Mamma's eyes. "But you told us—"

"On the night of the buggy accident, I got my answer. I'm ready to be baptized. But I want to join the church in Ohio. More than once, Hannah has invited me to live with her."

"Leibe, why do you want to go to Ohio with your sister? So far away from your family?" Mamma said.

"I cannot close my eyes to the truth. Nathaniel has made his feelings clear about my part in Jared's death. I have lost him forever, and I cannot bear to be near him."

"You would not have to see him. We have no reason to invite him into our home ever again."

"No, Mamma. I would see him everywhere. At gmay and auctions and barn raisings, at Ada's house… And I would see him even where he is not—strolling around Barker's Pond, leaning on our porch railing, playing baseball with the kinner. I could not even confine myself to the house, he's been there so many times."

Dat reached across Mamma and took Kate's hand. "The wound is still fresh. Time and the Lord Jesus will heal everything."

"But the wound would tear open every time I saw his face. I cannot bear it, Dat. Please don't ask me to."

Dat tilted his head. "You think one summer with you was plenty for me and Mamma? It would crush your mamma to be without you again."

Mamma nodded, her eyes brimming with tears.

"You could come visiting. I could come visiting," Kate said.

"That is not good enough," Dat said. "You need to be near your family. We can help you heal."

Kate thought of Ada's smug expression as she described Sarah's triumph. "Please do not force me to endure Ada's gloating and Aaron's lectures. Let them exult over me from a distance." She looked at her mother pleadingly. "I cannot endure it, Mamma."

Dat rubbed the back of his neck in frustration. "Nathaniel is not the only worthy man in the community. In time you will find another."

"What would you do if, heaven forbid, you lost Mamma?" Kate said.

Dat closed his eyes. "I know what you want me to say. Of course I would..." He sighed in resignation and patted Mamma's hand. "I would not be able to put two words together to form a sentence. But I would accept God's will."

"Can you imagine me being reminded every day that the man I love is lost to me forever?"

"We could ask Ada and Aaron to move to La Crosse," Dat said.

Both Kate and Dat burst into bitter laughter at the same time. Mamma, who sat between them, didn't see the humor.

"Do you think they would agree?" Kate said.

Dat stood up and pulled Mamma with him. He held out his hand to Kate and helped her up as well. "You may go for a visit. But when summer comes, I want you coming home for good."

"But—"

He held up his hand. "None of this talk of staying in Holmes County. We've already let an Ohio boy take our Hannah. I won't lose you too."

Kate reached into her pocket and fingered the photograph of Maria and Alex before handing it to Dat. "Will you keep this for me? It will help you remember."

Dat took the picture and fixed his eyes on the small image. "This will not take your place." He slipped the photo into his wallet. "Just till you return."

Kate nodded and managed a noncommittal shrug. It would be easy to plant herself in Ohio. Harder for Dat to uproot her.

She breathed in the fresh air of liberation. It was time to go.

Chapter Forty-Three

With his hands buried in his pockets and his face hidden behind the top flaps of his coat, Nathaniel stomped across the yard to Aaron's house in the dim light of a cloudy sunset. Ice crystals blanketed every tree, transforming the orchard into lace. Indents made by Aaron's heavy boots in the mud had frozen over with thin sheets of ice. No snow lay on the ground, but everything from Nathaniel's breath hanging heavy in the air to the frosted windowpanes on the Weaver home bore witness to the imminent winter.

Nathaniel knocked and heard a scuffle as several of Aaron's boys fought for the privilege of opening the door.

Even through the wall, Ada's voice pierced the air. "Giddy, stop bothering your brother. You'll be the death of me. The death of me yet."

She gave up screeching when she opened the door and pushed her boys out of the way. Her face lit up. "Nathaniel. Come in. We wasn't expecting you."

"I am come to see Aaron. Is he in?"

"Out to the stable tending the horses. I will have Giddy fetch him."

"Do not trouble yourself," Nathaniel said. "I will find him."

"Wait." Ada bustled to the kitchen and returned with a napkin folded around four cookies. "Take these for the two of you."

"Denki," Nathaniel said. "They smell gute."

"My favorite recipe from Mamm Weaver. She knows a barrelful about cooking, even if none of her daughters got the skill. Mary can't make a cake to save her life. And Kate never tried hard enough."

Nathaniel wished that once, just once, the mention of Kate wouldn't send pain coursing through his veins. He cleared his throat and turned to leave. "Denki for the cookies."

"I saw her yesterday," Ada said.

"Who?"

"Kate. She was dressed up all fancy with orange shoes. Can you believe, orange shoes?"

"Is she...is she in Apple Lake?"

"Nae, silly goose. She wouldn't show her face here. Mamm and Dat Weaver went to Milwaukee to visit her, and I went along. Mamm and Dat saw her opera. Bought a ticket and walked right in like they was Englisch. I warned them not to. My fater will have to be told of their sin."

"Is she well?"

"Who, Kate?" Ada folded her arms. "You will never guess. She told Dat Weaver that she wants to be baptized in Hannah's gmay. According to Solomon, she got on the bus this morning for Ohio."

Nathaniel furrowed his brow. *Baptized? Why would Kate be baptized?* He tried to make sense of that piece of information.

Ada had probably heard wrong.

Unless there was trouble.

Nathaniel almost asked Ada if she had noticed bruises on Kate's face. Even though Kate had rejected Nathaniel, the thought of that other man hitting Kate made Nathaniel want to put a hole through the wall. Kate had fled her violent boyfriend once. What if she needed another escape and didn't dare try to pull off the deception again in Apple Lake?

"I told Aaron I do not know why Kate would be baptized. The fancy life suits her well," Ada said. "The girl cannot even sew a tiny stitch."

What about her baby? Had the poor child been passed to yet another stranger so Kate could continue her deception? Nathaniel shook his head to clear it. How had he been so blind?

He nodded, took his stack of cookies, and left Ada standing on the porch.

Although small, Aaron's stable was a fine, sturdy structure. Nathaniel knocked lightly before turning the handle and slipping into the relative warmth inside.

Aaron was brushing one of his chestnut mares before bedding her in the stall. A bright propane lantern hissed by his side as he carefully smoothed the rough hair at the horse's neck.

"Are we playing Scrabble tonight?" Aaron said, glancing at Nathaniel out of the corner of his eye. "Ada didn't mention it."

"Nae," Nathaniel said. "Sarah is baking pies for the Herschberger wedding tomorrow."

Aaron led his horse to the stall. Smiling and lifting an eyebrow, he said, "I expected you to be preparing for a wedding for yourself by now. What's the matter? Can't convince Sarah to say yes?"

Nathaniel swallowed the lump in his throat and forced a smile. "Mamm would need at least two years' notice to prepare for my wedding."

"Let's hope not. You aren't getting any younger." Aaron closed the stall door and slapped Nathaniel on the shoulder. "Come inside where it's warm. Ada made cookies."

Nathaniel held out his hand. "She gave me some. Do you think we could stay out here yet? I need to discuss something with you."

Aaron raised his eyebrows. He studied Nathaniel's face then retrieved two three-legged stools. "Then sit," he said, placing the stools next to each other beneath the tall propane lantern.

"I went to Milwaukee to see Kate," Nathaniel said.

Aaron clenched his fists and the muscles around his jaw tightened. "When?"

"September."

"That long ago?"

"I had to see for myself," Nathaniel said.

Aaron knitted his brow together and stared as if he were trying to see the back of Nathaniel's head from the front. "And you talked to her?"

"I didn't have to. I saw her across the street with her boyfriend."

"The one who came to fetch her?"

"Jah, I'm sure of it. And there is something else." Nathaniel scooted his stool closer to Aaron's, feeling the need to whisper even in the isolated room. "But I must have your assurance that you will tell no one of this."

"How can I help?"

Nathaniel took a deep breath, still wondering if it was wise to share such a secret with Aaron. Was Nathaniel any better than the gossips who wagged their tongues and rejoiced over other's misfortunes?

He didn't rejoice over this. The knowledge weighed so heavily, he thought it might crush him.

His heart beat angrily. "In the two years she was gone, Kate had a baby."

Whatever Aaron was expecting, it wasn't this. His mouth gaped open in shock. "Are you sure?"

Nathaniel nodded. "The girl at the academy told me. Then I saw Kate and her boyfriend with the baby." Nathaniel's mouth went dry. He saw it all again in his mind, his reaction as raw and bitter as when it actually happened.

Aaron smiled widely, jumped to his feet, and threw his hands out as if praising God. Not the reaction Nathaniel expected. "I warned everyone," Aaron said. "Kate brought only wickedness into our home. No one saw her for what she was."

Nathaniel stared at Aaron.

"Now people will know who was wise and who was deceived," Aaron said.

"You rejoice over your sister's downfall?"

Aaron remembered himself before his rejoicings turned rapturous. He confined his hands to his pockets and put on a stern countenance. "Elmer and Mamm and Dat thought I judged too harshly, but now they will see I was justified in my suspicion of her, that I had good reason for my actions."

Nathaniel reached out a hand and grabbed Aaron's arm. "Nae, Aaron. No one must know. No one."

"But why? The community will realize how wise you were for seeing her as she truly was. And they will know that I was right all along."

"Someday Kate might feel sorry for what she has done. She will need our understanding, not our judgment. People would think badly of her if they knew. I will not allow that. When she is ready, she will come forward with the truth. Until then, I will not shame her."

"She has shamed herself."

"I will not compound that shame."

Aaron whirled around to face him. "Then why tell me?"

"Because I can trust you and because it has been such a heavy burden." The emotion overcame him like a brutal, invading army. He wrapped his arms tightly around his stomach to keep from shaking.

Aaron moved behind him and rested his hands comfortingly on Nathaniel's shoulders. "Her memory still has power over you. I am sorry. She was once a gute girl. I understand why you loved her. I am truly very sorry."

Nathaniel breathed deeply in and out, willing the gaping chasm in his chest to shrink and the violent pounding of his heart to cease. Why did his heart go on beating at all? Now that he had unburdened himself, things would surely get better. Surely Aaron and the rest of his community would help him find the will to go on living.

Time would heal everything. *Must give it some time.*

If he waited long enough, time would turn him to dust and the wind would blow him away.

Chapter Forty-Four

Nathaniel reached over and patted the milky white calf. "She's a beauty, ain't not? Gute color and bright eyes. No swelling in the knees."

"Jah," Davie Eicher said. "From Dat's best milker. She'll fetch a good price. You looking to buy?"

Nathaniel lifted each hoof and examined it. "May so. I ain't sure yet."

"I brought seven for auction. Lots to choose from." Davie pointed down the row of stalls. "Have a look."

Nathaniel raised his head just as Sarah Schwartz appeared at the pavilion door with her hands on her hips. "Nathaniel King, this habit of wandering away without telling me has got to stop. I spent the better part of twenty minutes searching you out."

With a look of embarrassment, Davie turned his back and busied himself with a knot in his rope.

Nathaniel stuffed his hands into his coat pockets and looked at the floor so Sarah wouldn't notice the resentment in his eyes. "I'm looking at buying a milking cow for Mamm."

"Your mamm has no need for another cow. Your milker still has plenty of good years left in her."

"This one's a wonderful-gute—"

"Not another word. I declare, if I weren't around to keep you in check, you'd be spending every cent of your money on things you don't need."

On tiptoe, Sarah ventured a few feet into the livestock pavilion and reached out her hand to Nathaniel. "Cum. Your tables are about to go up for bidding. You want to see how much they bring, don't you?"

Nathaniel glanced at Davie, who was doing his best to pretend he hadn't heard the conversation. "I'll be back," he said under his breath. Davie gave a barely perceptible nod.

With Sarah in the lead, Nathaniel tromped over to the warm east pavilion, which was outfitted with tables and folding chairs—and where buyers were already bidding on the last of his three walnut tables. Nathaniel and Sarah slipped into the back row.

"I told you, you shouldn't have disappeared," Sarah hissed. "You missed it."

"Not all of it."

"Most of it."

Nathaniel had always loved auctions—the excitement of watching the price of his item rise with every bid, the thrill of competition to be the highest bidder. He enjoyed browsing the goods and livestock that Englisch and Amish alike brought to sell.

His favorite memory was the time he'd threatened to buy Kate a quilt she knew he couldn't afford and watching her eyes grow to saucers as he pushed the bid past six hundred dollars. He knew precisely when to stop so he wouldn't actually have to buy the quilt, and she had cuffed him several times for putting her through such torment.

The thought sobered him now. How could he take pleasure in the memory of something that wasn't real?

"Seven hundred and twenty-five dollars!" Sarah clapped her hands. "Did you hear that? People love your furniture, Nathaniel."

"A gute price."

"Gute? Excellent, I'd say."

A beautiful quilt of emeralds and reds came up next. Tiny appliquéd flowers twined around the border, and a bouquet of roses graced the center.

Nathaniel folded his arms across his chest and grinned. "How about I buy that for you, Sarah?"

"You'll do no such thing. I can make thirty of my own for the price you'd pay for that."

After two bids were placed, Nathaniel raised his hand. "One hundred."

Sarah's horrified expression did not deter him. "Stop this at once," she scolded.

"Two hundred," Nathaniel yelled after waiting for a sufficient number of bids.

"Nathaniel, you will quit this foolish game right now, or I will have to remove you from the room."

"Two-fifty." Nathaniel looked smugly at Sarah, whose piercing stare could have sliced him in half.

Jumping to her feet, she plucked the hat from his head, clutched one of his suspenders, and pulled him toward the exit. He had no choice but to follow. She would have wrenched the trousers right off his legs.

As they emerged under the overcast sky, Nathaniel could hear guffaws and sniggers echoing through the pavilion. He felt his face flush hot—with anger or embarrassment, he could not tell.

"What in the world were you doing? I want to bury my head, I'm so embarrassed," Sarah said.

Nathaniel glared at her, every unkind thing he could think of at the tip of his tongue. With his heart pounding, he clenched his fists and tried to smother his temper before it got the better of him.

He snatched his hat from her fingers and jammed it firmly onto his head. Without a word, he wiped all expression from his face and stormed away from her.

"Nathaniel, come back. I didn't mean to…"

His resolute strides carried him behind the pavilion to where the livestock trailers were parked. Most people kept to the warmth indoors. It would be difficult for Sarah to find him here.

He should be so lucky.

He immediately rebuked himself. Sarah had no fault in this. How could she know he was teasing her? He thought she would find his game amusing, like...other people might.

Leaning against a large trailer, he closed his eyes and willed himself to calm down. The incident was trivial. Why had he reacted with such anger?

Nearby laughter caught his attention. He stuck his head around the corner of the trailer to see five young men standing by another trailer and carrying on an animated conversation. He thought about joining them until he spied Elmer Weaver in the group.

The friendship between Nathaniel and Elmer had completely dissolved with Kate's absence. Elmer made it plain that he thought it despicable that Nathaniel had abandoned Kate, accusing him of being unduly influenced by Aaron.

"Why would you volunteer for that?" one of the boys said.

"They're not even married," said another boy, ribbing the boy next to him.

"So? Marriage shouldn't give a woman permission to walk all over her husband." The speaker turned his head so Nathaniel could see his profile. Davie Eicher. "Better it is to single live, than to the wife the britches give."

"You make that up?"

"No," Davie said. "It's in Proverbs."

Nathaniel had decided to return to the livestock pavilion when he heard his name. "Everyone sees it but Nathaniel."

He plastered himself against the trailer and held his breath.

"Maybe somebody should warn him."

Nathaniel heard Elmer loud and clear. "Nah, he deserves what he gets with that one."

"If you ever want to know the definition of 'henpecked,' watch Sarah with Nathaniel," Davie said.

"Oy, anyhow," Elmer said. "If you ever see me being led around by the nose like that, hit me upside the head with a two-by-four."

Nathaniel felt as if all the breath had been sucked out of his lungs. Is this how they saw him? For more than three months he had lived in a perpetual stupor. Had he really let things sink so low with Sarah?

"I liked your sister better," Davie said softly.

Someone kicked the gravel. "Mamm says she's gone to Ohio."

With Ada as his informant, Nathaniel had heard that news before just about everyone else when Ada returned from Milwaukee three days ago. Joe Weaver had the nerve to ask Nathaniel if he would seek out Kate now that she had decided to be baptized.

We will see, Nathaniel thought.

"She's living with my sister Hannah," Elmer said.

"Is she coming back?"

Elmer's voice went very quiet. "I do not think so. She wants to be baptized in Ohio."

"Nathaniel would have been better off with Kate, I think," one of the boys said.

"She's better off without him," Elmer said, bitterness oozing with every word.

"He is a good man...and a man of God has to draw the line," Abner Burkholder said. "I'm sorry to offend you, Elmer. I would not want anything to do with a girl who gets in trouble with an Englischer and then has his baby."

"What are you talking about?" Elmer said.

"Her baby. Kate's baby. Had I been Nathaniel, I would have rejected Kate too."

"What do you mean, Kate has a baby?" Elmer said.

Nathaniel groaned inwardly. It was not right for Elmer to find out this way.

"She has a baby. You...you didn't know?"

Nathaniel heard a *thud*. It sounded like a body being shoved against the wall of the trailer. "That is a damnable lie. Who told you this?" Elmer said.

"The...the whole community knows," Abner grunted.

"Who told you?" Elmer said, his voice rising in outrage.

"Let go of him." More shuffling, more gravel crunching.

"My dat heard it from Ada, I think. Or maybe Aaron."

Aaron? Nathaniel wanted to jump out from his hiding place and call Abner Burkholder a liar. But deep down he knew Abner was not making it up. Exploding with fury, Nathaniel ran toward the pavilions instead. He stormed through the livestock area, scanning faces for Kate's eldest brother. How could Aaron have betrayed his trust?

How could Aaron have been so disloyal to his own sister?

Ada stood outside of the smaller pavilion, her arms wrapped around herself against the chill.

She caught sight of Nathaniel. "Sarah is looking for you. She says she's real sorry for making you mad, and she'd be pleased and proud if you still want to buy her a quilt."

"Where's Aaron?"

Ada shut her mouth then opened it again. "Did you hear what I said about Sarah? She's awfully—"

"I must speak to Aaron."

"He went with Sarah to find you. Oh, there he is."

Aaron stormed around the corner of the pavilion with Sarah hanging on his arm. Annoyance was etched on his face. He caught sight of Nathaniel and nudged Sarah in front of him. "She's sorry for whatever it is she did. Now can we finish with this nonsense?"

With no regard for propriety, Sarah threw her arms around Nathaniel. "I didn't mean it. Please forgive me."

All but ignoring the tearful girl, Nathaniel pried Sarah away from him and glared at Aaron. "You broke your promise."

Aaron's annoyance increased. "What promise?"

Nathaniel didn't have a chance to answer. Elmer appeared, charged Aaron, and thrust him roughly into the side of the pavilion, pinning his back against the wall.

"What are you telling people about Kate?" Elmer yelled, tears glistening on his cheeks.

Aaron struggled to break free, but at almost twenty years old, Elmer had grown taller and stronger than he.

"Tell me!" Elmer yelled again.

Aaron scowled, but it was clear he knew exactly what Elmer accused him of. "I told no one."

Elmer released him with a shove. "You're lying."

Aaron looked like he wanted to shove Elmer back. Instead he retreated a step and kept his voice low. "I told no one." He directed a sharp eye at Ada. "Except my wife. I do not keep secrets from her."

Ada clapped both hands over her mouth.

Elmer barely glanced in Ada's direction. "You let her spread it around for you."

Aaron stood with his feet apart and folded his arms, making a show of indignation. "Ada, who did you tell?"

Ada shook her head in mute distress. All three men stared at her.

Sarah pushed them aside and put a protective arm around her sister. "Don't pick on Ada. She hasn't done nothing wrong."

"I didn't mean to," Ada said, her voice grating on Nathaniel's ears like cheese curds on his teeth. "It just popped out." Her hazel eyes brimmed with water.

Aaron shrugged his shoulders. "Ada means well. Sometimes things slip."

Elmer gave his brother a black look. "You told her because you knew she'd repeat it. You wanted her to repeat it. She has the biggest mouth in the community."

Ada puffed out her chest and huffed at Elmer.

Aaron glared right back at his brother. "The truth was bound to come out sooner or later."

"The truth! Where is an ounce of truth in this?" Elmer said. "Did you think it would make Nathaniel love Sarah? Or did you want revenge for Kate's disrespect last summer?"

Aaron shook his head. "I did not make it up. Nathaniel first knew about it, and he shared it with me."

"Nathaniel! Nathaniel *knew*?" Elmer yelled.

A group of curious onlookers gathered around the center of conflict.

Nathaniel reached out his hand and took Elmer by the shoulder. "I am sorry you had to hear the news this way."

Before Nathaniel had time to react, Elmer shot out a fist and pounded it solidly into his mouth. The blow sent Nathaniel tumbling to the ground in utter astonishment.

Many in the crowd cried out in dismay. Sarah screamed and tried to run to Nathaniel, but he motioned for her to stay away.

He touched his lip. Blood trickled from the side of his mouth. He wondered if he should have felt some violent emotion at being mistreated like this, but he didn't. Even sitting in the dirt with a throbbing jaw and a bloody lip, he couldn't feel any worse about things than he already did.

"Elmer, stop this!" Dodging bystanders, Elmer's dat ran from the pavilion and grabbed his son by the collar. "You forget yourself."

Elmer wasn't contrite. He pointed an accusing finger at Nathaniel. "Do you know what he's been telling people?"

Ignoring his son, Solomon reached out a hand. Nathaniel took it. "Forgive Elmer for his bad behavior," he said coldly, pulling Nathaniel to his feet. "He has shamed the Weaver family."

Nathaniel grimaced at the man's aloof tone. He obviously didn't approve of how Nathaniel had handled things with Kate. But what could he do? Kate had made her own choices. Both she and Nathaniel had suffered the heartbreaking consequences of those choices.

Solomon pulled a handkerchief from his pocket and handed it to Nathaniel.

"Thank you," Nathaniel said. He dabbed his throbbing lip, soaking up the plentiful blood. Elmer had hit him hard.

"But, Dat, he told Aaron that Kate got pregnant and now she has a baby."

With jaw tight and body rigid, Solomon studied Nathaniel's face as if to discover the truth of his son's words. "Why would you say this?"

Nathaniel spit the blood from his mouth and wiped his chin. Unexpected despair washed over him as he thought of Kate and what he had lost. "It is time to tell the truth."

"And what do you think the truth is?" Solomon said through gritted teeth.

Nathaniel kneaded his forehead. The pain of remembrance saturated his senses. "Kate had a boyfriend in Milwaukee, and she has a child by him. A beautiful brown baby like his father."

Upon hearing this, some of the onlookers gasped, while others seemed unsurprised.

"I was deceived above everyone else," Nathaniel said. "But how could any of us have guessed her true character? She seemed so modest and pure."

Solomon altered his expression slightly and stared at Nathaniel. "Who told you this?"

"I went to Milwaukee. I saw them with my own eyes."

Elmer pinned him with a ferocious glare. "You saw nothing."

Solomon's hands began to shake uncontrollably. He turned slowly in a wide circle, surveying the faces of his closest neighbors and friends. "And none of you thought to come to me for the truth?"

Some of the men hung their heads.

Solomon turned to face Nathaniel in the way a convicted man confronts his accuser. "My daughter...," Solomon said, voice trembling, "my daughter is as pure as the driven snow. The baby is Maria Trujillo's. Jared, the man who beat Kate, was the father of Maria's baby."

"I saw her with a dark-skinned man and the baby."

"Carlos," Solomon said. "Maria's brother. He and Kate are friends. They took care of the baby when Maria worked."

"People saw them hugging," Nathaniel said, grasping for anything to justify himself.

"The Englisch are different from us that way. But you have made something ugly out of nothing at all. My Kate has done nothing to defile herself." He pulled a small wallet out of his pocket and retrieved a wrinkled photograph. "Here is Maria and her baby. *Her* baby. Not Kate's."

Struck dumb, Nathaniel barely looked at the picture. His mind couldn't even wrap itself around what he had heard. Where was the truth?

"You knew her the whole summer and you still believed she was capable of such a thing?" Elmer said.

Solomon wiped his hand across his mouth and lowered his voice so only Nathaniel could hear. "Because of you, our family has lost her. She's not coming back." He swallowed his next words and turned away.

Elmer jabbed his finger into Nathaniel's chest, fire blazing in his countenance. "Do you have any idea what you have done to her? I saw her. I know. She trusted you, and you crushed her. You crushed her."

Aaron stood frozen with his arm around Ada. Solomon had words for them too. "My son, I have kept away from you for three days. I have prayed for guidance before I acted. Now I ask you to examine your soul. There is no end to the damage you have done with your lies. You will proclaim your sins before the church or I will do it for you. Make all things right, or you are no longer my son."

Whatever his offense, Aaron showed no contrition. His father turned from him.

Then, with one grief-stricken look at Nathaniel, Solomon trudged away with Elmer close behind.

* * * * *

Nathaniel forgot how to breathe. He stood like a statue and watched Solomon and Elmer walk away. The crowd of spectators dispersed.

"Well," Ada said, puffing air into her cheeks and straightening her shoulders, "that was the biggest overreaction I have ever seen. All I did was tell a few friends—something I thought was true, mind you—and Elmer goes around smacking people."

"Gossip is a grievous sin," murmured Nathaniel.

Ada flicked her wrist in the direction Solomon had gone. "It's not gossip if it's true. Don't you think so, Sarah? If you think a story is true, then you're not gossiping by retelling it. Gossip is when you say something false about somebody to ruin their reputation."

The irony of Ada's words buzzed in Nathaniel's head like an angry wasp. He did not reply to her absurd logic. All he could hear was Elmer's voice echoing in his head. *"You crushed her. She trusted you, and you crushed her."*

Sarah offered her lacy handkerchief to Nathaniel, as if Solomon's was somehow not good enough. "Oh, sis yusht! Look at your mouth. You need some ice." She touched his jaw, and he recoiled as if she had burned him.

She pretended not to notice and stuffed the handkerchief into her apron. "Where could we get ice, do you think?"

Aaron patted Nathaniel on the shoulder. "Give them time to calm down. In a few days we will all apologize to each other and get over it. Elmer is childish and deerich. I think we can all forgive someone so young."

"Jah, he has always been Kate's champion," Ada said. "Even when she didn't deserve it sometimes. It is good he isn't baptized. That kind of behavior could get him excommunicated."

Nathaniel searched for something, anything, to justify his conclusions about Kate. Nothing came to mind. He pictured Kate as he had last seen her.

Maria *has a baby.*

Faces, buildings, noises—everything around Nathaniel vanished. Solomon Weaver's words spiraled around him in slow motion, filling his mouth and nostrils, suffocating him. He couldn't tell how long he stood there, not blinking, not breathing, not knowing whether he was dead or alive. It was her friend's baby? It was her friend's sin?

With perfect clarity, Nathaniel recalled Kate's voice on the phone.

"I want you to hear the whole story about Jared."

"I know about what happened with the boyfriend."

"But I want you to understand."

He staggered as the weight of the world flattened him. Did Kate think he had rejected her because of Jared's death? Because she had defended herself and saved a life?

She had phoned him. She had tried to explain, to make things right, and he had washed his hands of her before she could even speak. His reaction had been swift and cruel.

Why, after everything he'd done to her, would Kate choose baptism?

The answer charged at Nathaniel like a wild bull. *The buggy accident.* He had been helping Elmer with the injured horse when Kate's gaze had compelled him to look up. His heart raced at the memory. Light had surrounded her entire being. He recalled her glowing countenance with vivid, bright clarity. Her lips formed the words "I love you," and he had never experienced such elation in the midst of chaos. She had received an answer to her prayers. And he had crushed her very will.

Nathaniel felt his soul crack. "Kate, oh my Kate, what have I done?" His mouth formed the words, but no sound came out.

Aaron glanced at him. "Did you say something?"

Ada and Sarah fussed over Nathaniel's bloody lip without touching him. They wrung their hands and wondered if he would need stitches and did their best to convince him that he should retreat indoors where it was warm and he could elevate his feet. He brushed them aside and strode away with long, purposeful steps.

"Is this the thanks I get?" he heard Sarah say behind him—but he no longer had words for her.

He panted as if he ran a long, tortuous race. Not caring which way he went, he trudged on, aching for a place to hide, to flee where the iron hand of guilt could not seize and smother him. When he came to the edge of an empty field, he quickened his pace. A single drop of water slapped the back of his neck. Still he pressed forward. Soon the icy rain speckled his royal-blue shirt and began dripping off the brim of his hat.

He halted and looked around. With the rain falling sharply, the pavilions became blurs in the distance, and he remained the only human being as far as his eye could see. He bowed his head as despair overpowered him. Then he looked up into the sky and wept bitterly.

Chapter Forty-Five

"Three weeks. Three whole weeks you've been in Millersburg, and you haven't gone to one singing," Hannah said, clearing the plates from the table like a seasoned busboy.

"Sit, relax," Kate said. "I'll do the dishes."

"I'm pregnant, not crippled."

Kate turned on the water and began to fill the sink. "You'll wear yourself out. We want to keep the little one in the oven a bit longer."

Hannah's husband, Vernon, had tucked in two thick pork chops and four helpings of corn before kissing his wife and trudging out to the barn to help his dat finish the milking.

Hannah eased herself into a chair to supervise while Kate scraped the plates. "Like as not, the small brush will work better," she said, pointing Kate to the bottom drawer. "I've got six more weeks yet and I already feel bigger than a house. I can't even turn over in bed without Vernon giving me a push."

"You look beautiful. You're practically glowing."

It seemed Hannah couldn't supervise the dish washing from the vast distance of five feet. She climbed from her seat and stood by Kate. "Like this," she said, showing Kate for the tenth time how she liked the sink filled. "*Die youngie* have their crowd tonight at Rabers'. Three or four boys have asked Vernon about you. They think you are pretty." Hannah went back to the table for the dirty silverware. "Vernon could ask one of the boys from the factory to take you."

"Dat made me promise not to go to any youth groups."

"He did not," Hannah said.

Kate sunk the plates into the soapy water. "He doesn't want me to marry a Holmes County boy who will keep me in Ohio for the rest of my life."

Hannah's eyes sparkled, and she shook her head in mock indignation. "That would not be so bad."

Kate's younger sister had fallen in love with an Ohio Amish boy—a great misfortune, according to Dat—and she now lived quite contently "back East somewhere," as Dat often reminded them. Hannah's residence was a small apartment connected to her in-laws' house and, with her expecting her first child, it was just right for a young family starting out.

"A pretty girl like you attracts attention. It's not fair to the boys to keep to this house like a hermit." Hannah brushed the crumbs off the table and into her hand. "Use the blue rag for the flatware. I'm sure Ben Hostetler would bring the buggy around for you. He is only seventeen, but he knows all the older boys."

Kate couldn't keep up the cheerful façade. She slumped her shoulders and sighed. "I'm not ready."

Hannah grabbed a dish towel from the drawer. "How long before you are ready?"

Kate shook her head.

"Oh," Hannah sidled over to give Kate a hug. "You need to try harder with the boys, that's all." Hannah set the dish towel on the counter and cupped Kate's chin in her hand. "I miss the old Katie who used to sing all the day and bury herself under the sheets and giggle with me late at night when we were supposed to be asleep. Or the girl who used to put on secret shows for me and Elmer and the puppies. Remember how we scrambled up to the loft and hid if we spied Aaron coming?"

Kate nodded. "I still do that."

"Like as not, the youth gathering would cheer you up. You have lost your spark. It is almost Christmas, and you have no Christmas cheer."

"Mrs. Crawford will give me more hours at the store if I want."

"You work plenty already, and you are a big help with the house-work. You clean gute. Like as not, once you get married, you'll get better with the cooking."

Kate wiped the table and counters while Hannah put away the clean dishes. She wouldn't even entertain talk of marriage. With Nathaniel lost to her, finding another boy was out of the question. Who would measure up?

Tears stung her eyes as she vigorously wiped every surface in the kitchen. Why had she let Nathaniel wander into her thoughts? She could function perfectly well if he stayed locked away in her memories. Unfortunately, he escaped several times a day to torment her. She wished his life had never touched hers. Better to be ignorant of what might have been.

"I'll get it," Hannah said as she hurried to the front room.

Kate hadn't even heard a knock.

She rinsed her rag in the soapy water and wiped the windowsill above the sink. Hannah wouldn't find one speck of dirt in this kitchen.

"Kate, you have a visitor."

Kate turned. Standing there, as if he had materialized simply because she was thinking of him, was Nathaniel King. Hannah took one look at Kate's face and, without a word, tiptoed down the hall and into her bedroom.

For an eternal moment Kate and Nathaniel stared at each other, and Kate's heart disintegrated into a million pieces all over again. Turning her back on him, she covered her mouth with her hand to stop a sob that threatened to escape her lips. Why had he come?

"Please," he said, so softly she wasn't altogether sure she had heard it. "Please, Kate," he repeated. "Do anything but turn away from me."

Kate could never refuse anything Nathaniel asked of her. She slowly turned to face him, with tears spilling down her cheeks.

His glacier-blue eyes with his shaggier-than-usual hair and day's growth of dark beard pierced her defenses. He was even more handsome than she remembered.

While she'd been away in Milwaukee, she had pictured him wearing the eternal smile that could melt her down to her toenails. He was not smiling now. He looked like a man who had walked through perdition— beaten down and broken beyond repair.

For a minute, Kate wondered if he was going to say anything. He gazed at her, a thousand different tragedies reflected in his eyes. "I'm so sorry." His deep voice wavered, but it was still the most beautiful music Kate ever heard.

She folded her arms and stared down the hall where Hannah had disappeared. "The damage has been done. Why open the wounds again?" Or did he want to inflict new ones?

His voice spoke of anguish. "I can never atone for the pain I have forced on you, but I beg your forgiveness anyway."

Kate could barely find the composure to speak. "If the thought of being with a woman who has killed a man is disgusting to you, I cannot blame you."

"Kate, I thought... How can I tell you this?" Nathaniel reached out his hands then dropped them to his side.

Kate still loved him, heaven help her. She still loved him more than life itself, and she couldn't bear to watch him suffer. "If you came to do penance, I wish you wouldn't have. I just want to forget you."

He looked as if she had slapped him across the face.

"How can I ever be whole again when the mere sight of you rips a fresh wound in my heart?" Kate said. "Please go away and don't come back."

"Kate." Her name burst from his lips. "Will you hear what I have to say?"

Kate brushed an imaginary crumb off the cupboard.

"And then I promise to trouble you no further."

Kate wrapped her arms tightly around her chest to shield her heart against his crippling influence.

Nathaniel anxiously fingered the hat in his hands. "There were rumors and gossip. I shouldn't have listened. Someone saw that man from Milwaukee touching you."

"Carlos?"

"Jah. I came to town to find you, to find the truth. I saw you with him. I thought he was your boyfriend and the baby was your baby. I could not bear the thought." He ran his fingers through his hair in frustration.

"You believed I had a baby?"

Nathaniel hung his head. "I am ashamed at how ready I was to believe."

She backed away from him. "I tried to call you to explain. Why wouldn't you listen?"

"I feared that if I heard your voice, my resolve to do right would weaken. I cannot resist you." Nathaniel hung his head. "You cannot understand how my sins have tortured me. This is my doing. I confess it all, even though the confession might make you hate me forever."

Kate could not bear to watch his torment one more minute. "How could I ever in a million years hate you?" She kept her gaze steadily on Nathaniel's face. "I forgive you. Don't be troubled by this anymore. You can go back to Wisconsin with a clear conscience."

And marry Sarah and have children and live a happy life. Without me there.

"How can I to return to Wisconsin without you? I love you, Kate."

Kate pressed her hand against her cheek as she felt the blood drain from her face. Her fingers were ice-cold. She swayed unsteadily and, in alarm, Nathaniel rushed toward her and wrapped his solid arms around her. All thoughts of guarding her heart vanished. She didn't care the reason. It felt glorious to have him close again. Savoring his powerful presence, she regained her balance, but he did not release his hold.

His mouth was close to her ear when he whispered, "Kate, can you ever love me again?"

Nathaniel did not seem to mind that Kate was soaking his clean white shirt with her tears. "I have never for one day stopped loving you," she said.

She felt his arms tighten around her. "Then will you have me? Again and forever?"

"Even though I killed someone?"

"To save another. That would never stop me from loving you. I want you more than ever. Even if you don't want me."

"Of course I want you. I would do anything for you, Nathaniel King."

She looked up. *There* was the smile she ached for. He slowly lowered his face to hers. Their lips met with a tenderness Kate had not dreamed possible. The weeks of heartbreak and uncertainty, the pain of wasted days, and the despair of unfulfilled dreams released her like winter surrenders its ruthless grip on the frozen earth in early spring.

Did every first kiss hold such promise? Well, technically the second kiss, but it was decidedly better than the first.

Nathaniel pulled away to catch his breath. "I have wanted to do that for eleven years. This time I did not have to chase you around the playground." He flashed his white teeth. "It was better than I ever imagined."

She wrapped her arms around his neck and tugged him nearer to her heart. "Me too."

"How could I have been so foolish? I almost proposed to Sarah."

"Jah, I heard."

"I am so ashamed. I made her believe something that could never be. It was cruel of me to pretend. She was hurt, badly hurt."

"Poor Sarah. I know how it feels to lose you. It is horrible."

He shuddered and tugged her closer to him, if that was possible.

Kate nuzzled her cheek against his chest. "Ada must have felt it keenly. She had such high hopes."

"Ada and Aaron had their own troubles. After your dat made known to everyone what he did, Aaron was shunned. He will not embrace humility willingly, but I hope in time he will want to make amends for his grievous sins. I have to reach deep in my heart to forgive him for lying to me and then betraying my confidence about the baby I thought was yours. But forgiveness is easier now that I have you again. In my happiness, I have almost forgotten his transgressions. And I will forget every misery if you say you'll marry me."

Without hesitating, he boldly kissed her a second time, lifting her off her feet to bring her closer. Kate felt like soft and wobbly tapioca pudding in his arms. How could a kiss throw her completely off-kilter? *Intoxicating* couldn't begin to describe the feeling.

"I think I'm dreaming," Kate said.

"I know I'm dreaming. Happiness like this cannot possibly happen in real life."

"Yes, I will marry you, Nathaniel King. I could not want for one more thing to make me perfectly happy."

Nathaniel drew her to him for a kiss more heart-stopping than the first two. When Kate gathered her scattered wits, she said, "That's three kisses. Aren't you getting a little carried away?"

"I am making up for lost time. If we were back in Apple Lake, we'd be married already." In exultation, he lifted her off her feet and twirled her around the kitchen. "I know I don't deserve you, but not even Shannon can talk me out of keeping you now."

"Shannon?"

"Yes, your academy friend, who thinks she knows more about me than I do. She called me a 'jerk' about twelve times."

Kate looked at Nathaniel in astonishment. "You talked to Shannon?"

Nathaniel reached into his pocket and pulled out the business card that Shannon had given Ada. "Ada gave me this the day she returned from Milwaukee. 'The way of a fool is right in his own eyes.'"

"Did the passage make you angry?"

"No," Nathaniel said. "I thought it was a message for Ada. I almost threw the card away, but by the grace of God, I stashed it in a drawer in my desk and forgot about it. Then Elmer literally knocked some sense into me and I needed help and didn't know who else to call. I was desperate to talk to you, but I knew if I set foot on your property, Elmer would break my nose."

"Elmer would never do that."

"You'd be amazed what he will do when sufficiently provoked. He can be quite fierce when defending the honor of his sister. I called Shannon. After she cataloged all the reasons why I don't deserve you, she took pity on me and agreed to drive me the ten hours to Ohio."

"Shannon drove you here?"

"First she made me grovel to the dust, and then she told me I would have to wait three weeks before she could miss a class. I tried to put the extra time to good use."

"But Shannon actually drove you here?"

"She spent eight of the ten hours lecturing me on how a man should treat a good woman. By the time we drove over the Ohio border, I felt worse than I ever had in my entire life. I don't know how that guy puts up with her."

"That guy?"

"Shannon recruited Carlos because he has a truck."

"Why did you need a truck?"

"I brought you a present," Nathaniel said, instantly downcast. "If you would be kind enough to accept it from a fool."

Kate took his hand and laid a kiss on each knuckle. "Cum, show me."

With his arm firmly around Kate, Nathaniel led her outside into the frosty evening. A beat-up red Chevy pickup stood in the lane, a blue tarp secured over the truck bed. Shannon and Carlos sat uncommonly close in the front seat, sharing a pair of earbuds plugged into Shannon's phone. When Shannon caught sight of Kate, she slid out of the cab and hugged Kate enthusiastically.

"Kate," she whispered, "Carlos asked me out the night after the opera closed."

Kate squeezed Shannon's hand and smiled widely. They were a perfect couple.

Nathaniel busily untied the rope anchored to the truck. Carlos jumped out to help him.

"Hello, Kate," he said. "It's good to see you again."

She grinned. "It is very good to see you too."

"I didn't see your smile much in Milwaukee. You're even better looking when you smile."

"Carlos," Shannon said, "don't say that. Her boyfriend is standing right here."

"A guy likes to know that other men think his girlfriend's hot. Isn't that right, Nathaniel?"

Nathaniel glanced at Carlos. "Don't need anyone else telling me what I already know."

Nathaniel unwound the rope and pulled a tarp away from an exquisite rocking chair. He studied her face with hopeful anticipation.

She gasped with pleasure. "Oh, Nathaniel, it is beautiful. It's…it's the finest rocker I have ever seen."

That attractive smile of his always stole her breath. Nathaniel gently put his hands around Kate's waist and helped her climb into the truck bed for a better look. Her fingers explored the feather-soft armrests and the intricate design carved into the headrest. Then she sat down and rocked slowly, savoring the smooth motion that made her feel as if she were floating. This rocker was no assembly line, mass-quantity piece of furniture. Nathaniel must have invested countless hours and extreme care to craft it.

Kate looked down at her hands and quickly laced her fingers together. She was actually trembling.

"What's wrong?" Nathaniel jumped into the truck and knelt beside her. "Are you upset?"

Kate wiped a tear from her cheek. "I don't deserve this. How can anyone be worthy of such a man?"

Nathaniel put his hand over hers. "I will strive my whole life to be worthy of you," he said, raw emotion in his throat. "This is only my first attempt."

She put her hands on either side of his face and kissed him eagerly. He responded by raising her from the chair, embracing her properly and thoroughly, and kissing her into distraction.

Carlos's voice intruded on their bliss. "That's not a real good place if you're looking to be discreet. You've got three Amish people staring at you from that house." Carlos motioned in the direction of Hannah's bedroom window. Hannah ducked from view as she saw Kate look her way but then, deciding she had been caught, reappeared and waved enthusiastically at the two couples. Two of Hannah's nieces in the main house peeked out an upstairs window. They couldn't be heard outside, but it looked as if they giggled hysterically.

Nathaniel helped Kate from the truck, and Kate motioned for Hannah to come outside. She appeared a minute later, wrapped in her shawl. "What do you think you are doing out here in this weather? You'll catch your death of cold."

"Hannah," Kate said, unaware of any temperature but the warm glow inside her, "these are my friends, Shannon and Carlos."

"Nice to meet you," Hannah said, keeping her eyes glued to Nathaniel.

"And this," Kate said, taking Nathaniel's hand and pulling him forward, "is my fiancé, Nathaniel King."

Hannah squealed in delight and threw herself into Kate's arms. Kate almost toppled onto the gravel. Nathaniel's mouth would not fit on his face if he smiled any wider.

Hannah couldn't catch her breath. "Ach, the trouble you put us through! Kate has cried herself to sleep every night since she's been here, and she's barely eaten anything. I thought we might lose her."

Nathaniel's face clouded over and he turned his back on Hannah. Hanging his head, he rested his hand on the truck and kicked the gravel at his feet.

Shannon glanced at Nathaniel and frowned. "We've been hard on him," she muttered to Kate. Then her countenance brightened and she turned to Hannah. "Can we see your house? I've never been inside an Amish home before."

"Sure enough," Hannah said in delight. "There's shoofly pie waiting. It's the best thing you ever tasted, except for my bread pudding."

Kate watched the trio stroll to the house then rested her hand on Nathaniel's arm.

He fixed his gaze down the lane. "How will I ever make up for the pain I've caused you?" he said.

"You could give me a kiss for every tear ever shed," she teased.

His mood did not shift. "I almost lost you," he said. "In a hundred ways, I almost lost you. That knowledge tortures me every second. I dreamed of you and waited for you and loved you for eleven years, and in one moment, I almost lost it all."

Kate lifted his arm and put it around her shoulders. Then she wrapped her arms around his waist and nuzzled her cheek against his chest. He responded by bringing his other arm to the small of her back and resting his chin on the top of her head. They stood motionless, eyes closed, their senses saturated with each other.

Kate started to sing. "'Be still, my soul; the hour is hastening on when we shall be forever with the Lord, when disappointment, grief, and fear are gone, sorrow forgot, love's purest joys restored. Be still, my soul; when change and tears are past, all safe and blessed we shall meet at last.'"

"You are the music of my life, Kate. Promise me our song will play forever."

He brought his lips to hers before she could respond. She kissed him back with every bit of love and life her soul possessed.

He had his promise.

About the Author

JENNIFER BECKSTRAND grew up with a steady diet of William Shakespeare and Jane Austen. After all that literary immersion, she naturally decided to get a degree in mathematics, which came in handy when one of her six children needed help with homework. When daughter number four was born, she began writing, and between juggling diaper changes, soccer games, music lessons, and dinner preparations, Jennifer finished her first manuscript in just under fourteen years. *Rachel's Angel*, a historical western, won first place in two writing contests. Soon Jennifer turned her attention to the Forever After in Apple Lake series, about three cousins who find love in Wisconsin's Amish country. Her debut novel, *Kate's Song*, is the first book in the series, and two more books, *Rebecca's Rose* and *Miriam's Quilt*, will release in 2012 and 2013, respectively.

Jennifer has two Amish readers who make sure her stories are authentic. No matter the setting, she hopes to pen deliriously romantic stories with captivating characters and soar-to-the-sky happy endings.

A member of RWA, Jennifer is the PAN liaison in her Utah RWA chapter. She lives in the foothills of the Wasatch Front in Utah with her husband and two children left at home. She has four daughters, two sons, one son-in-law, and one grandson.